A GHOST OF SPRING

BOOK TWO OF THE PERTH PARANORMAL SERIES

A.B. HOOSER

Printed in the United States of America

First Printing, 2024

Paperback isbn-978-1-962019-11-8

The Henlo Press

P.O. Box 1694 Ashland, KY 41105

www.thehenlopress.com

For my mother, who raised two teens in the 90s without ever knowing where they really were at any given time.

1

You'd think that being shot at, breaking up a Ponzi scheme, and solving the forty-two-year-old murder of a child would grant you some extra coolness points in the eyes of the local teenage population, but it doesn't work like that. My sister, my twin, the good one, the prep, the quiet kid with straight A's... was now a pariah. Pansy Bellafini was an outcast. And I, Geraldine? Well, I was still a ghost.

Despite earning the censure of our senior class for being involved in "weirdness," our adventures over the past winter had brought about a few wins. For one, because of the excellent press coverage they'd received, the Perth Paranormal Society, the motley crew of amateur ghost hunters that investigated homes and businesses in our small town, had investigations booked for the rest of the year. Second, Pansy and my BFF, Bagel, had declared a truce and were being nice to one another. He'd even joined the PPS and gone on several investigations with us over the last few months.

"Here, Dario, pull the blue cable closer to the wall." Pansy still refused to call him 'Bagel,' and honestly, I think he liked it. In the twelve years that we'd been friends, it had never once occurred to me to call him by his given name, and I suspected he appreciated that separation. She looked like me, her voice was mine, but it was an audible reminder that she was not me.

I floated behind them, watching, waiting, and being my normal useless self. It was April, which may mean mild temperatures and colorful spring flowers for most of the country, but here in Colorado, it was still cold. Mother Nature reserved her right to drop two feet of snow on us whenever she felt like it. The cold didn't bother me - I was dead after all - but every living person running around the investigation site was wrapped up in winter coats, scarves, gloves, and knit caps. The old hospital we were investigating had working electricity but no heat, and I wondered for like, the third time, why they hadn't waited until summer to work this case.

I mean, it certainly *looked* haunted. If you'd wanted to make a movie about a haunted hotel then Chivington Sanitarium, or The Castle as the locals called it, would have been the perfect location. The five-story stone monstrosity was located off County Road 12 about an hour west of our hometown of Perth. The property came complete with an imposing wrought-iron gate at the bottom of the hill and a crumbling driveway that wound up through an overgrown pine forest. At the top of the hill, the broken asphalt formed a circle around a three-tiered marble fountain, blackened with mold and rotting leaves. The east and west wings were set back at forty-five degree angles to the center section, giving the impression that the entire building was ready to leap forward. It was, like, totally creepy.

According to Blake, resident historian and researcher for the PPS, the sanitarium had originally opened in the 1880s to care for tuberculosis patients. At the time, doctors thought that the high-altitude, Colorado air was a magical cure-all, or something. In 1918, the sanitarium had briefly opened their doors to Spanish Flu patients during the height of the pandemic. The sanitarium remained in business until the fifties when some philanthropist dude bought the property and turned it into a nursing and rehabilitation home. I hadn't quite understood what had been done with the existing patients. Maybe tuberculosis had been cured by then, but I couldn't exactly pull out a volume of the Encyclopedia Britannica to confirm that.

Less than thirty years later, the nursing home was bankrupt and closed its doors. Again, I wondered what they'd done with all the residents. Did they give them a bus ticket and five bucks and hope for the best? Call their families to come pick them up? Either way, some investment group had bought the building in '84 with the plan to turn it into a retirement home. That sounded like a nursing home without nurses to me, but they'd only managed to upgrade about half the wiring and none of the plumbing before they'd run out of money. And so, the Castle had sat moldering for the last decade until a few months ago when a new owner arrived with visions of creating a luxury hotel. I hoped their checkbook survived the experience.

When we'd first arrived, I'd taken one look at the decorative carved granite and impressive two-story tall windows spanning the entire bottom floor of the main building and expected to float through the front doors into something straight out of the movie, *The Shining*. I was sorely disappointed. There was no furniture or even a front desk, just saw-horses holding up half-stained beadboard paneling, scaffolding erected along half-painted walls, and five-gallon buckets setting around everywhere. Twin staircases spiraled up from the back corners of the room, the dim lighting revealing cracked wooden railings and missing newel posts. There were no grand lighting fixtures hanging from the ceiling of the two-story lobby or fancy sconces attached to the walls. Cords dangled at regular intervals from the ceiling, each holding a single bare lightbulb that barely illuminated the floor below it. There were a few construction lights set up on tripods, but even they couldn't fully penetrate the darkness pooling in the corners of the large space. We were definitely going to need flashlights on this job.

"Anything yet, Gerri?"

"Nope. But they only have lights on in a few rooms so far." Being unable to see in the dark really hampered all the cool ghost things that I thought I'd be able to do once I got used to the idea that I was no longer breathing. I was essentially useless in the dark.

"Anything?" Bagel asked her. Having to go through Pansy to talk to me had irritated him at first, but I think he was getting used to that, too.

"Not enough lights on."

"Well, go turn them on for her. I'll finish taking care of this camcorder."

He really was a good friend. "Up or down?" Pansy asked me while still facing Bagel in case anyone walked by and thought she'd lost her mind.

"Start with up." Christopher, the first ghost that we'd encountered after I'd made my post-death reappearance, had been living in the attic of his former residence. He'd preferred it because it was quiet up there, and that seemed like a good place to start.

We left Bagel in the second-floor hallway of the east wing unwinding a spool of coaxial cable towards a supposedly haunted room. Randy, a professional exterminator who moon-lighted as the President of the PPS, was already in there setting up a video camera. As far as I could tell, there wasn't anything haunted on the second floor, at least in this wing. I followed Pansy up the stairs, her long black braid swinging back and forth as she climbed. On the third floor, a bare bulb lit the hallway and the doors to the individual rooms stood open with nothing but darkness and peeling paint on the other side.

Pansy's flashlight revealed that renovations had yet to begin in these rooms. They were empty of furniture and had been stripped of flooring and fixtures, with the occasional scrap of carpet foam or tack strips left behind. While the upgrade to the electrical system could be traced in spackled lines on the drywall downstairs, the wall art in these rooms, supplied by the local teenagers judging by the number of spray-painted penises and pentagrams, was largely uninterrupted. Huge chunks of the ceiling had either fallen out or been removed, and I began to wonder about our asbestos risk. The whole place seemed like a giant insurance claim waiting to happen.

"Wait, did you see that?"

"See what? Where?" Pansy swung the flashlight in every direction but the one I was pointing. I moved into the hallway and caught another glimpse of the staircase and what had clearly been an adult-shaped person passing by. It didn't look like anyone with our group.

"I swear I saw someone walking up the stairs."

"A ghost?"

"I don't know, ghosts just look like regular people to me. Let's go see." I was already floating ahead, grateful that the dangling bulbs on all levels of the stairwell were already on. I didn't have to wait for the mortal half of my Nancy Drew detective team to catch up. I reached the top floor without spotting anyone, ghost or not. Confused, I floated straight through the floor to where Pansy had arrived at the fourth-floor landing.

"I don't see anyone. Maybe I'm going crazy."

"So it was a ghost?"

"Not necessarily. They could have turned down this hallway and I didn't see them."

We both turned to stare down the darkened hallway. Nothing moved and no lights came on as we waited.

"Well, we can start here if you want. Check every room."

She was flashing her light around but my attention had already turned to the man coming up the steps behind her. I definitely hadn't seen him go down. To me, he looked like a living, breathing, elderly black man, bald on top with a fringe of white on the sides, his light blue pajamas decorated with white pinstripes. His feet and legs were moving like he was climbing the stairs, but they weren't moving at the same rate that his body was actually progressing up the stairs. It was like when the TV station messes up the sound and video feeds and they're out of sync by a second or two.

"I'm going to go out on a limb here and guess that you can't see this dude coming up behind you." Pansy jumped against the wall so fast that I worried she'd fall, but her frantic head bobbing as she looked up and down the stairs proved to me that she couldn't see the man.

"Sir," I said. "Can I bother you for a moment?" He didn't seem to hear me and continued past us, never slowing. "Rude," I said.

"What did he say?"

"Nothing. He acted like he didn't see me at all. He didn't even pause, just floated right past us."

"Well, that's weird."

"Talking to yourself, kiddo?" Greg asked as he came up the stairs behind us. Greg was Randy's right-hand man, the licensed plumber of the group, and was determined to make looking like a lumberjack a fashion choice. He was currently carrying a kerosene heater up the stairs like it weighed no more than his lunchbox.

"Well, you know, sometimes I need expert advice," Pansy replied with a laugh. This was the third time this month I'd heard her use that line when someone caught her talking to me. There was little chance that her reputation was ever going to recover at this rate.

"Hey, when you get a chance, can you bring me up another spool of RCA cabling? I'm going to set up an extra camera near the heat source and see if we get anything."

"Cool beans. I'll go do that right now." Pansy started down the stairs and I watched the old man in pajamas float through both of them as he slowly made his way up the stairs again. At no point had I noticed him going down.

I spent a few frustrating minutes trying to interact with the old man, but eventually gave up and floated down to the lobby. Progress had been made setting up what the group referred to as Grand Central Station. Folding tables had been erected and banks of monitors had already been hauled in and set up. Several cameras were already live, their grainy black and white feeds coming through on each 13" screen. The crew took turns watching the live feeds so that if something paranormal showed up on camera, a team could be directed via walkie-talkie to investigate in real time. So far, I'd seen them put a lot of effort into investigating dust and the occasional flying insect.

I figured that if Pansy just told them that she could talk to me, we could save them a lot of work. It was exhausting watching them lug all of this stuff around every other week. Besides, I hadn't seen a legit haunted house since old Mrs. Garcia and the ghost of Christopher, who'd poofed out of existence in January. Unfortunately, I didn't know exactly why or how, and the kid hadn't stopped to explain what he was seeing or feeling before simply saying, "oh," and dissolving in a flash of light. As a case study, it left a lot to be desired.

Chandra passed me in the lobby and the beam of her flashlight illuminated another mysterious figure in a darkened corner of the room. A gray-haired old white lady floated in a sitting position rocking back and forth without the aid of a rocking chair. I considered this to be a really good indicator that she was not, in fact, alive. Judging by her hand motions, she thought she was knitting or doing some kind of crochet project with invisible needles and yarn. The old-fashioned nightgown she wore indicated she'd surpassed her expiration date by a few decades.

"Hello? Ma'am?"

She didn't acknowledge me, even after I tried to touch her. When Lee, my unwilling ghost mentor, and I had occasionally shared spectral space, I could feel a change where we touched. It was like a low level increase in current, but my hand slid through these unresponsive ghosts with no change. Nothing. Nada. Zip.

This was getting weirder by the minute. My ghost lessons had included nothing about ghosts who couldn't see or hear me.

Since Pansy was on a mission to fetch the cable for Greg, I couldn't explore the fourth or fifth floors. I floated down to check the basement, but it was also still dark. Looking for something interesting to do while I bided my time, I made my way through the once magnificent double front doors and scanned the front drive which was currently full of our vehicles.

Randy, who looks like Friar Tuck from that Robin Hood movie that everyone watched because it showed Kevin Costner's naked butt for two whole seconds, was at the rear of the equipment van talking to someone I didn't know. He was a short, cocky little dude with a buzz cut that didn't disguise his bald spot, and a crooked front tooth. He wore a suit and tie which struck me as deeply strange because that was not normal investigation attire. Randy, who was dressed appropriately in his insulated Carhart overalls, was looking agitated, so I went over to be nosey. I mean, as a ghost, it was what I did best.

"It doesn't work like that, sir. It's either haunted or it's not, but we have a code to uphold."

Do you, Randy? I thought. *Was there really a paranormal inves-*

tigator's code? I'm pretty sure I would have noticed if Pansy had been required to take a test on it or if the group recited it before meetings or something.

"Look, construction costs are eating me alive and I need investors. People go nuts over anything haunted, so just don't say that it's *not* haunted. Three hundred dollars"

This must be the owner. I wished I could tell them it was one hundred percent haunted, but the whole being dead thing really got in the way, sometimes.

"For all I know, it really is haunted, but I can't tell you anything yet. We haven't even finished setting up for goodness' sake. On the other hand, you could have an entire raccoon army hiding in your rafters and not a single paranormal entity. It's too soon to say. I won't be going public with any information, either way, so that's entirely up to you."

"Well, as long as you don't say it's not haunted, I guess we can work around you."

"Work around me? We who?"

"The Channel 3 News crew. They should be here any minute." *Ahh*, I thought. *This explained the suit.*

"We haven't consented to being on the news."

"You're on my property. I can film you if I want to."

"Look, I'm not an attorney so I'm not going to argue with you. We're doing this investigation because the history indicates the potential for paranormal activity. We'll see what we see."

Randy, carrying a tote full of who-knows-what, walked away from the smaller man. I could practically see him resist the urge to push the dude out of his way as he moved past him. The owner wanted the hotel to be haunted? That seemed like a bad business model to me, but what did I know?

I started to follow Randy back inside, but changed my mind when I noticed Owner Dude heading towards an idling truck with another man in the driver's seat. After climbing up into the passenger seat, Owner Dude immediately held his bare hands in front of the heating vents to warm them up. I went full Gladys Kravitz and put my head through the front windshield to listen in.

"Did he take the money?" the stranger asked. He was wearing a dark blue sweatsuit and tennis shoes. Not exactly camera ready.

"No, the jerk said he has a code or some nonsense."

"A code? Did you tell him that we have investors that are only interested in unusual properties? We need this to be haunted." *We? Were they partners?*

"Yes, I told him. He didn't care. He said they'd investigate this property like they do every other and we'll see what we see."

"It's almost nine. The news crew should be here soon."

"Yeah, he didn't like that either. Said his group didn't consent to being on the news."

"What'd you say?"

"That it was my property and that I can have the local news come film on it if I wanted to. He didn't like that one bit and stormed off."

"These people need to understand that they work for you, not the other way around. We make the rules." The way he ran his hands through his dark hair made me think that this wasn't the first time they'd had this conversation.

"That's right. I make the rules." He looked like he was trying to convince himself of that when the tops of the pine trees surrounding the driveway lit up as a pair of headlights drew closer. "Look here, that looks like a news van coming now."

I pulled my head out of the truck cab and sure enough, there it was. A gleaming white van with a miniature dish on top and a red News Channel 3 logo emblazoned down the side.

It came to a stop alongside Summer's baby blue Volkswagen Bug.

Doors slammed as both the driver and passenger stepped out of the van. The side door slid open, revealing a third person behind a bank of monitors and equipment that looked like a more high-tech version of what the PPS was using. By reaching into the van and grabbing a huge camera and microphone boom, the driver suddenly switched roles to cameraman. The passenger removed his quilted Broncos jacket, revealing a suit and tie as he transformed into newscaster mode. I was pretty impressed with their efficiency.

I went back inside to find Pansy and Bagel, and after a few minutes of floating through floors, finally found them setting up a camcorder in the basement. The basement was one large open space that seemed to be the length and width of the lobby. The ceiling was low and both the exposed pipes overhead and the stone columns that supported the floor above were coated in multiple layers of drippy gunk and spider webs. All of the discarded furniture that filled the room was equally disgusting. I had the overwhelming desire to tiptoe through it and keep my arms pulled in tight so that I didn't touch anything, which was ridiculous. I reminded myself not to scream if I saw a spider.

"Hey, do you remember what the owner's name was? And was it just one guy or, like, some kind of property group or something?"

Pansy looked up from the screen on the back of the JVC camcorder. "Why, is there going to be a pop quiz later?" Even in the dim light she could tell her sarcasm wasn't welcomed. "I think it was Brown, or Bruin, or something like that. I don't remember it being a group, but that doesn't mean it's not. Why?"

"Is Gerri back?" Bagel asked, and received two identical expressions of 'well duh', although he could only see the one.

"The *reason* is that the dude that I thought was the owner was arguing with Randy out front. But, then there was another guy who also acted like he owned the place and I was curious because I didn't actually read all of Blake's report." I rarely did.

"Why was he arguing with Randy? Randy's a teddy bear. Who argues with a teddy bear?"

"He wanted to pay Randy to make sure that he says the place is haunted and Randy wouldn't take the money."

"Well, that's weird."

"That's what I said. Oh, and Randy was also mad because Channel 3 News is here to film you guys while you investigate."

"What?! The news? I cannot be on the news dressed like this." Her silver puffy coat was open, revealing a ratty sweatshirt and a pair of my black jeans. Her long dark hair, normally straightened and sleek, was in a sloppy braid under a hot pink toboggan that had a poofy yarn ball at the end. A matching hot pink scarf and gloves completed the look. It was a great look... when we were twelve.

"Why is the news here?" Poor Bagel, always two steps behind in the conversation.

"Gerri said the owner called them because he wants to prove the place is haunted."

As Pansy removed her toboggan and tried to smooth the static from her bangs, I caught a movement from the corner of my eye. Turning, I saw another ghost making her way towards the camcorder. She wore an ankle-length white dress with a white apron pinned to the front. Her brown ankle boots and little white hat gave me the impression of 'nurse', but I had no idea what era she was from. I fully expected her to be on some kind of loop like the others, but after giving the camcorder the once over, she looked me straight in the eye.

Oh, this one was different.

2

"Pansy, we have company."

She looked around, confused. "You mean a real one?"

"Yeah, like me, a tall red-head in an old-fashioned nurse's uniform."

"The living can hear you?" Our new friend looked back and forth between us with interest. "You're twins, I take it?"

"Yes. And yes, Pansy can see and hear me."

"Can she also see me?"

"No. As far as we know, it's just me."

"What's she saying?" Pansy asked. I waved a hand at her, indicating she would have to hold her horses. She grumbled, leaning one arm across the top of the camera and settling in to wait.

"There are so many people here this evening, and they are all carrying the strangest contraptions." She looked over the camcorder before giving me the same head-to-toe eyeball treatment. "Were you a soldier?"

I was confused for a minute because to the best of my knowledge there weren't any armies rocking Green Day concert tee shirts and ripped jeans as a part of their uniform. I realized she was looking at my combat boots, the coveted Doc Martens in ox blood red that my grandmother had bought me last year for our birthday.

"Uh, no, not a soldier. I'm still, well, I *was* still in high school. We're here with a group of paranormal investigators from Perth, a little town about an hour east of here. The equipment that you've seen helps them look for ghosts."

"Ghosts. And they think this...equipment, can help them see us? Hear us?"

"They think it does. I mean, they haven't seen or heard me yet, but I've only been dead for a few months. Maybe I just don't know how to ghost very well." I shrugged and pointed towards the camcorder. "The thing you were looking at there is a video camera. Like, to make movies, but for people to use at home."

"A movie camera? Truly? It's much smaller than those we used during the war," she moved closer and looked at it again. "You do not have to crank it by hand?"

"Definitely not." I wasn't sure which war she was referring to but I also couldn't think of a polite way to ask. "My name is Gerri, by the way."

"Apologies. Where are my manners? I am Nurse Daniels. Jessica was my given name."

"Do you mind if I ask how long you've been here?" I decided on a direct approach.

"She's asking the other ghost how long she's been here," I heard Pansy whisper to Bagel.

"Decades, I suppose. I truly do not know. It was '19 when I caught the flu. I had survived two years of war as a nurse stationed in France with the Red Cross before my transfer here. I lived through Zeppelin raids and flying bullets only to succumb to the flu, of all things. It is positively galling, if I can be honest."

"Well, that sucks." She looked confused at my slang and I wondered when she'd last spent time with modern living humans. "It's 1996 now, so you've been dead for almost eighty years. So like, uh... do you ever leave this place or do you just hang out here by yourself?" Surely she could have found her way to Denver if she'd tried. It would have to be more entertaining and way less depressing than this pile of rocks.

"At first. When I was still curious and had hope that I could continue on to the next world. It became apparent early on that this is not a condition that everyone must suffer. But I have long since given up on that happening. Now, I remain here and tend to my patients."

"Your patients? Um, it's just, you know, there haven't been patients here in years."

"Oh, is she a doctor or a nurse?" Pansy asked. We were going to have to work on her having some patience of her own. I gave Pansy the basic rundown to keep her occupied for a few minutes.

"Don't give up just yet," I said, turning back to Nurse Daniels. "I met a little boy a few months ago. He moved on."

"Interesting. So it is possible?"

"It is, although I can't explain the why or how. Do you have any theories about why you've remained here? Maybe there was someone who wronged you and you're seeking revenge?" That was a popular movie myth and I figured we should start with the obvious.

"Excuse me? Wronged me?" She laughed then, a beautiful tinkling laughter that made me think of well-bred English ladies from period movies. It was a world away from my signature cackle. "Do you mean, besides the Red Cross and every doctor who dismissed me because I was a woman and therefore could not possibly understand how the human body worked?" She was right, she'd been a woman with a career at the turn of the century. Her list of wrongs was probably infinite.

"Ask her if she's the one haunting the hotel."

Oh, yeah. The actual reason that we were here.

Nurse Daniels looked at Pansy, her face pinched. "What do you mean?"

"She means that the new owner thinks the hotel is haunted because the workers say they feel cold spots and experience the sensation that they're being watched. Some say that things keep getting broken with no explanation. Are you messing with them or is there another ghost around here like us? You know, one that's like, actually aware of its surroundings. The other two I've seen don't seem like they'd be able to break out of the weird patterns that they're in long enough to move things."

"I actually have five patients in residence, but I am the only other being here that is, as you say, like us. I may have moved some minor items in the hopes of frightening these people off. It's not safe for them here."

"Well, the guy that bought the place thinks that it's haunted, which," I gestured at her with one hand, "is obviously correct, but his master plan is to turn this place into a hotel. He thinks it's close enough to the ski resorts to appeal to high-end clients who don't want to stay in the ski towns."

"So Chivington would be full of the living, again?" She seemed disappointed.

"Well, yeah. The dead don't exactly pay the bills. He wants to keep the ghosts, though. In fact, the more haunted, the better. He thinks people will pay more to stay in a haunted hotel."

"This seems like an unorthodox view."

"Yeah, you could definitely say that. I'm sorry if this is a breach of like, ghost etiquette or anything, but can you move things?"

"Things?"

"Like in the living world. Turn lights on and off, flip switches, throw things."

"I can."

"Good. Great. Look, we've got these cameras set up all over the place and I know that this guy really wants to show that it's haunted, so if you've ever wanted to like, put on a show, tonight is the night. I can't move anything, or I'd help, but trust me, the living here tonight? They'll eat it up."

She cocked one head to the side and seemed to think it over. "I can try, but surely they will see the Other."

"I don't think so. These people never see me, and I actually try to interact with them. I don't think they'll pick up the other ghosts on camera or anything."

"I am not speaking of the patients, their souls moved on long before their hearts stopped. I am referring to the Other, the entity that exists here. Referring to him as a ghost seems incorrect, for he is not like you and I."

Well, wasn't tonight just jam-packed full of firsts? Fantastic. "So, it's not like the ghosts who run on repeat, but not like us, either?"

I heard Pansy whispering to Bagel behind us.

"Not like us, no. He is..." her brow creased as she struggled to find the words. "Evil is the only word I can think of, and it is woefully inaccurate. His energy does not come from a human soul, it is made of... rage and revenge."

Well, that sounded less than ideal. "Pansy, according to Jessica, there's another spirit running around here that doesn't have a body, and she thinks it's evil."

"Evil? What does that mean?"

"Evil? What's evil?" Poor Bagel.

"Uh, so does this thing only *feel* evil to you, or have you seen it trying to hurt people? Not that there are usually many people around here."

"I... I cannot say how he came to be here. When I took on this form, I could then bear witness to his atrocities. When there were so many sick and dying, he would... feed on them."

"Like a vampire?" I asked and heard Pansy make a squeaking sound behind me.

"I am sorry, what?"

"A vampire, like Dracula. Big fangs, drinks blood from people's necks?"

"Oh, like Stoker's ridiculous novel. No, nothing so grotesque. It is more that he hovers near the sick and then absorbs their energy, their... very life force. Their suffering seemed to strengthen him, but there were so many old ones that his damage went unnoticed. A hotel with healthy clients would be too tempting for him, and the resulting weakness in so many would draw attention."

"What does he look like if he isn't like us?"

"When he chooses to take form, he is still shaped somewhat like a human, but there are no features. I don't see him like I see you, with your strange clothing and youthful face. He... it has no face, just a vague form of... energy would be the best word to describe it, I suppose." She paused and paced a bit while she looked for the words to describe this 'Other.'

"When I was young, a traveling circus came through the town in which I lived, and one attraction was a glass ball with lightning trapped inside. If one touched it, all the hair on your body would raise. Again, it was not until after I had passed that I could see him, but when he hovers over a person, to be near him, it is like that ball of lightning. The brightness of his form increases in intensity until his victim passes on."

Not terrifying at all. Not.

"Can it hurt the other ghosts?" *Or me*, I thought, although I didn't say that out loud, mostly to keep Pansy from freaking out.

"I do not believe so, or at least, he has never tried. But I do not want to leave them, just in case."

"Do you think there's any way that we can get rid of it?"

"I do not know, but this link that you have to the living makes me wonder if we could not somehow find a way."

A link to the living. Yeah, Wonder Twins powers, activate!

"While I was living, I vowed to protect my patients and keep them safe. That did not change after I had passed. I have accepted that my role is not to rescue, but to watch over these lost beings. Until this point, I have gone about my duties without questioning my fate, but I'm afraid that your being here is giving me that most dangerous of all things, hope."

No pressure or anything.

"Okay, but like I said, I'm still new to all of this, so like, let's not get our hopes up too high, okay? I mean, the truth is out there and all that, but like, I really need to talk to my friend Lee before we make any plans."

"My dear girl, any hope at all is more than I have ever had before."

I was busy giving Pansy the Reader's Digest version of the conversation when we were interrupted by the news crew and Owner Dude.

"Now, we haven't made many updates down here, but I think this will give you the creepiest footage for your B roll." The owner led them through the maze of low-hanging pipes and abandoned furniture like a little kid showing off their bedroom to visiting strangers.

"Mr. Browning, I appreciate the tour, but we're really here to interview the Paranormal Society." The newscaster seemed thoroughly repulsed by the creepy atmosphere of the basement. On the other hand, the cameraman immediately had his lens three inches from a cobweb and was trying to shoot through it for effect. The world was made up of very different people.

"Well, here's two of them right now. Interview them."

"Oh crap," I heard Pansy whisper as she maneuvered herself behind Bagel. I cackled out loud, and Jessica looked on with confusion.

The newsman carefully stepped around some old desks and held out his hand for Bagel to shake. "Josh Smith, how are you doing?" Smith was a regular on the local news and had been Channel 3's man-on-the-scene for several years. He was bald on top, maybe in his forties, and of average height and weight. His one distinction was the ridiculous blond ponytail he wore at the nape of his neck. I'd often imagined that if he took his hair down, he'd look like a better fed version of the butler in Rocky Horror.

Bagel looked around like he was looking for a hole to crawl into. There was one behind the stack of chairs over in the corner, but I decided not to point that out to him. "Uh, fine, I guess."

"Awesome, awesome. So, if you don't mind, I'd like to ask you a few questions and my cameraman here, Mike, he's going to film. Is that okay?" I'd never seen the cameraman before. As he looked like someone had dressed a stick bug in human clothes, it made sense why he was on that side of the camera.

"Uh, sure."

"Awesome. Okay, so we'll get you set up next to this camcorder here and get started."

"Just be yourself, you'll be fine," I offered, not that he could hear me.

Smith maneuvered Bagel next to the PPS camcorder and Cameraman Mike took up a position that allowed him to film over Mr. Smith's shoulder. Bagel frantically motioned for Pansy to join him but she shook her head and retreated a few steps further back. Bagel rolled his eyes and dusted the stray cobwebs off the sleeves of his coat. His dark hair, cut short on one side and hanging past his chin on the other, slid forward to hide half his face.

"Okay, so why don't we start with you telling the audience your name and how long you've been working with this ghost-hunting crew?"

"Uh, my name is Dario Ventura and I've, uh, I've been a member of the Perth Paranormal Society since February of this year. I joined right after Pansy," he motioned to my mortified sister with a gleam in his eye, "found out about those guys who tried to rip everyone off with that fake diamond mine and then found the body of Christopher Fairchild."

Well, you know what they say about paybacks.

Cameraman Mike's focus swung to Pansy.

"Oh my, I didn't even recognize you. This is awesome, you're the one!" Mr. Smith exclaimed. The one *what* was left up for interpretation, but Pansy was now almost as pink as her beanie.

"If I assist you in demonstrating that Chivington is haunted, you will help me find a way to dispatch the Other?" Jessica asked, pulling my attention from the two worst choices of inter-viewees.

"I can't promise that we'll find a solution," I assured her. "But we'll try to the best of our abilities."

Jessica gave a single nod of her head. Then she pushed a stack of wire hangers off the top of the filing cabinet directly behind Pansy while the camera was still pointed in that direction.

"Oh my God, did you catch that?" Smith was practically jumping up and down and Cameraman Mike gave him a thumbs up. Bagel and Pansy turned to stare at the pile of hangers on the floor behind them and Jessica floated up through the ceiling.

"Beetlejuice. Beetlejuice. Beetlejuice," Cameraman Mike said with what I swear was a giggle at the end. Almost immediately, I heard a crash upstairs and several screams. Nurse Daniels wasn't wasting any time.

"We made a deal. She's going to put on a good haunting," I said to a shocked Pansy before floating up to see what the commotion was about. I found the lobby in chaos. A bucket of paint had fallen from some scaffolding and barely missed Chandra's head. Unfortunately, it had busted open when it hit the floor and she was now covered in white paint from her knees down.

I had popped up between Randy and Greg, who had just ran down the west stairs and paused to stare at the mess before leaping into action. Running to either end of the folding table, they quickly lifted it and moved the monitors and equipment away from the spreading puddle of paint. "I should have taken Browning's money," Randy told Greg, as he kicked a spaghetti pile of cables back under the table. "I'm starting to think that proving this place is haunted will be a cakewalk."

"It's tempting, but if you take money, someone somewhere is going to claim it's all fake." Greg went back to move a tote out of the slowly spreading puddle. "Look at Ed and Lorraine and that house in Amityville. No one believes them because they made money off the book and press tours. You've got to be smart about it and not give anyone a reason to doubt your word."

By the time Pansy, Bagel and the Channel 3 News crew made it up out of the basement and to the lobby, Summer had pulled a roll of paper towels out of one of the totes and was trying to wipe the paint off of Chandra's jeans. Cameraman Mike was taking it all in, a huge grin on his face. Summer still held her EMF detector in one hand and as I watched Jessica near the two of them, it started beeping faster and faster. Mike was on it, swinging his camera towards the sound and Shawn grabbed the camcorder from the tripod in the corner so that he could record, too. I had never been able to set the EMF detector off. How was she doing it?

"Could he be faking it?" Greg asked Randy, pointing to Mr. Browning. Browning looked like he'd just struck gold.

"I don't see how," Randy replied, looking around at the chaos. The construction lights were dimming and brightening in a slow progression between the two states, throwing dramatic shadows over the scene. One of the overhead light bulbs began swinging in slow circles, although I didn't see any ghosts near it. Jessica, I saw, was clear on the other side of the room knocking a cup off the table. She was watching the light with a frown, and I floated over to check in with her.

"Are you doing that?" I asked, hope in my voice.

"No, that would be the Other. It seems he has decided to join in the fun."

Great. I looked around and noticed Summer heading out the front door while the rest of the crew had stopped to look up at the lights. All five bulbs were circling now. I had just enough time to complete the thought that it probably wasn't a good thing when all of the construction lights and handheld flashlights dimmed to almost nothing. Suddenly, all five of the overhead bulbs exploded at one time, raining glass down on everyone below. It sounded like a slumber party full of twelve-year-old girls when everyone screamed at once.

"Please tell me that someone got that," Randy asked. I could hear him smacking his flashlight against his palm. "I just put fresh batteries in this when we got here," he mumbled.

The construction lights came back up to normal brightness and I could see Cameraman Mike shaking his head as he examined his camera. "Right before everything exploded, my battery died. I've never had a battery die on me while filming on site."

"My battery is dead, too," Blake said, shaking his EMP detector.

"This camera was hard wired in since it's so close to our monitoring station," Shawn said, rewinding the footage he'd caught. "I've got it all." There were a few whoops and hurrahs before Randy's booming laughter echoed across the room. Browning followed, and soon they were all laughing. They had a legitimately haunted structure here, and they'd caught it all on film. The only one not laughing or celebrating was Jessica.

"How bad is he, really?" I asked, not sure that I wanted to know the answer.

"The living are in danger and I don't know how to protect them."

Great.

3

After five hours of filming what was clearly a haunted hotel, the PPS packed up. The tapes and cassettes were stored in their cases, the cameras were packed, and miles of cable were wound onto giant plastic spools. Pansy usually carpooled to investigations with Summer, but since Summer had left early and there were only two seats in the equipment van, that meant that she, Bagel, and Blake rode home squished into the back seat of Shawn and Chandra's Saturn. If the hour-long ride was uncomfortable, no one cared. They were all talking a full octave higher than I'd ever heard them before, every other question beginning with, "Did you see…?" Being nosey, I bounced back and forth between the van and the car because I didn't want to miss anything.

It was four in the morning by the time we made it back to Sycamore Plaza, where everyone had met up at the beginning of the night. The Plaza was the newest construction that our small town of Perth had seen in the last decade, housing Blockbuster and Spin Time Records, as well as the bowling alley, and a few other small businesses. Ten miles north of the New Mexico border, three-and-a half hours south of Denver, our one-stop-light town was named for the Perth Canyon that created the western border of the town. It was centrally located in the middle of nowhere.

After a few minutes of goodbyes and final plans for who would review which crate of evidence, the crew broke up and went their separate ways. Pansy left her new (to her) Geo Tracker in the parking lot and Bagel drove her home so that she could finally relay my conversation with Jessica in its entirety. Since it was a brief trip from 'downtown' to our neighborhood, she still wasn't done by the time he pulled up to our house.

"That's crazy," he muttered as she concluded her story.

"I know, so that makes three different types of ghosts or spirits, all in one place. I know the PPS is excited, but do you know how hard it was for me not to just blurt out what was really going on? They would absolutely flip if they knew every-thing we know."

"It is kind of unfair to them, isn't it? I mean, they brought us in and showed us these methods they've been using for years, and we just waltz in with a ghost of our own and skip all the hard work."

Pansy was silent for a minute. "It's not like I can assign everyone a ghost interpreter so that they can get a play-by-play."

"If I could stand up at a meeting and give a speech, I would," I offered, not that Bagel could hear me or that Pansy bothered to translate.

"Yeah but, don't you think we should tell them? I feel like we'd have more luck figuring out what this dangerous entity is with their help? I mean, like Randy? Dude LIVES for this kind of thing. Surely he's read something somewhere that could help us."

"I..." Pansy was shaking her head. "I can't tell them. I like them. I don't even think that they would treat me differently, or not a lot, anyway, but... what if they tell other people? After Gerri died, everyone acted so weird around me. They'd stop talking when I entered a room, they'd avoid eye contact with me. It's like I brought doom and sadness with me everywhere I went. And then after Christopher? It's like someone has stacked bricks on my back and it's now my job to carry them without complaining, and everyone else pretends not to notice them. If this got out? It wouldn't be adding a few more bricks, it would be like adding an entire house on top of it all. I can't carry that."

Bagel nodded, the wedge of black hair falling into his face, again. "I promised you both that I'd never tell anyone about Gerri. And you know, I understand about not wanting to stand out. It's totally your call."

"Speaking of not standing out..." Pansy said before twisting in her seat to punch him in the arm.

"What was that for?" he asked, rubbing one hand over the other bicep. He'd shed his coat off as soon as he'd gotten behind the wheel of his Bronco, leaving his arm unprotected by the thick winter coat.

"I got sidetracked by the ghosts and forgot that I was mad at you for tossing me to the wolves with that reporter."

Bagel laughed and pointed his finger back in her face. "I'm sorry, who threw *who* to the wolves? If you could have crawled into that filing cabinet, you would have left me there to fend for myself. Uh-uh. Homie don't play dat. If I've got to be inter-viewed, so do you."

She had to concede his point, and after promising that he'd pick her up the following afternoon to review tapes and pick up her Tracker, they said their goodbyes. Our parents had been asleep but woke when they heard the front door open, meeting

Pansy downstairs in the kitchen. This had become the regular after-investigation ritual because they knew she'd be too excited to go to sleep immediately. Mom would make the three of them some Swiss Miss and they'd sit around the dining room table while Pansy told them about our adventures. The G-rated version, at least.

When I'd first returned, we'd decided not to tell them about my sudden reappearance. We didn't want them to think Pansy was crazy, but we also didn't know how long I'd really be around. After my death, they'd sent Pansy to therapy because they didn't think she was grieving enough, and Pans couldn't tell them why. Ironically, while they'd insisted on therapy for her, they'd thought that they could handle their own issues all on their own. They'd failed miserably.

Once we'd made the big reveal after Christmas, they'd agreed to start family therapy, which meant Pansy still had to attend with them every Saturday, but at least now the sessions weren't spent with Dr. Noonan accusing her of being on drugs or asking about her love life the whole time. Granted, being the sole person your dead twin can still speak to is enough to make anyone act weird. Now medicated, Mom still had moments of sadness, but she no longer resented Pansy's lack of grief. Knowing that I was still there, still with Pansy, had made things easier for her and she'd even started a part-time job doing nails at the local salon. For Easter, Pansy had received chocolate and a new purse, but Mom had set out a small basket with a hand-drawn heart in it for me, which had made me feel super loved.

"Oh my gosh, you are not going to believe all the things we saw tonight," Pansy began as soon as she saw them coming down the stairs. "It was absolutely insane, there were so many ghosts!" Pansy was already filling mugs with water for the hot cocoa, so excited that she needed to be in motion.

"Is that a good thing?" Dad asked.

"Well, yes, and no." She filled them in on the story, how the owner wanted to have his own haunted hotel, brushing away their questions about why anyone would want to stay there. "I know, I know. We don't get it, but this guy is convinced that it will be a big draw and he'll be able to charge more money for it.

"Anyway, so Gerri can see these...things. I don't know what they are, but we're calling them loop ghosts. She can see them, but they don't talk or interact with anything and they just do the same things over and over. Like one guy is walking up the stairs. Never down, just up. Then he disappears and starts over again. And there's an old woman who thinks she's rocking and knitting, but there's no rocking chair or like, yarn or anything. She found a few others, but it's just really weird that they're all here together in one place."

"Well, that sounds like an awful way to spend eternity."

"They also don't put out any kind of electrical signal. There are no EMP changes even when I was standing there testing while Gerri told me that the guy who paces up and down the fifth floor hallway was walking right through me." The microwave dinged and Pansy ripped open a packet of hot chocolate, spilling it over her hand and onto the counter.

"Here, let me do this. Go sit down." Mom shooed her out of the kitchen towards the table.

"Okay," she said, perching on the edge of the chair like she was ready to sprint at a moment's notice. "So, by the time we wrapped up, she'd found five of these loop ghosts, but she also found a real ghost who used to be a nurse there." We'd already decided not to mention the 'entity' to the parents. No reason to worry them about something that we didn't understand how to explain yet. Baby steps.

Once questions were answered and hot chocolate

consumed, Pans had finally retreated to our room. I repeated my conversation with Jessica for the third time before she finally fell asleep.

As soon as she was snoring, I left her to go in search of Lee. A quick search of the police station and the Loaf 'N Jug, his two favorite places to pick up local gossip, left me wondering where else he could be. The house he'd lived in when he died had been torn down a few years ago and I was at a loss as to where he could be. He hadn't mentioned going on a ghost vacation or anything. I wandered back over to the police station to spend the early morning hours. The beige block building sat on Main Street across from the internet cafe and really was the best place to pick up all the juicy gossip about our neighbors. When I noticed the morning sun shining through the plate-glass windows, I figured that my family would be up and about. Not Pansy, she'd still be unconscious, but Mom and Dad would be drinking coffee and reading the paper.

Before heading home, I made a quick trip south, floating over the wash at San Isidro Creek, which drained into Perth Canyon on those rare occasions it held water. I continued south on Sepulveda Boulevard until I spotted the two-and-a-half-story house on the right painted a bright Pepto Pink. Most properties down here were spread out over hundreds of acres of flat dusty plains, and the houses were not visible from the road. The Garcia house was very visible. Our family had always used it as a landmark when traveling home from trips to New Mexico - when we saw the pink house we were almost home.

Mrs. Garcia was a shriveled prune of a lady who enjoyed her Andy Griffith reruns and whose gnarled hands could still crank out a crocheted blanket faster than I could untangle a ball of yarn. Although someone from a local church took her grocery shopping every Saturday morning, she was alone for the rest of the week. Since Christopher was no longer haunting her, I made it part of my daily routine to stop by and check on her.

At this time of the morning, she was almost through her first pot of coffee and was settled into her recliner with a lap full of yarn. I was concerned for a second because she had her entire hand in her mouth, picking at something towards the back. I looked at the battered TV tray next to her - it usually held the remote, both new and used tissues, and the TV Guide. This morning there was a half-empty Whitman's Sampler on top of the pile. Next to it, her teeth were soaking in a glass. With some tongue swishing and lip-smacking, she finally dislodged the chocolate candy stuck to her gums and continued her crocheting.

The old woman showed no changes in health or happiness, and I left her to search the house and make sure that Christopher's naked butt wasn't floating around anywhere. He'd been gone for three months now, and I hadn't seen a glimmer of him. He really was gone.

Finished with that task, I floated home, flying over my neighborhood of cookie cutter split levels and two-story houses. Every house had a one-car garage, although I'd wager most were filled with random crap instead of vehicles, judging by the number of cars parked on the streets. It was a quiet, suburban neighborhood, a three-minute drive into the booming metropolis of Perth. Mom and Dad were exactly where I thought they'd be, at the dining room table, the Easter pastel tablecloth still covering the oak tabletop, and two steaming cups of coffee, black, set in front of them as they traded sections of paper. It made my non-functional heart happy to see them like this after the drama of the winter.

Pansy woke up about five minutes before noon and had time to shower and get dressed before Mom was yelling up the stairs that Dario was here to pick her up. If our mother thought it odd that my former best friend was now spending a lot of time with my sister, she never mentioned it. And it wasn't because she thought that either of us was or had been dating him. I'd overheard her tell Dad years ago that she'd known Bagel was batting for the other team since kindergarten. She'd also had some pretty choice words about Bagel's dad and how he treated his son, so I knew that she'd accepted Bagel as a fourth child a long time ago. I could tell that it made her happy to see him and Pansy getting along so well.

"Dario, sweetie, do you want some coffee? Juice? I've got some leftover cinnamon rolls here if you're hungry."

"No, ma'am. We're going to go get lunch at the Firefly before we head over to Summer's place to review tapes from last night."

Bagel was intentionally keeping it vague as to where, exactly, we were going because we still hadn't told Mom who Summer was. Mom knew she was a member of the PPS, but she didn't know that she was also the owner of Wild Harmony on Main Street. Although my family wasn't religious at all, she would have balked at letting them hang out in that 'occult' shop, as she called it. In fact, she'd strictly forbidden us from going to Wild Harmony when it had opened a few years back. Set on Main Street across from the elementary school, when the entire brick facade was painted in a shade called Violent Violet with glossy black and white trim, our sleepy little town had been shocked and appalled. The shop was mostly a bookstore that sold otherworldly knick-knacks like tarot cards and Ouija boards, with a yoga studio in the back. The yoga studio stayed pretty busy with classes, so obviously not everyone in town thought Satan was operating in a purple book store, but we didn't have the energy to attempt convincing Mom that Summer was harmless. We avoided the topic altogether.

"Did you have fun ghost-hunting last night? Pansy told us

you'd found some new ghosts." Despite the events of the winter where Pansy had been chased by a man with a gun who had every intention of shooting her and tossing her body to the bottom of Perth Canyon, our mother believed ghost hunting was harmless fun. The reason she thought this was because we hadn't told her what had really happened. Mom and Dad got the newspaper version - that Pansy had been trying to find her lost kite (in the dark) and had gone down a path to a cave on the edge of the canyon where she'd discovered Christopher's remains. She'd innocently and completely, by accident, found an injured man on her way back up and gone to call for help. Besides the dude who'd dropped his gun into the canyon when Christopher had shoved him off the ledge of the cave, Bagel was the only other living person who knew the true story.

While Pansy and Bagel were driving the few blocks to downtown Perth, I made another check of the Police Station and the Loaf 'N Jug to see if Lee had shown up yet, but no dice. I made it back to Sycamore Plaza at the same time Bagel was pulling in next to Pansy's bright yellow Tracker. As if being a retina searing shade of yellow wasn't enough to stand out, Bagel had hand painted Tweety Bird onto the spare tire cover for her. It stood out in a crowd.

The two walked the two blocks south on Main to the Firefly Cafe. Chandra owned the cafe and made a killing feeding teenagers since it was directly across the street from the high school. The whole place was decorated with a 1950s soda fountain aesthetic, complete with red vinyl booths, lots of chrome accents, and a black and white checked floor.

I spotted Chandra instantly, her brilliant cranberry bob practically glowing under the lights. She was leaning against a booth and it took me a second to notice the headphones she had pressed to one ear. Shawn and Blake were sitting in the booth, an array of food and micro-tapes spread on the table between them. Pansy made a beeline to their table to check in with the group.

"Hey guys, did we get lots of cool EVPs?"

"Duuuuuuude," came Blake's response, twirling his head phones by the metal band. "We have some insane noises caught on tape." Blake Casey taught history and some other history related stuff at the community college in Trinidad and was a hobbyist photographer. He was in his early thirties, single, short, had blond swoopy hair that parted in the middle, and was easily the biggest nerd we'd ever met.

"But are they voices or just noises?" Shawn asked, pointing a half-eaten fry at Blake. Shawn Bailey was married to Chandra and was the electrician of the group, an important job since often what people thought was a haunting was really just faulty electrical. Where Chandra was barely five feet tall, he was well over six. Her skin was so white she practically glowed in the dark and his was a fabulous shade of polished mahogany. Visually, they were an interesting pair. They'd been together for over a decade and it was obvious to anyone who met them that they were still head over heels over one another. Shawn was also the second biggest nerd we knew, and he and Blake could spend hours talking about video games and science fiction movies. Everyone in the PPS knew to never, under any circumstance, bring up the Star Wars franchise to either of them unless you wanted a two-hour conversation about the special effects.

Chandra took the headphones off and handed them back to her husband. "I can't tell if it's really saying something, but I feel like it's definitely a response to the question."

"That's what I'm saying. I'm not hearing actual words," Shawn replied.

"Are you two heading to Summer's?" Chandra asked, turning to Pansy and Bagel.

"Yep, but we needed a milkshake first." Blake began to make room for them, but Pansy stopped him. "No, no, we have some, umm, homework that we needed to talk about so we'll just sit over there," she pointed to an empty booth closer to the counter in the back of the dining room space. "We don't want to bother you."

"Yeah, we have some history to discuss," Bagel piped in.

"Well, if you need any help, I *am* a history professor," Blake offered.

"We'll keep that in mind," Pansy said before leading the way to the other booth.

The waitress took their order and had their milkshakes on the table before Pansy had located her favorite pen at the bottom of her purse. "So, what do we know about dangerous ghosts?" Pansy asked. She tapped the pen against the open notebook in front of her, making the neon green hair of the baby troll on the end wave erratically.

"Poltergeist," Bagel and I said at the same time.

Pansy looked back and forth between us before sighing. "Okay, what do we know that doesn't come from a Hollywood movie?"

"Did she say..." Bagel began.

"Of course she did," Pansy cut him off and pointed the troll at each of us. "You two are just alike."

Bagel gave a triumphant smile and I smacked his hand with mine since I couldn't give him a proper high five. Bagel was one of the few people I'd found who were sensitive to my touch, feeling what he described as a coldness whenever I touched him. We'd worked out a once for no, two for yes communication system over the last few months.

"Besides Hollywood, I know exactly nothing." Anne Rice hadn't prepared me for this kind of issue.

"Maybe we'll have to call in an exorcist, like that little old lady in the movie," Bagel offered between sips of chocolate shake.

"Again, Dario, Hollywood movies are make-believe. I can't look up an exorcist in the Yellow Pages and send one out to the hotel."

"I don't know why you're stressing out over this so bad. We're not even in charge of this investigation. We have real live adults for that. Let them figure out how to fix it."

Pansy leaned forward, lowering her voice so that none of the other customers could hear. "Except our real live adults don't even know what's really there. They think it's a regular ghost, don't they? Besides, the living person who owns it doesn't think there's a problem. It's the ghost who lives there that is asking for our help."

"Oh look, it's the freaks. Aren't they so cute together?"

"Oh my god, get a room already."

Bagel blushed as Danielle Newhouse and Andrea Lopez, who both thought that they were all that and a bag of chips, made their way to the counter, noses in the air like they hadn't just insulted my sister and best friend. I'd gotten used to it long ago. Bagel, too. This was new to Pansy, who'd turned so red that she looked like someone had physically smacked her across the face. Somehow, she'd made it to seventeen without ever having someone be an absolute jerk to her. Although she didn't have my mouth, so maybe that made sense.

I had hoped that Pansy could finish out her senior year before the other kids turned on her. She was pretty, smart, well-behaved, and had gone from being the preppiest of preps to being that girl who'd killed her sister and who now hung out with the lone goth kid. Oh, and the whole 'hunting ghosts' thing didn't improve the situation. I mean, there was no chance that she was going to make it out completely unscathed, but we only had two months of school left.

"Well, the Barbie's are here, Ken's won't be far behind," Bagel said, wiping his face with a paper napkin before tossing it onto the table next to his empty glass.

"You're not going to say anything to them?" Pansy was still sputtering and not thinking logically.

"Would it help anything? No. Will it get me beaten up later by one of their boyfriends? Possibly. Time to go, Pans. Don't forget your purse." He tossed some cash onto the table and picked up his jacket before scooting out of the booth.

I watched as Danielle looked back to see how her rude comment had hit, and Bagel rolled his eyes at her. Pansy was literally shaking. Grabbing her by the elbow, Bagel pushed her out the front door, the little bell jingling on their exit.

Wild Harmony was a few doors down and Pansy hadn't even begun to calm down before she was pushing through the glossy black door. I no longer possessed the power of smell, but Pansy had assured me that the store smelled heavily of sandalwood. I could see the little smoke trail from the incense holder on the counter and hoped it was something calming. Sarah was behind the register and looked up from the book she was reading, brushing her dark brown hair behind her ear before nodding towards the back room when she saw who it was. The one-eyed orange tabby was perched atop of a display of wind chimes and watched me closely as we made our way through the beaded curtain in the back.

After the first beaded curtain, we crossed a small space that held Summer's desk and boxes of extra inventory before passing through a second beaded curtain and into the yoga studio. The afternoon light streamed through the clerestory windows on the back wall, reflecting in the mirrored wall and honey colored wood floors and making the whole space glow. It was one of my favorite places to hang out in the daytime while Pansy was in school. Summer had a card table set up in the corner by the doorway where her TV/VCR combo held a place of honor. It's where she usually watched the videos from investigations between classes, and that's where we found her sipping on a cup of tea.

"You must be feeling better if you're already starting without us?" Pansy asked as she and Bagel pulled up folding chairs.

Summer was wearing a colorful pair of palazzo pants and a tank top in the overly warm studio, her long brown dreads pulled up in a bright scarf that in no way coordinated with the pants. "Yeah, Randy dropped these through the mail slot on his way home this morning and since I felt bad about flaking out last night, I couldn't wait to get into them. I'm glad you're here, though."

"You're not contagious or anything," Pansy asked, looking her up and down. She looked fine to me.

"No, I just had a migraine set in, probably the flashing lights. I had to get out of there."

"You missed quite a show," Bagel told her.

"I thought you had to work today?" Summer asked him.

"Not until four, so I wanted to see what kind of good stuff we got before I go." The three arranged their folding chairs around the table so that everyone could see, and Summer resumed playing the video she'd been watching.

"Randy left me the tapes of the basement, and the west and east wing videos for the second and third floors. This is the second tape of the evening for the east wing, so it begins a little after midnight and the only thing I noticed on the previous tape was strange fluctuations in the recording, like, the picture stutters. It took me a while to notice at normal speed, but you can really tell when you speed it up that it's like there's an occasional power surge or something."

"That could be Jessica," I said.

"Do you think it has anything to do with the place being haunted or just bad electrical?" Pansy asked.

"I'm not sure, to be honest. I wrote down the timestamps and it was really precise." Summer pulled out her notes. "Every two minutes and twenty seconds. How weird is that?"

"The camera was out on the landing pointed down the hall," I said. I wondered if it was the staircase ghost messing with the power. I tried to calculate how long it would have taken him to float all the way to the top and then appear at the bottom again. He was really slow. Two minutes sounded right.

"I documented it so that I didn't have to watch it again, but I thought maybe it was a bad tape or something, but this one is doing it, too. See." The film glitched, not like when I walked through a camera and screwed up the film, but like the camera had experienced a power surge.

"All the cameras were set up on the landings. I wonder if all of them were doing this?" Bagel asked, giving Pansy a very obvious stare. We were going to need to work on his poker face.

"Yeah, I don't know. Here, let's check one that wasn't from this stairwell." Hitting eject, Summer waited for the machine to spit out the tape and popped the west wing tape in. We gave it five minutes, but there was no glitch. "So maybe there was something wrong with that camera. Hang on," she ejected the west wing tape and pulled out one from the basement. We could hear Shawn and Chandra talking, although they weren't visible from the angle of the camera. We watched for ten minutes as they worked on EVPs and there was a whole lot of nothing going on with the tape. "Well, that rules out my tape heads needing to be cleaned. It could be something with that particular camera, but it's not the VCR. Let me check the footage from the east wing of the third floor."

A few minutes later, we'd confirmed that the footage went wonky every two minutes and some change on both the second and third floor, but only in the east wing. While I suspected the pajama ghost was the culprit, I had no way of proving it. Even though I'd watched him walk through the cameras in real time, I had no more answers than Summer did. Why didn't he overexpose the film like I did when I went through it?

I had questions and needed a better ghost to talk to, a more professional ghost. I needed Lee on the case. Where in the blue blazes was he?

4

Bagel eventually left Summer's to go to his job as a bag boy at Foodarama, but Pansy had stayed until they finished reviewing both of the east stairwell tapes. The next morning, with Pansy and Bagel both in school, I floated out to check on Mrs. Garcia before swinging by the Perth branch of the Las Animas County Library. At least once a week I'd stop to see if there were any new and exciting books on How To Be the Best Version of Yourself when You're Dead, or maybe a scientific treatise on the subject of ghosts. The library didn't have anything that we hadn't already read, so that was a bust, but there were a few volumes in the dedicated 'local history' room that looked like they may mention the Chivington Sanitorium, and I made a note to have Pansy follow up later.

I swung by the police station to see if Lee was back, but he still wasn't there and I regretted my inability to leave a note. I left, wandering aimlessly down the street, looking for something to do. At night, Pansy would leave the television on the channel that played reruns of Jerry Springer all night. We figured that since I was dead I couldn't rot my brain any more than it already was, but the daytime hours could get really boring. I considered flying out to The Castle and snooping around, but it was a long way and I wanted Lee to go with me. The fact that Jessica, who was the oldest ghost I'd met, seemed to be afraid of 'the thing' and that it could harm people creeped me out a little.

I could have floated through the school, spied on some classes, maybe even learned something, but Pansy didn't want me in there because she was afraid that someone would notice her talking to me. Or notice her watching me and think she was seeing things. And I was happy to let her believe that that was the reason I didn't go inside. I actually avoided the school because knowing that I'd been six months away from gradua-tion but would never walk across the stage with my diploma, even after years of pulling straight A's, well, it hurt too much. I missed my friends and my art teacher, and being inside those familiar halls made me wish for things I could never have. No one needed a melancholy ghost hanging around whining about her afterlife. So, I did the same thing I usually ended up doing, hanging out in Summer's yoga classes and trying to memorize all of the poses. I'd been going every day for the last four months. If I'd had a real body I imagined I'd be very limber by now.

Summer's two o'clock class was finishing up their Shavasana when I heard the church bells hit three and knew it was time to float down the block to meet Pansy. She pulled her cell phone out of her purse and pretended to make a call as she drew closer to me.

"I want to crawl into a hole and die," was her conversation starter. Must have been a good day at school.

"What happened?"

"Apparently our little news interview was on the six o'clock news last night. Mrs. Ventura was kind enough to make me a copy because she thought I'd be excited. We can see how bad it is, later."

Bagel's mother, bless her soul, had her VCR set to record the news every evening just in case something exciting happened. As we lived in Perth, that didn't often happen.

"I mean, how many people actually watch the news?" I gave her my attempt at emotional support. "I didn't even know the news came on on Sunday nights."

She sighed as she power-walked down the sidewalk. Maybe she didn't know that either. "Everyone thinks I'm a freak now."

"Well, honestly, if we define a freak as a person who speaks to her dead sister, you totally qualify." With the amount of side-eye she was shooting me, I guess she wasn't in a joking mood.

Her stride was fueled by rage and embarrassment and we were entering Wild Harmony in record time, the cheerful sound of the little bell over the door a stark contrast to Pansy's mood. She looked like she was ready to cry.

Pansy waved to Sarah as she stalked past her before knocking the beaded curtains aside. She practically threw herself into the plastic folding chair when she got to the table. Summer was still rolling up yoga mats from her last class and paused to give Pansy an odd look.

"What's up, Pansarooni? You look like you want to stab someone."

"Several someones, thanks. Ugh," she sighed, propping her elbows on the table and hiding her face in her hands. "Did you see the news last night?" the question was muffled by her hands, but Summer heard her.

"No, I never watch the news, it's too depressing."

"Well, apparently I was on it. Actually..." she leaned over to dig through her book bag that she'd thrown into the floor at her feet. "Dario's mom recorded the news and she made a copy for my mom. Do you mind if I watch it real quick to see how bad it is?"

"Knock yourself out," Summer said with a wave toward the video setup.

Pansy pulled the VHS out of its little cardboard sleeve and popped it into the slot. It started with the tail end of a commercial coming across the screen before changing back to the news desk.

The editors had started with a few spooky shots of the exterior that I'd watched Cameraman Mike filming before they'd gone inside, and then it cut to an interview with the owner. A shot of Bagel and Shawn doing EVPs flashed across the screen before it changed to an interview with Randy who was introduced as the founder of the group. Then they cut to a clip of Summer and Chandra setting up the monitors downstairs before going to a clip where paint cans were being knocked off a scaffolding and exploding their contents across the floor.

"Looks like Chandra and I made the news too. This is just local, right?"

"Yeah," Pansy confirmed. "Oh, here we go, this was his second attempt to interview me," Pansy said, pointing to her own image on the screen. Since the first attempt had ended in a pile of hangers on the floor and ghosts causing a ruckus in the lobby.

"You may remember this face from earlier this winter when we interviewed Pansy Bellefini after she discovered the body of a child who'd been missing since 1953." Pansy sat up straighter to watch. "When asked if she thought that her recent brush with death only a few months prior had brought her closer to the spirits of the dead, she had this to say,"

"Oh sure, absolutely," the on-screen Pansy was nodding. The real-time Pansy stood up so quickly that she knocked the plastic folding chair over.

"He asked me if I enjoyed investigating with the PPS, not if I communed with the freaking dead. What a liar!"

"Do you think the PPS helps people?" the newsman continued.

"In a lot of cases the help people need is really with their electric or plumbing, or sometimes wild animals, and we have an expert in each in our group, so yes, I think we help a lot of people." This was followed by a clip of one of the hallways where moaning sounds could be heard and the news anchor making a quip about what kind of wild animal might be making that sound.

"Holy crap, I look like a crazy person."

I gave her some side-eye and she started to sit back down before remembering that her chair had gone flying. Turning it upright, she brought it back to the table and slumped down into it with a sigh. "No wonder everyone was avoiding me today. I am now trash. Crazy, ghost-talking, trash." She laid one arm on the table and buried her face in the crook.

Summer patted her on the shoulder and looked like she was trying to make a decision. "Pansy, can I show you something? On the tapes from the castle?"

"Sure," Pansy mumbled from the depths of her elbow.

Summer walked to the end of the table and picked up a different VHS and traded out the tapes. She fast-forwarded, rewound a bit, and then hit play.

"She says the ghost's name is Jessica and she was a nurse here at the Sanitarium."

Pansy's head popped up and my mouth fell open. It was one of the tapes from the basement. Apparently , it had already been recording while we were talking with Jessica.

On the video, you could barely see Pansy's elbow and neither Jessica nor I showed up, but the audio portion was going to be hard to explain. The elbow disappeared. "So, she died of the flu in 1919 and has been here taking care of her patients ever since."

The elbow comes back into frame and then she asks, "Is she the only one here besides the ghosts that you said were on some kind of loop?"

The elbow disappears, "Gerri says, 'yes.'"

Summer hit pause and turned to Pansy. "I didn't flag this part as a clip to be shown to the whole group, but I wanted to ask you about it. What am I watching here, Pansy? Did you, I don't know, have a stroke and Bagel is playing along, or is there something you'd like to tell me?"

"Can I choose option number 3 and run away to hide for the rest of my life?"

"You can, but I'd rather know what I'm seeing here. Because it looks to me like you're talking to Gerri, and then relaying the information back to Bagel, who is fully aware that you're having this conversation and is totally cool with it."

Pannsy sighed and put the tape of the news recording back in her backpack, zipping it up as slowly as she could.

"Tell her," I urged. "It's Summer. If our parents can handle it, she'll be no problem."

After a moment of silence, she looked at me and muttered, "Fine." Summer looked back and forth between Pansy and my general location twice, her eyes wide.

Pansy sighed deflating in her seat before turning to face Summer. "What if I told you that she came back, okay? Gerri. Three days after she died, she showed up in our bedroom again."

"Actually, I showed up at the bridge and then went home from there."

Pansy rolled her eyes. "She wants me to clarify that she showed up at the bridge where she died and then went home from there. That's just where I first saw her, again."

"So, you think that she's here, like, right here, beside me?" Summer had a mildly panicked tone to her voice.

"She's actually kinda there at the end of the table," Pansy pointed at me and I waved. It was awkward. For a moment or two, the only sound was the ticking of the second hand on the clock above the doorway.

Summer reached for the chair next to Pansy's and slowly sank down to sit facing her. She drew a deep breath and let it out slowly. "Okay. I mean, I asked. I should have been prepared for the answer. Right?"

Pansy looked at me and I shook my head, this seemed to be a rhetorical question probably best not to answer her.

"So, you said she came back three days later, that would mean she's been with you the entire time that you've been with us doing these paranormal investigations." Pansy nodded. "And I would assume that she went with you on at least some of those investigations?"

"All of them."

"And we never saw her."

"She goes to the meetings, too, sometimes. As far as we know, I'm the only one that can see or hear her. Bagel can feel her. Chandra can too, but she doesn't know what it is yet. When Gerri touches them they feel a coldness."

Summer was quiet for a minute and Pansy fidgeted in her seat waiting for the next round of questions.

"On the video, you said Gerri was talking to another ghost, right? So there are more ghosts out there?"

"There are, but not many, and Gerri is the only one I can see or hear. She can talk to the others, but up until the Chivington Investigation, Gerri had only met two other ghosts. Do you remember the first investigation that we went on with you guys? The McAllister's house?"

I saw Summer mouth the word, 'we' and blink a few more

times. Then she shook her head and thought about the question, "Mom, son, and daughter, house out on Briarwood Lane? We found a few unexplained orbs on the videos for that one. Was it haunted?"

"No, there weren't any ghosts but Gerri staked it out to find out what was really happening. One night she sees their dad taking the ladder they kept behind the garage and using it to crawl through the attic vent. Apparently, he liked to get drunk and then go try to scare the kids so they'd think the house was haunted. We figured out that his goal was to get the kids so scared of their own house that they'd want to live with him, which is just as screwed up as it sounds. I lied and told Kaitlyn that I saw his truck parked along the road down from their house and thought it was weird. And then I, like, casually mentioned that I'd also noticed some weird marks on the ground under the attic vent that I absolutely never saw, and suggested that she may want to mention it to her Mom. Apparently, she did because her mom set a bear trap in the leaves behind the garage and caught him."

"Omigosh, I saw him in a cast at the grocery store and wondered what had happened. That's crazy!"

"That wasn't really the response we were going for, we thought maybe she'd just move the ladder into the garage, but..." Pansy shrugged. I smiled at the memory, that had been an exciting night at the Police Station.

"Wait, were any of the places we investigated actually haunted then?" She seemed kind of heartbroken and when I considered the sheer amount of time and effort each investigation took for all of them, I could see where this would be really disappointing to find out you were wasting your time.

"Well, the Garcia house down on Sepulveda was haunted by the ghost of Christopher Fairchild. He was killed there but was never brave enough to leave the house. But, he's the one that told Gerri about the men that were trying to scare Old Mrs. Garcia into selling her house so they could get their mining permit."

"I remember that you found that box under the bed."

"Christopher saw them put it there and told Gerri. She told me. It's like a really complicated game of telephone every time we meet another ghost."

"So the whole story about you looking for your lost kite and then you just happened to stumble onto an illegal mine…"

"A lie."

Summer nodded. "I wondered why you would be flying a kite down there when there are at least twenty other places closer to your house if you wanted to fly a kite."

"I haven't owned a kite since I was eight years old."

Summer paused, still taking it all in. "You said you knew two ghosts, who is the other one?"

"His name was Lee Bradley and he used to be an investigative reporter with the Perth Gazette back before it went out of business. He mostly hangs out at the Police Station. Lee died in —what was it, Gerri?"

"1983."

"1983, do you remember him?"

"No, I've only lived here for a few years."

"Well, like I said, he used to be a reporter and he enjoys snooping so he helped us a lot. He volunteered to watch those real estate guys while they were in their motel rooms and read through the files he could see. Lee really enjoyed reading their emails over their shoulders."

Summer looked a little concerned and Pansy rushed to assure her. "I don't want it to sound like they're running around putting their nose in everyone's business, but we already knew those guys were shady, but we didn't understand the goal of their shadiness."

I rolled my eyes, that almost made sense, right?

"But... that's it? All of those investigations and only one of them had a real ghost?"

"They seem to be rare. And Christopher's ghost is gone, now."

"What do you mean, gone? Where did he go?"

"Well, that's the million-dollar question. When I was running from the security guy, Christopher showed Gerri where the path down to what he called his 'cave' was. She followed him and then I followed her. When the guy found us and aimed his gun at me, apparently Christopher shoved him off the ledge." Summer looked startled and Pansy explained. "The older ghosts can touch and move things, Gerri can't do that yet. Anyway, when I turned the flashlight on and found Christopher's body, Gerri said he just went, poof." She made explosion motions with her fingers. "She said his ghost got really bright, like a flash of light, and then he disappeared. I didn't see anything at all, so I can't really tell you more than that."

We were back to listening to the second hand make its way around the clock face as Summer processed all of this. "This is incredible," she finally muttered.

"You're not going to tell anyone else, are you?" Pansy asked. "Everyone already thinks I'm a freak, I can't handle more right now."

"No. No, of course not."

"But you believe me? When we told our family we had them pull cards out of a deck and then Gerri read them over their shoulders so that they believed me."

"There is more to heaven and earth, Horatio, than is thought of in your philosophy," Summer muttered, more to herself than anyone else. She reached out and held Pansy's hand and looked her in the eye. "I absolutely believe you. You finding those real estate guys, and that boy's body, it all seemed like a crazy coincidence. Having Gerri with you is really the only way any of it makes sense. Now, tell me everything you actually know about Chivington and the ghosts there. The curiosity is killing me and you can't hold out on all the juicy bits."

Pansy laughed, and I was happy to see that having someone accept her for the freak she was, especially someone she looked up to like Summer, made a big difference.

5

On Tuesday evenings, Summer's yoga classes ran every hour and a half until eight o'clock, so Pansy and Bagel had agreed to meet at the library. Pans had packed Blake's summary report about the history of the Castle in her bookbag that morning and we were hoping to fill in the finer details by looking through the books I'd found the day before. We wouldn't be allowed to check those books out, but she'd also packed plenty of nickels to make copies of any pertinent info.

They were both flipping through some of my preselected options when a movement by the front desk caught my attention. Turning, I saw Lee floating through the front door, his brown robe open and floating behind him. If I squinted, I could sort of imagine it as a trench coat and him as Humphrey Bogart, but only if I squinted really hard. Unfortunately, even squinting did nothing to hide the coffee stain that spilled down the front of his blue and white striped pajamas. Every time I saw him I was happy that I hadn't dropped food all over me the night I'd died. Fear of embarrassment was going around, it seemed.

"Lee, I've been looking for you for days! Where have you been?"

"Lee's here," Pansy told Bagel.

"Finally," Bagel said.

Lee floated over before responding, even in death he'd never shout in a library.

"Dude, where have you been? Saturday night's investigation is a story you're going to want to hear."

"Sorry. If I'd known it was going to take me so long to find the body I would have told you where I was going beforehand."

"Ex-squeeze me? You were finding a body? What body? A body belonging to whom?"

"What body?" Pansy perked up from the book she was reading.

"What what?" Bagel looked at her. I swear we needed to invent a ouija board with a party line.

"Geez, Kid, give me a second to finish the story. So, about a decade ago, I found a body out on the eastern slope but, for obvious reasons, I couldn't do anything about it. Now that the snow is melting off, I thought it would be a good time to go find it, again. Since you have a link to the living," he gestured to Pansy, who was staring a hole through me waiting to be filled in on what was going on. "I figured that your crew here could go and I don't know, discover it, or something. Get the local authorities involved to help find out who it is. Who knows how long they'd been out there before I found them the first time."

"Oh, well that sounds doable. It's not like, in a canyon we can't access unless we're in a helicopter or anything, right?"

"No, it's right off the regular trail, about a hundred yards down a deer path towards the creek."

I nodded and turned back to the two breathing members of our party. "Okay, so Lee said he found a body out on the eastern slope a long time ago and wants to know if you guys can go and like, 'discover' it for the local authorities so they can get an investigation going and figure out who it is."

"Oh, wow. Of course. We'd be more than happy to go discover," she made air quotes," a body in the woods. I bet that poor person's family will love to know what happened to them."

"Gnarly," Bagel whispered.

"You're good kids," Lee said as Pansy relayed the mission to Bagel. "Sorry I was gone for so long, I couldn't remember where I'd found it and there isn't a whole lot left."

"I hope it's enough to identify them."

"They had a bag with them, it's still there, just rolled a little further down the slope. My hope is that it contains some kind of identification."

"Okay, how far away is it and can we do it this Sunday? We've got a PPS meeting on Saturday that we can't miss. We're going over all of the crazy from Saturday's investigation."

"Saturday was your investigation at the Chivington Sanitorium, right? Is that crazy nurse ghost still there?"

"Uh, yeah man, she is. Thanks for the heads up, by the way. So what? Do you already know about the evil thing that sucks people's souls, too?"

"Does that jerk already know about it and didn't say anything?" Pansy said, slamming closed the book she'd been flipping through. "Are we wasting our time?"

Lee held both hands up in surrender, although Pansy couldn't even see him. "I only know about the nurse. I visited once or twice but the whole place is... unsettling, so I avoid it."

"He said it gives him the creeps and he's as clueless as we are."

"That's not exactly what I ..."

"Close enough," I said, cutting off his protest. "Look, we talked to Jessica and she wants us to help her figure out how to get rid of this thing before it hurts someone else. The owner really wanted his hotel to be haunted, but I feel like he's leaning more towards flickering-lights-and-creaking-doors, and not sucking-out-the-guests'-souls end of the spectrum."

"I've never heard of such a thing. Outside of Hollywood, of course. Did it move things while you were there?"

"Dude, it rocked the casbah."

His confused look reminded me that while he'd been alive in the early eighties, he was strictly a country music kind of guy. References to The Clash weren't going to get me anywhere. "It was crazy. Once Jessica started knocking stuff over and making things move, this other thing joined in and started trashing the place. It made lights explode, threw things across the room, groaning noises, the whole nine yards."

"I'm assuming that your ghost-hunting group caught all of that on tape?" He sighed, shaking his head. "That's only going to attract the lunatics."

"I mean, yeah. That's the whole point. Owner Dude wants people to think that it's haunted because he says that people will want to stay in a haunted hotel. It will appeal to a certain sector of the population."

"Yeah, the lunatics," Lee grumbled.

"You were a journalist, you should know that everyone wants to see things like that with their own eyes. They want to prove or disprove it themselves, but no one is going to sign up to be sacrificed to this thing. At least, not knowingly. And it wasn't just the PPS that caught it on tape, Owner Dude called in the local news too. They caught everything. Well, I mean, except for the lights exploding, but Cameraman Mike put a new battery in and caught everything else after that."

"So, what have you learned about it?"

"Umm, absolutely nothing. We're calling it a poltergeist

because we don't know what else to call it. And we have no idea what to do to get rid of it."

"Sounds like you're making great progress."

"We were planning on starting at the beginning, finding out more about the history of the property and then looking for any records about patients to see who would have been a big enough "bad guy" to leave this kind of energy behind when they passed."

"Good grief, kid, are you planning to go through the history of every patient that ever stayed there? First of all, good luck finding those kinds of records, and second, even if those records survived the last hundred years, those two don't have the life span to locate and then go through all of them. Besides, just because this entity is there now doesn't mean that it died there, it could have come from anywhere."

"Well, then what's your plan?"

"I don't have one as of yet, but step one would be to go check it out for myself. Do you want to come with me?"

"Now?"

"There's no time like the present."

"Pans, do you mind if Lee and I go take a look through the hotel?"

She didn't look up from the book she was flipping through. "Right now? It's pouring rain."

I stared at her and it took her a full second to process what she'd said and look up from her book."Uh, yeah. Go ahead, then. It's not like I can assign you to microfiche or something."

"Ha. Ha. Ha." It was true, there was nothing to make you feel more useless than being dead.

As we started out of the library, my first instinct was to ask Lee if he wanted to go home and get some rest before starting out on a new adventure. He'd just returned home from a long trip, after all. But that was how living people thought. We had no need to, or even a way to, rest. We didn't need to shower, eat a good meal, or relax in front of the boob tube to reset our brains. We didn't even have to make phone calls to check in with our friends and family and let them know we were home safe. Lee had no one to check in with except for me, and as I left the library, I couldn't help imagining a future where my family got old and died, leaving me all alone.

We started the journey west, floating at speeds much faster than a car could travel, especially in the rain. We flew as the crow flew, unconfined by the winding roads. In no time at all we were crossing the sweeping front lawn of the hotel.

As we paused by the fountain, a crack of lightning split the gloom and made me jump. Lee chuckled, looking up at the impressive stonework. "Well, if any place looks haunted, this place wins. I remember now why I never made it past the lobby."

"Chicken. Wait until you see the basement."

I was pretty sure he muttered, "great," under his breath as we crossed into the foyer. The construction workers were wrapping up for the day so the lights were still on. That worked out for us because with the rain, the floor-to-ceiling windows weren't illuminating anything.

"Jessica! Are you here?" I yelled as loud as possible, hoping she'd be somewhere nearby. Apparently, she wasn't.

Shrugging, I pointed down and Lee nodded, following me straight through the marble tiles and into the basement level to begin our search for clues. The lights were on and there were two guys throwing all of the old, rotting furniture and moldy junk into a rolling bin. They must have been at it all day because they'd managed to clear one corner, but the bin filled quickly. It wasn't long before they were wrestling the oversized garbage can up the stairs.

I looked behind me to see Lee examining a wall full of graffiti. "Veritable poets, weren't they?" he asked, pointing at the badly spelled scribblings someone had made with a Sharpie on the stone wall.

"And wannabe Satan worshippers, or something," I said, pointing out the multiple variations of pentagrams spray-painted on all four walls. Some were better than others and a few were surrounded by strange symbols. I figured the artist's attempts at mystical runes were probably as misspelled as the rest of the graffiti.

"Jessica!" I yelled again. If Jessica ever came to my house, a thought that made me uneasy, I'd at least want her to announce herself before barging in. It was hard to be polite when you can't call first or ring a doorbell. Lee was already moving on, floating straight up through the ceiling while I was still trying to decipher spray painted cuss words.

"Lee, where'd you go?" I had no intention of running around all evening shouting for ghosts.

"Up here," it sounded like he was in the lobby. "Come take a look at this."

Not having to walk up and down stairs was definitely in my pro column. I found him in the back corner of the massive room where the ghost of the old woman was rocking and knitting. Or crocheting, or whatever it was she thought she was doing.

"Do you think that she believes that she's making progress?" he asked, fascinated with the behavior.

"I don't think she thinks about anything. That's the problem. Not her, or the old man going up the stairs, or the other old man who wanders around on the top floor, or the old woman on the fourth floor pacing in her room, none of them have any idea... well, that's just it, isn't it? They don't have ideas. They don't think. I know that our current goal is to get rid of the poltergeist, but do you think if we can talk to an exorcist or something, we can help these people too?"

"And do you know any exorcists?" Lee asked.

"Well, no, but I feel really bad for these people. How can they enjoy their afterlife if they don't even know they're here."

"I don't know. I've never actually seen anything like this before. Although, I make a point of not hanging out in places with this much death attached to them. Maybe all places like this have these kinds of spirits inside."

I'd been examining some purple wax spilled on the tile next to a charred spot on the wall, but looked over at Lee. "Have you never been to the hospital in Trinidad? I haven't gone there myself, but it's on my list of places to visit and check for ghosts."

"Oh, there are ghosts there. Diane, my wife, died there." He paused, looking around the room and for a second I thought he was going to leave it at that. "She spent several months dying there, and if I had never stepped foot inside again it would have suited me just fine. After I came back... I had to go look, you know, just in case. When I arrived there were three other ghosts hanging around the nurses' station, but none of them had ever heard of her."

"And you never went back? You never got lonely?"

"No, I had no good memories of that place. I turned around and came back to Perth where it was nice and quiet. Familiar. Besides, I like being alone. Christopher never left his house and Thomas doesn't come into town very often. Even when he does, he's not exactly chatty."

"Who the heck is Thomas?" I had a vague recollection of Christopher mentioning the boy once, but I'd been distracted with something else and had promptly forgotten about it.

"An Arapahoe kid. Not very talkative, stays in the woods most of the time. I figured I'd introduce you next time he came through, but I haven't seen him in months."

I gave him some serious side-eye and was about to ask how

many other ghosts he knew about when a shout echoed across the lobby behind us, followed by the sound of breaking glass.

"Call 911!" one of the workers yelled to another as he rushed out the front door. A ladder was leaning over, the top wedged in the frame of one of the floor-to-ceiling windows, and I could see boots sticking out of the overgrown shrubbery outside.

"Does anyone have a cellular phone?" The worker's question was met with several hardhats shaking a negative and since the front desk where phones would eventually be installed still didn't exist yet, there wasn't a landline in the building.

"I'll run over to the carriage house and call from there," one man volunteered.

"Please," the first worker said from the broken window. "The shrubbery seems to have broken his fall, just a few little nicks from the glass, but he seems groggy. He might have a concussion." The volunteer ran through the doorway that led to the west wing which exited closest to the small carriage house behind the hotel. Lee and I watched as the man who seemed to be in charge of this work crew hauled his comrade from the evergreens and carried him back inside out of the rain.

"Did it fall on him?" I asked, looking at the overhead wires dangling from the ceiling. It looked like the man had been trying to install a heavy light fixture that was now spread in a few hundred pieces across the tile.

"It's possible," he looked over the mess on the floor but I noticed something else catch his attention. "Ah, I believe that would be your nurse friend, Jessica." he pointed towards the other end of the room where Jessica was indeed floating across construction debris towards us.I looked from her to the man outside in the rain, shaking glass from his overalls, my suspicious mind working overtime.

I hadn't seen her do anything, but I also hadn't been looking at the ceiling. I read an article once that stated that there were two things that humans will never instinctively do unless they've been taught specifically to do it. The first was that they will never gouge out another person's eyes (even though it's a very effective method of stopping an attacker) because the thought of it is so terrible that even in mortal peril, people won't do it. The second was that they never look upward when searching for danger. Danger comes from below, behind, from the side, but we never look up. I made a mental note to start looking up.

6

"Jessica," I said, moving towards her, "looks like you're having an exciting time."

"Yes, I am afraid that after so many years with no one to feed on, the Other has been glutting himself on these workers."

"Workers, plural?" I asked. "So, this isn't the first accident?"

The woman even snorted delicately. It was irritating how prim and precise she was. "Hardly. One would think they would understand the danger by now, yet they persist."

"Well, they don't get paid until the job is over, so they're probably just trying to finish and get out as fast as they can. How many other accidents have there been?"

"Well," she tilted her head to one side while she took count. "Yesterday, a man fell down the stairs and nearly broke his neck. He was rushed by ambulance to a hospital. Then earlier this morning, another man collapsed while using an electric sawing machine. His friends indicated that they were going to take him to a nearby clinic."

"Nurse, uh...?"

I turned to see Lee was done inspecting the wiring and was floating over to join the conversation.

"Daniels."

"Ah, Nurse Daniels, it's nice to see you again. My name is Lee Bradley. I used to be a reporter for the Perth Gazette, and Gerri's been filling me in on your situation here." It had never occurred to me that my new ghost friend may want to be called by her actual title. I guess I thought that being dead automatically put you beyond such formalities, but here was another example of something I could learn from Lee.

"Yes, I recall meeting you once many years ago, Mr. Bradley. Will you be assisting our young friend, then?"

"That is my hope. Gerri and I have worked together on a previous case, and she's asked me to help subdue this entity. If you don't mind, I have a few questions."

"I would certainly appreciate any help you can provide. As you can see," she swept one hand to the broken window, "the *entity*, as you say, hovers near a living person and seems to draw their life's energy from them. It makes them quite weak."

"That's very interesting. I've never seen anything like it. This entity, have you ever heard it speak or use words?" I watched Lee, waiting for him to pat his front pocket, looking for the notebook that no longer existed. I'd seen him in reporter mode enough to know it was coming.

She remained still, hands clasped in front of her like she was awaiting orders, but I could tell she was flipping through her mental files. "No, not to my knowledge."

"But you've seen it?"

"In a manner of speaking. It is not like us, or even like the lesser entities in residence here. The shape is vaguely human, but it isn't solid, like we are. It seems to consist only of energy."

"And the living can't see it?"

"No, not that I have ever witnessed."

"And where is it now? Would I be able to see it?"

"Now? Oh, I do not know," she scanned the room. "He pulled the energy from that man installing the light, causing him to fall. But is he still here? He is constantly moving about the building in search of unsuspecting prey and is never in one place for long."

"Interesting." There it was, the pocket pat in search of a notebook that wasn't there. I watched him shake his head, remembering he was dead, but he didn't miss a beat with the questions. "And how often would you say that you see it, say, on average, for a typical week?"

"Oh, I hardly ever see it. Really, it stays hidden most of the time. When there were people here and, well, I hate to sound crass, but when it could feed regularly, it only made its presence known every few weeks. But he has gone hungry for years and I am afraid he has built up quite the appetite."

I watched four men carry large sheets of plywood into the lobby. Together, they began covering the broken window, blocking the cold and rain.

"Gerri tells me you succumbed to the flu in 1919? Was this entity active when you were still a nurse here?"

"There were several unexplained deaths in the months leading up to my death. Patients who were fully on the mend one day would be found dead in their beds the next. As I said, the living do not seem able to see him, so I can not say for certain that he was the cause."

"And you say that it hovers over a living person and removes what? The electrical impulses from the body? Do I have that right? Wouldn't a lightbulb be easier?"

She looked offended. "For what reason would I know why it does what it does?

"It sounds more like a vampire than a ghost," Lee muttered.

"That's what I said. Please tell me that vampires aren't real." I wasn't ready for that.

"Don't be impertinent, child. Of course, there are no such things as vampires."

Impertinent. Pardon me, a ghost having a conversation with two other ghosts about magical creatures that couldn't possibly exist. Whatever, man.

Lee seemed to agree with her. "It's highly unlikely, Kiddo. We don't need to contact Buffy just yet." I was surprised that he knew the movie, but I didn't want to interrupt his process to ask him when and where he'd watched it.

"Nurse Daniels, one more question, if you don't mind. Actually, sorry, I have two. First, if there were any kinds of records kept for the sanitarium, do you know where they would have been moved to? And second, do you happen to know where the current owner lives?"

"I am almost certain that all of the original records were burned when the sanitarium was sold. Patient information should be a private matter, after all. As to your second question, that rude little man and his harridan of a wife have moved into the carriage house." She pointed towards the back of the building.

"Well, that will make snooping through their things just that much easier, won't it? Come along Gerri, I doubt we'll find anything interesting in this building."

Wide-eyed, I followed Lee through the back wall of the lobby and across the weed-infested patio that stretched between the two wings. There were still several rose bushes struggling to grow in the stacked stone beds, but both the beds and the walkways were crumbling and there was nothing inviting about the space. It was certainly on theme for the rest of the property.

"Why are we snooping through the owner's stuff?"

"The question is, why wouldn't we snoop through the owner's stuff? We're already here. Why not take a peek and look for anything suspicious?"

"Anything suspicious? Nothing vague about that. I hope they left all of their important clues laying out in the open." Lee could flick a light switch and move papers around, but rifling through filing cabinets or drawers would be an incredible and constant use of energy.

"We'll see what we can see. Again, we're already here. What's it going to hurt?"

"Uh, it's not polite?" I looked behind me to see if Jessica was coming with us, but she'd apparently stayed to oversee the cleanup of the glass in the lobby.

"Polite? We're dead. Who's going to tell him?" Lee's very loose system of morals was probably what had made him such a good reporter back in his day.

The carriage house was easy to locate since it was still intact and there was a humongous black Chevy Suburban parked in front. The stone building squatted next to what had probably been the stables, which had, at some point, been converted into a dilapidated row of six separate garages. There was zero chance the Suburban would have fit inside any of them. I made a mental note to ask Pansy if Blake's report had mentioned any activity inside the carriage house.

Instead of using the front door, we entered through the side wall of the building, floating straight into a bedroom. This was why I usually only enter buildings by the front door so that I could avoid walking in on someone undressing. If I was stuck in this state of in-between for eternity, there were certain things that I absolutely did not need stored in my memory.

The bedroom appeared to be a spare as there were no knick-knacks or clothes to be seen in the open door of the closet, just random boxes stacked inside and a few smaller boxes across the top of the dresser. The bed frame and mattresses were leaned against a wall and a rocking chair was wedged between the mattress and the dresser, two side tables and what looked like a set of plant stands randomly shoved into the room. I guess they'd moved from a larger place and only had room for so much. The honey oak hardwood floors ran into the hallway and as we floated further into the house, I could see that they'd been laid throughout. All the walls were painted the same shade of ecru. It was a study in oatmeal.

"Uh huh, I see." I heard a woman's voice coming from what had to be the owner's bedroom. Curious, I floated in to see who she was talking to. The woman was suited up in a Day-Glo pink and purple track suit, the nylon rustling with her every move-ment. She was putting away laundry while chatting on a cord-less phone she had wedged between her ear and shoulder. This bedroom was no larger than the spare and was crowded with a full-sized bed and two nightstands against one wall, a highboy and a dresser with a large attached mirror on the other. Even the comforter was beige.

The woman slammed a drawer shut, making the mirror sway with the force. "Okay, but this is my third call today. If you don't know, then I need you to connect me to someone there that can give me some answers." Holding the phone with one hand, she straightened up with one hand pressed against the small of her back and stretched. Leaning her head from side to side, her lacquered helmet of ash blond never moved. She had to be twenty years younger than Mr. Browning, I thought. Maybe she's his daughter? As Lee and I watched, she went back to the bed where clothes had been sorted into stacks and picked up another pile of folded nylon before stuffing it into a different drawer. Maybe she was a housekeeper?

"I understand that the future isn't clear, but you'd think for the money I've spent on your Psychic Friends Network over the course of the last two months, I could be put in touch with Dionne Warwick herself. My husband insisted on this move and I need someone to tell me when we're getting out of this backwoods money pit and back to Miami where the people with taste live. I need to be back in civilization. Are you listening to me? The people here wear flannel for god's sake. I can't take this anymore, I need to know when!" Her voice was going up a few notes with every word until she was screeching by the end, loud enough that Lee also had to come and see what was going on.

"Is this the wife?" he asked. I nodded. "Who's she talking to?"

"I think it's one of those psychic lines that they advertise at two in the morning on the public access channel."

"It sounds like she's not happy with her current living arrangements," Lee observed.

She continued to put away clothes, the nylon swishing with every motion. At the rate she was going, she'd create enough static electricity to light the hotel all by herself. When she was done putting away the clothes, she stormed into the kitchen, phone still firmly clamped to her shoulder by her cheek. I heard the dishes rattle as she yanked open the door to the dishwasher. Apparently, she liked to rage clean while she talked on the phone.

Their living room was spotless. I tried to remember the last time the coffee table at our house had been completely clear and it was probably...no, even at holidays there was at least a bowl of nuts or hard candy, even when it didn't hold homework, college brochures, library books and Blockbuster VHS cases. The kitchen was also gleaming, and also beige. So much beige. Lee and I progressed to the dining room where, finally, we hit the jackpot. Since the six-room house was too small to have an office, it looked like Mr. Browning had taken over the dining room. Papers were stacked a foot and a half high on the table. Folders, journals, loose leaf, stacks and stacks, on every surface. There was only one chair that didn't have something stacked on it, and the space on the table in front of it was taken up by a huge desk calendar and a PowerBook. As I floated closer, I saw what looked to be construction notes scribbled into the calendar boxes, as well as phone numbers for subcontractors and vendors for their hotel construction.

"Well, this must make family dinners a little more difficult," Lee said.

"This is absolutely how I imagine you used to work."

"I had a real desk, I'll have you know. But yeah, I guess I wasn't the tidiest."

"I'm shocked. So, what are we looking for, exactly?"

"Anything suspicious."

"Sure, boss." Being unable to move anything, I could only skim over the top layer of the paper detritus. Still, it didn't take me long before I had a winner. "Hey, Lee, come look." Stacked on one chair was a book about seances and communicating with the dead.

"Interesting."

"Do you think they're trying to call the ghosts or get rid of them?"

"Maybe they were studying up before the investigation? Trying to see what they thought your friends were going to be doing?"

"I guess, but we've been in the paper enough that they should know we only document hauntings, not invite the ghosts over for tea." I eyed the rest of the stack. Every book was about ghosts, demons, or summoning spirits. "Get a load of these titles. Ghost Hunting for Dummies, and here's one called Demons, Devils, and Things That Go Bump in the Night by someone named M. S. Winchester." Nothing like a little light reading. "As for 'something suspicious,' other than their penchant for beige, this is the only thing I see that I'd call weird."

"Keep looking and quit whining. It's not like I've pulled you away from a hair appointment or anything. What else did you have to do?"

"I could be helping Pansy and Bagel do research."

"By reading over their shoulders? They're seniors in high school. Surely they can read their own books."

"Thanks for the reminder that I'm no help."

"You're helpful, just not in a conventional way. You haven't fully grown into you new skill set yet." He was moving through a stack of papers on the table. "Like now, this would fall within your realm of expertise. I've heard of MTV, but what is The Real World?"

"Uh, it's a reality show where they put strangers in a house and make them live together while they film them."

Lee paused, and I had a feeling he was waiting on the punch line. I shrugged. He shook his head. "I don't know if I should feel sorry for the people being filmed or the people who have to watch it."

"It's actually a really popular show. Why do you ask?"

"They have a sticky note here with an address for the production company. I thought it was more 'weirdness', as you call it."

I thought about it for a minute. "I wonder if he's pitching the idea of having a show set here at the Castle? If it was haunted and people were here all the time being filmed, a lot of people would watch that."

"And if a lot of people watch it, then that will make it a

popular destination for tourists. Have you ever watched that Kubrick movie, *The Shining*?"

I snorted, since that was the exact movie I'd thought of on my first night here. "Yeah, about thirty times."

"Then I'm sure you know they based that movie on The Stanley Hotel up in Estes Park. I did a piece on it not long after the movie was released. So many people wanted to stay in a haunted hotel that they were booked solid for the next year."

"So, he's not as dumb as he looks, is what you're saying?"

"Well, I haven't seen him, but I'd say it's a safe bet. If he could get this haunted hotel on television, it would be free advertising. He could probably charge them to film here and still get his hotel's name out nationwide."

I thought about *The Real World*; it was considered must watch TV amongst the high school crowd, every episode to be dissected in detail over lunch trays in the cafeteria the next day after airing. I was sure our small selection of teenagers wasn't an anomaly. If he could get the hotel livable, and then get MTV involved, well, the idea had potential. "I guess that means we need to get rid of the soul-sucking poltergeist before it kills off the cast and crew of an entire television show, then."

"That could be a tall order," Lee muttered, but nodded in agreement.

I heard the crunching of tires on gravel and for a moment I wondered if the ambulance had somehow missed the front entrance of the hotel and driven around to the back where the carriage house was located. I was floating toward the front door when it was flung open. A man stepped through the doorway and quickly closed it behind him, his rain soaked hair plastered to his forehead.

"How long?" he asked, taking his shoes off by the door.

"We have an hour and a half," said the wife seconds before she flung herself into his arms and began kissing him with what I can only describe as fervor. The nylon track suit added some interesting sound effects to their groping.

"Browning, I presume," Lee said.

"You would presume wrong. That, my friend, is the business partner."

7

While I had no desire to watch whatever craziness was about to happen in the carriage house, Lee volunteered to stay and observe for a few days. I didn't want to know how close he'd be observing, but I made him promise to meet us at The Buffalo Chip on Saturday night and if anything earth shattering happened in the meantime, he'd come tell me. The PPS met every other Saturday evening in the back room of the restaurant to review the recordings from the week before and to discuss upcoming investigations. Since Lee had missed out on all the fun, I thought he'd enjoy watching the tapes.

Pansy and Bagel spent Wednesday evening with Summer watching videos and marking obvious clips of ghost activity, but Thursday was officially declared a night off from investigating. Mom stopped at Foodarama on her way home from work to pick up a birthday cake and ice cream to celebrate our eighteenth birthday. We had a family party at home and our older brother, Robbie, made it home from his last class at UNC about five minutes before the pizza dude arrived. Pansy made a big show of scooping up one of the giant icing roses we used to fight over, staring me straight in the eye as popped the whole thing into her mouth, staining her lips purple.

"Pansy, stop teasing your sister," Dad told her between scooping out ice cream into bowls. While Pansy blew out our birthday candles by herself for the first time in our lives, I was ashamed to admit that I was jealous.

She was stealing a second rose when Dad stood up. "Okay, I can't stand waiting anymore. It's time for your gift. And we got something for both of you." He looked around the table, trying to include me without really knowing where to look. Pansy motioned to where I was floating next to her and Dad tried to direct his conversation my way. "Of course, Pansy will really have to do the work here, but we thought this was something that both you and your sister will enjoy."

It had been quite a few years since we'd wanted a pony, so I was excited to see what this mysterious gift was. Dad disappeared through the door in the kitchen that led to the garage and came back lugging a large wrapped box he must have been hiding in the back of his Silverado. I hadn't thought to look there when I'd been snooping earlier in the week. He set the box on the kitchen counter with a thud and stood back, grinning. Mom was practically vibrating and looked like she was three seconds from offering to help Pansy unwrap it.

Reaching out to get a good grip on the top of the box, Pansy pulled a piece of pink and purple birthday themed wrapping paper straight down the side of the box, revealing the Dell computer logo. We both gasped at the same time. A computer of our own? Like, for real?

"Oh my gosh, are you kidding me? Wait, this isn't a prank where the box is for one thing and then there's something else inside, is it?" Pansy asked.

"No," Mom assured her. "It's really a computer. And that's

not all! We also have a CD for AOL, so you'll be able to get onto the internet."

I thought Pansy was going to pass out. I was feeling a bit faint myself.

"But there are rules," Dad interjected.

"Exactly. If you're on the internet and either of us needs to make a phone call, we expect you to get off of it, immediately. No whining."

"Yes, absolutely, whatever you want. This is so amazing. I can't even process it. I think Gerri is hyperventilating, too."

"We know it's been a tough few months, and we wanted something that you could use together," Dad said, placing his arm around Mom's shoulders and giving her a squeeze.

"Well, let me go ahead and put an order in for my birthday, too," Robbie said.

"We can probably arrange that," Dad assured him with a clap on the shoulder.

Tired of Pansy standing there staring at the box, Robbie stepped forward and began tearing the rest of the wrapping paper.

Startled from the daze she'd been in, Pansy slapped his hands away from the box. "I've got it, move!"

Pansy had the rest of the wrapping paper on the kitchen floor and the top of the cardboard box torn open in no time. She was pulling the monitor out of its protective foam sheeting, fighting the static cling when Mom stopped her.

"You know what? Before you drag all of that out, why don't you have your brother carry it upstairs where you can set it up in your room? I'm sure he'll be more help connecting it than we will. Oh, and don't forget this," she opened the kitchen junk drawer and pulled out a splitter for the phone jack and a twenty-five foot spool of phone cable. "This will let you plug one line into your telephone and the other to the computer."

Robbie was so excited that he didn't even complain, lifting the box and jogging up the stairs to our room. Pansy and I had shared a bedroom since birth, and while there were still two of everything: beds, dressers, nightstands, and desks, we had very different ideas on how to decorate our halves. Pansy had gone with purples and framed Monet prints. I'd opted for forest greens and rock posters ripped from magazines. Since I certainly wasn't using it, we finally decided to set the computer up on my old desk. The tower, monitor, keyboard and mouse took up a considerable amount of space and this would leave Pansy's desk clear to do actual homework.

After ten minutes of reading directions and untangling cords and twist ties, we had the world at our fingertips. Robbie loaded up the AOL disk into the CD-ROM drive and after some screeches and squeals from the modem and a few minutes of discussion about what her screen name should be, the software was installed and Pansy had an email account.

"Just think, we never have to go downtown to Connekt again." She said, practically petting the keyboard. This was going to be so much more convenient than the internet cafe. Any time we wanted to look something up, we could do it from the comfort of our own room and it would only take a few minutes. Also, unlike at the computer "lab" at school, which had a grand total of four computers, there wouldn't be an adult watching over our shoulders to see every single thing we searched.

"Wait, I need to log back off so I can call my friends and let them know," Pansy said.

"Don't forget to get their email addresses," I reminded her.

She scooted over to her desk and pulled her sunflower-patterned address book out of a drawer and began making phone calls. By the third call, Robbie had lost interest in the squealing conversations between Pansy and her friends and had gone to take a shower. I wandered downstairs to see what the parents were up to and was heading towards the kitchen when I heard explosions coming from the TV. I detoured to the living room and found the 'rents cuddled up on the couch together, watching an action movie. Each held a glass of wine and they were debating the intelligence of the various movie characters, laughing about what they would each do in the same situation. They seemed happy, or at least able to laugh and interact with one another, which was a huge step forward. It did my heart good to see them acting so normal.

Eventually, Pansy yelled she was ready to log in, and the screech of the connection being made echoed all the way down-stairs. I floated straight up through the floor and avoided going through Pansy with a last-minute twist to the right.

"I really wish you'd use the door, like a normal person."

"Well, I'm neither normal nor a person, so suck it up. What are we going to look up first?"

"Hang on, and I'll show you." She pulled up WebCrawler and typed 'Chivington Sanitarium' into the search bar. "I think we need to gather more information about the Castle. I never dreamed I could do it from our bedroom, though. This is so cool."

"I thought we were going to avoid investigation work tonight?" I asked. Pansy stared at me like I'd lost my mind. "Okay, scoot over a little so I can see the screen."

"There wasn't a lot in the library about the specific people who lived or died at the Castle, just the people who built it and that hundreds and hundreds of people had died there. Unless the original owner has been haunting the place, but I didn't read anything that said he was a bad person or anything."

"If we assume that this Other really exists, I feel like we can assume he was definitely a bad person."

"What do you mean, if it exists?"

"I'm not sure I trust Jessica—she's hiding something. But hey, maybe we'll find something else online about the people who were there or someone famous that died there."

Pansy scrolled through the list of returned links, searching for anything that looked like it may be interesting. One of the first options was "The History of Col. John Chivington," and it looked like someone's history report that was being hosted through a University website. We'd come back to that one later. It may be interesting, but I doubted his ghost haunted a sanitarium that was named after him. There were lots of things in Colorado named after him, so if he was still floating around out there, he had his pick. There was a recent newspaper article from the Chronicle-News about the sale of the property to Mr. Browning and how he planned on turning it into a luxury resort, but there was nothing in it we didn't already know. In fact, it looked like Blake had used the article for a sizable chunk of the research he'd provided to the PPS in the pre-investigation report.

"What are we looking for?" Robbie asked from the doorway. His shoulder-length black hair was still damp, his face was freshly shaven and even in ratty old sweats he was still adorable. It was beyond infuriating. Fresh from the shower and in sweats, Pansy and I would look like drowned rats, but not Robbie. No, he had always been good looking, popular, the center of attention everywhere he went. He was charming in an effortless way that made people trust him, not least of all because he really was a good dude. Also, I had to hand it to him, he'd hardly ever balked at having to drag his little sisters around with him to every concert or event.

"We're looking up this haunted sanitarium that we just investigated."

"If you just investigated it, what's left to look up?" He pulled Pansy's desk chair next to where Pansy was sitting in mine and

Pansy gave him a quick rundown of our investigation. She filled him in on Jessica's request for help, under strict condition that he not breathe a word to Mom and Dad about the poltergeist. Or Other, or whatever was actually haunting the place.

"So, you left this other ghost dude there to snoop around? What do you think he's going to find?" Robbie asked after he'd been briefed.

"Well, we're still not a hundred percent convinced that there really is a poltergeist," Pansy told him. Scrolling further, we saw a link titled CHIVINGTON CASTLE IS HAUNTED and Pansy clicked on that one.

"Tell him about Jessica showing up immediately after that dude fell off the ladder Tuesday evening."

"Gerri said a guy fell off a ladder the other night when she and Lee were there and Jessica claimed the Other did it, but they can't see the Other and she was conveniently close by."

"So, you think maybe she's got multiple personalities or something?"

I mean, I'd thought that she was just lying because she was lonely and bored, but now that he mentioned it.

I shrugged, and Pansy did the same. "That's why Lee is snooping," she told Robbie. "Because we don't know what's really going on. Besides, he seems to enjoy it." She turned back to the computer monitor and snorted. "Well, that's interesting."

The website had finally loaded and a digital banner across the top of the page spelled out "The Seeker" in red letters on a black background. It had some sort of animated effect that looked like blood dripping from the letters in all of their eight-pixel glory. The site looked like it was entirely dedicated to the search for ghosts and paranormal activity. I'd thought the PPS was weird, but they had nothing on whoever was running this thing. Scrolling through the tiny, grainy photos of scanned Polaroids, we saw that each was labeled with a different, supposedly haunted, place that the author had visited, and below each photo was a link to another page that detailed their less than scientific investigations. The stories indicated it was a single person and not a group, and he seemed to favor abandoned places.

"I'm thinking that he only goes to abandoned houses because he's not asking permission to be there," Pansy said, clicking through the different photos.

"Well, he might be a complete amateur, but he has a website," I said.

"I'm going to bookmark this because I think Randy needs to see it. You're right, though, the PPS needs a website, too."

"I didn't realize that there were other groups out here trying to debunk or prove the existence of ghosts," Robbie said, squinting because the red text was really hard to read.

"Oh yeah, Randy and Greg both subscribe to a few monthly magazines about searching for the paranormal, and I know I overheard them talking about a chatroom for investigators."

"Oh, that's what you need. A place to ask questions where no one knows who you are," Robbie said.

"If only I could get that in real life," Pansy mumbled.

"You can," he said, throwing one arm around her and giving her a quick hug. "It's called college. There, you get a fresh start. You take classes with people you've never met, people who've lived different lives in different places and had whole other experiences than yours. No one there knows about the time you picked your nose in kindergarten or that time in third grade when you declared to everyone who would listen that you were going to marry Michael Jackson."

Pansy smacked his arm. "Good grief, don't remind me."

"Exactly, no one knows, so no one will remind you. Like I said, you get a fresh start. Why? What's up? Are the kids at school giving you a hard time?"

"And what if they are? Are you going to beat them up for me?"

"Psshh, you know I'm a lover not a fighter."

"Gag me with a spoon," I quipped from the other side of Pansy.

"You're making us nauseous, just so you know."

"I want it noted that you're evading."

Ignoring him, she turned her attention back to the website and continued scrolling through photos until she came to the one for Chivington Sanitarium. We read through the author's experiences there and had to admit that they seemed very similar to what the PPS had experienced Saturday night. It was when the author mentioned that the batteries in both his camera and flashlight went dead after only an hour of being there that I had an idea. A new experiment.

"Pans, do you think it's a coincidence that the batteries drain in the camera and flashlight for this dude the same way it kept happening to the PPS? Like, is there something about a Duracell that's easier to, I don't know, charge up the energy grid for a ghost than just the regular electricity floating in the ether?"

"I don't know. We have some spare batteries. Do you think they have to be actively conducting electricity to charge you up, or could you just float through some batteries that aren't doing anything?"

"We'd better go with functioning, just to be sure."

"What on earth are you two talking about?" Robbie asked, confused by the part of the conversation he could hear.

Pansy quickly explained before running downstairs for a flashlight and an extra set of "D" batteries. She turned the Maglite on and sat it on the desk, waiting for me to perform a magic trick for which I didn't have directions.

"Do you feel anything different when you're near it?"

"No. If you recall, I spent a month trying to turn this thing on and off when I first came back. I didn't notice anything then and I still don't."

"Okay, let's try this." She grabbed a Number 2 Ticonderoga from her pencil holder and set it on the desk next to the flashlight. "Don't push the switch on the flashlight. That takes a good amount of thumb strength, even for a living person. I want you to hold your hand where the battery is, and let it, I don't know, charge you for a few minutes. Then I want you to move the pencil on the desk."

Holding my hand directly where the battery was, I concentrated, trying to pick up any differences in how I felt. I felt nothing, and continued to feel nothing, but after about ten minutes, I noticed that beam getting weaker. The first few times we'd tried this I'd given up after about thirty seconds, so I'd never actually spent this much time with my hand inside the flashlight.

"Is that you?" Pansy asked.

"I don't know. How old are the batteries?"

"Uh, probably put them in the first time I went investigating."

"So, they could just be drained."

"Try to move the pencil."

With a sigh of resignation and feeling that I was destined to fail, I reached out with my other hand and tried to hit the pencil. It moved. Not as much as it would have if I'd been alive and hit it at that speed, but it did move. Just a little, rolling over twice on its little flat sides. Pansy screamed.

"Holy crap," Robbie whispered.

"Oh my God, it worked! We've just got to charge you!"

"Maybe there was a breeze." I wasn't ready to jump for joy just yet. It could have been a fluke.

"A breeze? It's forty degrees outside and there aren't any open windows in this house. That was all you. Do it again."

I tried again, this time concentrating harder, but the pencil only gave one turn. We all stared at it for a moment, contemplating what this may mean. Maybe the reason that none of the ghosts I'd spoken to could tell me how they moved things was because they didn't know. They weren't purposely seeking a charge, but they gathered more and more energy the longer they stayed in this weird plane of existence. And then, one day, through no effort of their own, they'd reach the threshold needed to move something. Lee had died thirteen years ago and could move light switches and shuffle papers. Although, come to think about it, he spent a lot of time sitting on the corner of Detective Crane's desk and kind of like, IN the lamp there, so maybe it was keeping him charged. Christopher had died in the 50s. He'd been able to throw a ball, and even pick a phone receiver up from the cradle. Jessica had died almost a hundred years ago, so it made much more sense now how she could do the things she could do. She was like, supercharged, or something.

Pansy replaced the batteries in the flashlight, and I held out my hand again. After about twenty-five minutes in which Pansy and Robbie continued to read through the website, the battery was finally dead. I moved to the light switch and heard Pansy giving Robbie the play-by-play. They both moved closer to get a better view. Blowing out a deep breath of air I didn't need, I reached for the switch. It moved, balancing at the midway point, but I couldn't push hard enough to flip it down. But this was progress. This was something that we could finally mark off the list we'd made when I'd first come back and we'd had no idea what I could or couldn't do.

Pansy looked at me with a cocky grin. "We're going to need a bigger battery."

8

I intended to leave Lee to his information gathering, but with Pansy at school, I quickly became bored. I had already checked on Mrs. Garcia, spent some time with the nine o'clock yoga class, which consisted mostly of the retirees, and quickly ran out of things to do. Besides, I reasoned to myself as I flew to Chivington, I had a neat new trick and a limited audience to whom I could demonstrate it. Besides, Lee would be interested in hearing my theory about gathering energy.

The day was bright and, according to the temperature on the clock at the bank, a balmy fifty-six degrees. Practically shorts weather. Confident that I knew where I was going, I skipped the roads and flew directly over the foothills of the Sangre de Cristo mountains to Chivington. I went around the future-hotel to the carriage house in search of Lee, hoping to avoid Jessica. As a fellow ghost, I wanted to trust her. Since we were so few and far between, there was, I guess you'd call it a kinship that naturally occurred and I naively wanted everyone in this boat with me to have the same caring, do-gooder spirit that I hoped to uphold. But I couldn't shake the feeling that she was hiding something, and her lack of forthrightness made my brain itch.

The carriage house was empty, so I entered the hotel proper, hoping to find him quickly and get out. I found Lee on the second floor landing of the east staircase, counting. He held up one finger as he saw me approach and continued to count aloud until the pajama ghost passed him. He stopped counting and grinned like the cat who ate a canary. "You can tell your friend Summer that I've counted it off, and yes, the disturbance on the tapes is caused by this gentleman walking through the camera every two minutes and twenty seconds."

"But he doesn't erase the tapes? If I walk through a camera or a camcorder, I ruin the film."

"Ah, but you are not the same as these folks." He looked up, although all we could see was the underside of the staircase above us. "Anyway, what's going on? I thought I was meeting you Saturday night? It's only Friday, right? Or did I miss a day somewhere?"

"No, it's still Friday, but I was bored and I learned a new trick, so I thought I'd checked in with you."

"A new trick, huh? Do tell."

"This way, kind sir," I said, leading him down to where the front desk was being built of two-by-fours, a sheet of plywood laid across the top to create a temporary desk. I remembered seeing someone's pencil lying on top of some blueprints there. "Watch," I said, and concentrated on touching the pencil. It rolled three times before wobbling and falling still again.

"Impressive. My baby ghost is growing up."

"Yeah, yeah. We figured it out."

"Figured what out?"

"Well, you'll see on the tapes tomorrow night how every battery in every device in this place went dead when Jessica, well, when Jessica said that the Other, was putting on a show.

Pansy and I found a website where some amateur ghost hunter had also investigated the Castle and he had the same thing happen to him. It occurred to us it probably wasn't a coincidence. So, Pansy had me hold my hand inside of a flashlight we'd turned on until I'd drained the battery, and well, this was the result. I could make a pencil move. Our theory is that the reason it takes so long for new ghosts to gain physical powers is that we are absorbing random electrical currents loose in the atmosphere, like static electricity, sun flares, that kind of thing. Eventually, we have enough stored energy to make things move. The longer you're around, the more powerful you become."

"I'd never thought about it, but it makes a certain kind of sense. At first, like you, I couldn't move anything and then slowly I could move smaller things. As time went by, I became stronger and stronger."

"But it wasn't a matter of just concentrating harder or finding some kind of inner zen, right? You could just do it. In the movies, it's always some external force that makes the hero mad or emotional and then suddenly their superpowers are unlocked. But I don't think it's that simple."

"Superpowers, huh? I don't know. It seems like a reasonable hypothesis. So what now? Are you saying you're going to hang out at the power substation and be the most powerful ghost in the area?"

"We'll save that for when I'm ready to begin my superhero origin story," I laughed. "I'm just happy the reason I couldn't move things before wasn't a failing on my part, but something I literally didn't have the juice to make happen. But…"

"But what?"

"But now I'm wondering if the reason I didn't show up on film or audio, or especially on EMF, is because I didn't have the juice. I hoped that since Jessica was so much more powerful, she'd show up on tape. We've seen a few lighter spots in the film that might be her, but they could also just be a glare on the lens. The tapes we watched at Summer's had a lot of things moving around, but none of the cameras caught Jessica lingering as a full-bodied shadowy figure or anything."

"Interesting," he said before shooting me his know-it-all grin. "But not as interesting as what I've learned. Would you like to hear what the wife and business partner of Mr. Browning are planning?"

"Do you even have to ask?"

"Well," he began, floating over to the front windows where we had a front row view of the fountain being pressure washed. "The husband, this Browning character, is oblivious to the fact that they're conspiring against him. From what I've seen and overheard, the business partner, Jed Dixon, has taken out an insurance policy on him and he and the wife are planning on taking him out, setting the hotel on fire with his body in it, then taking the money and running back to Florida."

"She's in love with the business partner?" the guy gave me the creeps. Not that Browning was Brad Pitt or anything.

"I think love is too strong a word," Lee said, giving me some serious side-eye. "It's more that she finds him useful at this particular moment in time."

"It must be a lot of money," I thought with a shudder.

"It's a big building with a lot of undeveloped property. I'm sure it'll be enough to pay off any debts and still afford a nice condo in Miami Beach."

"Do you have a timeline for this? I mean, not to sound like I'm agreeing with this plan, but if the hotel burned down, what happens to the Other? It won't have anyone to feed on."

"I don't know that there's any reason that would stop it from moving on to greener pastures. He could move into the nearest town."

"But it could have already done that and it didn't."

Lee thought about what I was saying. "No. When the nursing home closed, it would have been strong, fully fed, and if there wasn't something holding it here, it could have gone anywhere. But you're right, it didn't leave. I wonder why? What holds it here?"

"You are attributing human reasoning to the being," Jessica said from directly behind me, scaring the bejesus out of me. "He isn't human, just rage and hunger."

Lee must have seen her coming because he didn't jump like I did, but considered her words. "So, you think that it's devolved into these base instincts and even deprived of food, it wouldn't go out in search of more? Have you ever noticed the Other leaving the building?"

Jessica paused for a moment, searching back through her memory. "Not that I recall. Shortly after my death, I left to search for my family, find old friends. I have occasionally left for short periods, solely to see how the world has changed, but he's always been here when I return. I do not believe I have ever pondered his lack of wanderlust."

"Interesting," I muttered. Maybe Pansy and I would do some research on spirits that were locked in a single location. Maybe that could help us narrow down what this thing was and how to get rid of it. Speaking of things I would need Pansy to do, "Lee, did you notice if... Jeb?"

"Jed. The wife is Heather."

"Jed. Sure, okay. Anyway, did you notice if either of them left any proof of this plan lying around anywhere?"

"I didn't see anything in the carriage house, but I expect good old Jed is staying around here somewhere close, maybe in a hotel in town. I figure he'll show up around four again and I planned to follow him back to whatever hole he crawled out of tonight. Then I can do a little sleuthing and poke around."

"I know it's a hardship for you, having to go through other people's stuff. Okay, remember, six o'clock tomorrow night at The Buffalo Chip. I'll see you there. Jessica, we're not making a lot of progress, but knowing that he seems to be stuck here may help us search. At least it's something else to add to the list. I'll let you know if we find anything." And with that, I was out, floating home. A few hours later, I wished I'd stayed put.

To celebrate our birthday, Pansy was having a sleepover with her friends. Anne and Amber had driven over directly after school and the pizza dude was making an appearance for the second day in a row. Our kitchen counters were covered in bags of chips, cookies, and cans of soda, as well as the leftover birthday cake.

"Diabeetus," I muttered to myself as I floated upstairs, interested to see how things were going. Pansy hadn't participated in parties or sleepovers much since I'd died, and I realized that I desperately wanted her to have a good time. I floated up into a corner of our room, just enough of my head above the carpet to peek in and hopefully not be spotted by Pansy. I was hidden behind a trio of open Caboodles that had been left on the floor. The hair accessories and makeup items originally held within the brightly colored tackle boxes were now strewn across the carpet, mixed with issues of Bop and Seventeen, and even a few issues of Tiger Beat. I spotted a Delia's catalog under a selection of nail polishes. The three girls were also on the floor, an open box of pizza pulled up close and Robbie filling in as a fourth at a hand of gin rummy. Anne and Amber were flirting shamelessly with him, which he was eating up, and their laughter echoed through the house. Pansy had her back to me so I watched them for a while, pleased that she was having fun.

You only turned eighteen once, if you were lucky enough to make it that far.

Everyone was having a great time without me and as much as I wanted to sit in a corner and pout, and I really, really wanted to pout, I knew Pansy needed this time with her friends. If she saw me, she'd feel guilty. Even though I'd told her a hundred times that none of this was her fault, she was never fully convinced that she wasn't somehow responsible for my death. If only she'd not wanted to stay at the party so long, if only she'd turned the wheel sooner, if only, if only. It wasn't her fault.

I left them there playing card games and eating junk food. I wasn't in the mood for company, so I headed out to watch the full moon rise over the high plains by myself. Pansy wasn't going to need me tonight.

9

"Oh, good, you're back," Pansy said around a mouthful of sausage biscuit. I'd just flown back home to find her and Dad lingering at the breakfast table while Mom was loading the dishwasher.

"Daily check in on Mrs. Garcia, who I predict will live to be a hundred and ten. Did everyone already leave?"

"Yeah, Anne had practice and Amber had to open this morning at Spin Time. Anyway, heads up, Mom has some kind of surprise planned for this morning. She wants you to meet us on the way back from therapy."

"Just when you get done, or do I have to go to therapy, too? Because that sounds like the opposite of a fun surprise."

"Mom, do you want Gerri to go to therapy with us or just meet us afterwards?"

"She doesn't need to go, it would just distract you. Gerri, you can meet us after. That's fine. Are you sure you know how to get there by yourself? I can get the atlas out if you need to look it over before you go."

I rolled my eyes, and Pansy translated. "She's okay. She's been there before." I had. When you think about it, I'd been to a lot of places that I wouldn't have gone to if I'd had a corporeal body. When I first came back in this form, I was afraid of a lot of things and getting lost and floating alone across the country had been high on the list. Over the last few months, I'd gained a lot of confidence in my navigating skills. I could fly fast, high, and mostly straight, and that was something firmly in the win column for being a ghost.

I gave them an hour's head start before I floated toward Trinidad. The sun was out and I briefly wished that I could enjoy the warmth. Honestly, though, I knew that if I was suddenly capable of feeling hot and cold that I would do more complaining about it than reveling in it. I was at least that self-aware of my faults.

The Trinidad Carnegie Library was a stone block building that looked like it had been built in New York City and then airdropped onto a street corner in Trinidad. Pansy and I had been there many times over the years and I quickly located their selection of books on local history. Being a larger town, they had a lot more books than our branch, and several were dedicated histories of Chivington Sanitorium since they were also closer to the Castle. Their selections on ghosts and paranormal offerings, however, were no better than the Perth branch and I called my work there done, since I couldn't actually take anything off the shelf. Yet.

I tried to kill more time by floating through Trujillo's, the local ice cream parlor, and then a new arcade that was packed with teens on a Saturday morning. I considered checking out the hospital ghosts that Lee had talked about, but was too afraid I'd end up gathering a side quest from each of them. Honestly, we had enough on our plates without adding to it now. I floated over to the doctor's office, where Dad's Silverado was still in the parking lot.

Keeping my body in a rose bush outside the windows, I

poked my head into the office where my family sat in over-stuffed furniture being treated. I said Pansy's name to get her attention, earning me a brief glare. She turned her eyes back to the doctor who was speaking, but flashed her hand towards me twice, indicating they still had ten minutes.

I went shopping through a secondhand store to waste more time, making a mental note to make Pansy come back and buy a pair of vintage bell-bottom jeans with flowers embroidered up the sides. They looked like they'd be our size and would be adorable on her. The family was just loading into the truck when I got back to the parking lot.

"Okay, so there are some books in the library here about Chivington that you and Bagel could look through and there's a pair of jeans that are absolutely to die for in that shop over there. You need to call our boy and plan a trip."

"Uh, your boy and I already have a trip planned for tomor-row, if you'll recall. It'll have to wait until next weekend."

"Is Gerri here? What will have to wait?" Mom asked and Pansy updated her. While the two discussed tomorrow's sched-uled search for a dead body, Dad drove east on 25, occasionally interjecting warnings about snakes and twisted ankles, while I sang along to the REM cassette tape Pansy had shoved into the tape deck.

Pansy kept her eyes turned towards the small side window and did her best not to look my way as we drove home. I could float along at pace as long as someone was driving a steady speed, but every time Dad braked I'd go floating forward. After witnessing my body being impaled by a guardrail when we'd crashed our Cavalier, the sight of me floating through the wind-shield understandably caused her a lot of anxiety. When she was driving, I tried to float in the backseat where she couldn't see me, but that was a little harder to accomplish in the king cab truck.

A few minutes from Perth, Dad pulled off onto a side road that led to the cemetery and we both sat up straighter. My parents had, of course, been to the cemetery several times since my death but Pansy had me so psyched up with her conviction that if I saw my own grave, I'd poof to wherever was next that I was terrified that if I even got near the cemetery, I'd never see her again. Neither of us was ready for that cord to be snipped permanently and I considered floating out of the truck and going straight home, but then thought, why not? In books and movies, people always have the option to move on, right? They can move towards some proverbial light, or choose not to. Although, my memory dredged up the image of Christopher looking very surprised before he became a ball of light and was gone. He hadn't seemed to have had a choice.

"Are you okay with going in there?" Pansy asked me.

"I think we should see what happens. It's time to mark this one off the list, don't you think?"

"Has Gerri not been to see her headstone yet?" Mom asked from the front seat.

"No, we were afraid there might be some kind of door or portal or something that will take her to where she's actually supposed to be." Like every ghost wandering the earth was just terrible with directions and didn't know where the local cemetery was. Although, suppose you were an unidentified body? If there really was some way to pass at the cemetery, but it had to be the cemetery your body was in, what did people do who were kept in a morgue somewhere forever while they searched for a name and then were buried in a paupers grave? Did you just have to wander through every cemetery in the area until you were magically sucked away by a cosmic Dust Buster to the afterlife? No. No, I'd watched Christopher go. He wasn't raised in the air like he was being abducted by aliens, he'd just blinked out of existence. Was he gone because he'd been reunited with his body? Or did it have something to do with finding the baseball card? There'd been a brief moment where he'd looked so relieved that he'd found it before he'd lit up like a supernova.

"Is that a thing to be worried about?" Mom asked. "I know we all enjoy that she's still here with us, but didn't you say that it wasn't normal? Shouldn't she have moved on by now?"

"In theory. But I'm not ready for her to go yet."

"Well, I wanted her to see the flowers I bought for her grave for her birthday," Mom said, pointing towards the bed of the truck as Dad concentrated on the one lane gravel road leading to the cemetery. "If she doesn't want to go in, we can stop here and I can show her."

Perversely, her concern just made me more determined to try it. "I'm going to try it."

"I don't think you should. Didn't Christopher disappear when he saw his body?" Pansy said. Dad had slowed because of the ruts in the road, but the gates were just ahead.

"Yeah, but first of all, I'm not going to actually see my body. It's in a casket six feet underground, and I already know where it is. It's not like I was searching for it. I'm not finding anything shocking. I'm going to try it."

"Am I continuing or stopping?" Dad asked.

"Keep going," Pansy grumbled. "She's determined to mark this off her list."

The San Isidro Cemetery was on top of a small hill north of town and surrounded by pines that towered over the wrought-iron fence that encircled several acres of cemetery. While the fence was typical six foot high fencing with a brick base, the scrollwork that spelled out San Isidro over the gate looked like something straight out of a Tim Burton film and I was secretly thrilled that I was buried in a place with such a creepy aesthetic. The gates were open, and Dad drove forward, carefully avoiding the larger pot holes.

My eyes were closed and I was in the middle of doing some yoga breathing exercises as he drove through the gate, so I let out a yelp of surprise when I suddenly stopped floating forward. There was no wall, no feeling of hitting anything solid, but I could not move past the gate. Pansy whipped around in her seat as I was pushed out the back of the truck, and through the back window I could see her mouth moving. The truck came to a stop and three doors opened almost at once. I continued to float at the gate, hands feeling around in the air, looking for a way to push through it.

"What are you doing? This is the worst mime routine I've ever seen."

"I'm not trapped in an imaginary box, you dork. It's like a freakin' invisible wall. I can't get through it."

"Then go over it."

The parents were demanding an update and Pansy filled them in as I tried to go over the wall, but whatever kept me out created a dome shape. I could glide along the top, but I wasn't going through. It was like an invisible bubble surrounded the cemetery, and despite my best efforts, I couldn't even slide a hand into it.

Puzzled, I landed back at the gate where the family was still standing, the engine still on in the truck. I remembered reading something about ghosts being repelled by iron in one of the bazillion books on ghosts that we'd bought a few months ago. We'd tested it out with Mom's cast-iron skillet, but I hadn't noticed anything strange happening when she'd waved it through me. Was the ground here sacred? Blessed? Omigosh, was I like, ah unholy demon or something?

"No dice. Short of testing out every inch of the walls like that velociraptor in Jurassic Park, I'm stuck out here."

"Mom, you might as well show her the flowers now, she can't get in." Five minutes of discussion followed this statement, some of which was actually spent admiring the lilies that Mom brought for my grave.

"I wish I'd brought a disposable camera. We could take a picture of it for you," Mom said.

"Well, who would have thought this was going to happen?" Pansy said, throwing her hands up in the air. "Looks like we aren't marking this off the list today."

"No, we're adding more questions to the list," I grumbled. After promising I'd meet them at home in a bit, I shooed my family on their way and continued testing every part of the fence. It was a puzzle I couldn't solve. Yet.

"Geraldine, are you home?" Lee yelled from downstairs while Pansy was putting her hair into a French braid.

"Lee's here. I'll go down and talk to him while you finish getting ready." She nodded and I sank through the floor and found Lee in the kitchen with his nose in a pot simmering on the stove.

"I wish we could smell. Your mother's marinara looks delicious."

"I mean, I remember it smelled delicious, but I don't know. With the places we go? Sometimes I'm really grateful that we can't smell." Basements, cellars, falling down old buildings.

"That's a good point, but still…" he said, eyeballing the garlic bread that was ready to go under the broiler.

"Enough about dinner—guess where we went today?"

"I have no idea. Where?"

"To visit my grave at San Isidro Cemetery."

He chuckled and moved to watch Mom chopping veggies for the salad. "I may have forgotten to warn you about that. Let me guess, you spent an hour trying to force your way in?"

"I gave up after twenty minutes, but yeah. Do you have any idea what's going on there?"

"Well, best I can figure, it's something about the iron. A single iron object doesn't seem to have any power, but when you have a lot of it, connected all the way around in a loop, it acts like... what did they used to call it on Star Trek?"

"A force field?"

"Yeah, that."

"Do the bars in the jail cells do the same thing?" I'd never had a reason to go inside of one, so I wasn't sure.

"No, those are made of stainless steel. The only time I've ever encountered this kind of thing was at a few old cemeteries that were surrounded by an iron fence, and one house that had it all the way around their yard."

"Well, I was going to ask if maybe it's because the ground has been blessed or something, but I guess the house negates that argument. I may or may not have questioned if maybe we came back as demons and not ghosts."

"Kind of late to worry about your immortal soul now, isn't it?" He shrugged. "Yeah. I've never had a problem in an open cemetery or church graveyard as long as the fence only covers three sides. It's like it isn't a closed system unless it's uninterrupted all the way around."

I thought about the sign over the open gates, that ornate piece of iron across the top creating an uninterrupted 'system', as Lee referred to it.

"Why were you at the cemetery?"

"Thursday was our 18th birthday and Mom wanted to put flowers on my grave and wanted me to see it."

"It's nice that you still have someone to look after your headstone."

"Are you buried here, too?"

"Yep. Section 28. We picked out our plots when Diane was

first diagnosed with cancer, so I know where it is, I just can't see it from the fence." I made a mental note to make sure Pansy and Bagel went to search out his headstone and take a photo of it for him. Maybe take him some flowers every now and then.

"Don't look sad, kiddo. Eventually, everyone dies. It's just nicer when you have people to remember you." I hadn't begun to digest this bit of Mr. Miogi wisdom before he continued, his voice taking on that tone he always got when he was going to tell a particularly gossipy story. "Speaking of dying, I thought for sure that the wife was going to take out this Browning character today. They left together this morning to go into Trinidad, so I followed them to see what they were doing. He went to the bank to get a loan, and she went to do some shopping."

"Boring adult stuff, go on."

"The bank refused to loan him any more money. Apparently he's already taken massive loans out and they've heard stories about the injuries and unsafe working conditions. He'll have to find more investors if he doesn't want to default on the loans he already has."

"Good luck with that," I muttered.

Pansy stuck her head into the kitchen to announce that she was leaving for the PPS meeting, giving me a 'hurry up' look.

"We'll still be there before you will," I told her. She rolled her eyes at me and headed out the door. "So the wife wants to kill him, or I guess, kill him faster, because of the loan?"

"Oh no, when it became clear that Browning wasn't getting any money out of them, I tracked her down to a clothing store. She wasn't hard to find because I could hear her screeching at the cashier from two doors down. Her credit card was declined and the bank told the cashier to cut it up. Furious doesn't quite cover it."

"I bet that was a fun ride home." I almost felt sorry for Mr. Browning.

"She screamed and cried about how he embarrassed her all the way back to the Castle. He did some screaming and yelling back at her and almost drove off the edge of the canyon road twice on the way home."

"Well, I don't know if we can top that kind of excitement," I said, checking out the clock on the microwave. "But if you want to see what the PPS caught on film during the investigation, we'd better get going."

"You know I love a good drama," he said with a wink.

"I am aware."

10

The PPS held their meetings at a bar and grill called The Buffalo Chip that squatted on a dusty piece of land just over the East bridge. Imagine *Road House* with slightly less class but better food. A crusty taxidermied bison named Bill greeted visitors at the entrance and every table was occupied on a Saturday night. Used mostly for family gatherings and business meetings, the back room where we met every other Saturday night had been added on sometime in the seventies judging by the dark wood paneling that covered every square inch of the windowless walls. With some creative table arranging they could probably seat about fifty customers, which was funny because the PPS only had eight members counting Pansy and Bagel. We certainly didn't need that much room, but the owner was one of Randy's cousins.

Lee told me about following Jed back to a motel room as we floated to the restaurant. The business partner hadn't left anything incriminating lying around and it seemed that any and all office work the two conducted was done at the dining room table of the carriage house.

We passed Pansy's Tracker as she was crossing the east

bridge and we floated into the building without waiting on her. Greg already had the TV connected to the VCR, and Randy was futzing with his overhead projector. The pre-investigation reports that Blake had prepared for the next week's investigation were stacked on a table by the door, and Pansy picked one up as she entered a few minutes later. His reports usually consisted of a map, a list of previous owners, and information about any deaths that may have taken place on-site. They always contained a summary of the phenomena the family or owner of the property being investigated suspected of being supernatural.

The room was divided by two rows of long tables, all facing the front of the room where the TV and projector were set up. Pansy took her regular seat next to Summer, waving at Bagel, who sat at the table behind them. Shawn and Chandra were just a minute or two behind Pansy, and they sat in their normal spot at the table across the aisle from Summer and Pansy.

"Look," I told Lee. "They always sit in the same spots. Pansy sat down next to Summer at her first meeting and her butt has never graced another seat in all these months." She shot me a dirty look over her shoulder and I shrugged in response. I couldn't help that they were boring and never varied their seating arrangements. Even Randy and Greg sat in the same spots. As they took turns speaking at the front of the room, whoever wasn't standing usually perched a butt cheek on the edge of one of the front tables. Which could be why no one sat at the front tables. Blake, who, to the best of my knowledge, had never been on time for any meeting, took his seat next to Bagel just as Greg was hitting play on the first piece of video footage that they had queued up. Judging by the stack of VHS tapes, there were quite a few spots we'd be looking at tonight.

"We're going to do this chronologically tonight and see how much we can get through. Since this was such a massive job, I know that there are still some tapes no one has had time to look at yet, so we'll just keep working on them and review anything we haven't covered in two weeks. There's a reason we booked a small job for next Saturday," Greg paused, grinning, and I suppose waiting for someone to laugh. No one did, so he moved on. "Okay, so first up, this is Tape Number One from the camera on the left side of the lobby area. If you look right here," he said, pointing to the screen, "there's going to be an orb that comes across and then moves back and forth a few times before flying off to the right." His finger wiggled across the twenty-inch screen, mimicking the flight of what I felt for sure would be a dust orb across the paused image. Sure enough, a roundish ball of reflective light did a little dance on the screen before flying out of the shot. He rewound the tape and pressed play again. After the second viewing, everyone spoke at once and the opinions started flying like dust orbs.

"Obviously, it's just an insect flying around," Shawn said once the initial outburst calmed down.

"There's no way a bug would fly in a pattern like that. There's no directionality," his wife countered.

"Have you never had a gnat in your face? They just wander around in the most annoying way they can."

"You know what the criteria are: does it move in an unpredictable pattern or can it be explained by a reflection from something else moving nearby? If not, we can assume it's supernatural," Randy interjected.

"I'm voting bug," Pansy said.

I heard a hmmph from Lee as floated with his arms crossed. "If they only knew what was around them, they wouldn't spend five minutes fighting over a bug."

"I kind of wish I could tell them sometimes. It just seems like so much work carrying all of this equipment around, and even with all of it, they have no idea that I'm here. They've never noticed me. I can tell you if a house is haunted in the time it takes me to float through all the rooms. Presto, done. It would be so much more efficient."

"Looks like that's one of the moving item ones, there." Lee motioned to the screen where Greg had moved further along on the same tape to a shot where a construction light fell from a piece of scaffolding just on the edge of a shot. "Now, we know that none of us knocked that light down, but it's so close to the edge of the screen that we can't use this as proof because a skeptic could say that someone was just off screen and pushed it with a pole or something."

He looked at his notes and fast forwarded, played, fast forwarded, play, rewind, play. "Here, this was just after that paint fell all over Chandra, and even with everyone talking at once you can hear that EMF detector in Summer's hand going crazy and then it faded away again like something came close and then went away even though Summer doesn't move." The room erupted with comments, but Randy wasn't done yet. "Now, this one, there's no one that can explain this with anything other than paranormal activity. Okay, watch the Big Gulp on the edge of the table here." We all watched, fascinated, although I'd literally been standing right there with it when it had happened and Jessica had swept her hand across the table, sending several cables and the giant plastic cup flying off the edge of the table. No slow moving, incremental nudging for this video. No, it landed about three feet away, and the whole thing had been caught on film.

"Oh my stars, I heard you guys talking about this one," Summer said, "but I didn't realize it went that far. No one can say that a breeze made that happen unless there was a Category 5 that swept through the room and no one noticed." Everyone agreed, and we spent another hour watching things fall off from things they had no business falling from, and every once in a while I caught a flash of light, which may have been Jessica showing up on film. Or it could have been light bouncing off a lens, I couldn't tell.

The door opened and the noise of the crowded dining room entered a few seconds before the server and food runners came in, bearing trays of food. Randy stood up. "Guys, since we're pressed for time, I'm going to give you some time to get situated with your food, but while we eat I want us to go through some of the EVP's."

The group broke to grab their food from the trays but wasted no time getting back into their seats. Every person held a burger in one hand and an ink pen in the other, ready to write down what they thought they heard on the tape. Instead of searching for each event on all the individual tapes, these had all been dubbed into one tape, and Randy began playing them one after another. There were nineteen in total, and when they were done, he rewound the tape and started over.

"Why are they writing?" Lee asked.

"Well, because human brains are weird, and if you hear a strange sound, you might associate it with a spoken language, but maybe not the same words as someone else. However, if you say, 'hey, does this sound like it's saying, insert random phrase here,' then almost everyone will also hear those exact same words. So, to prevent, I don't know, cross contamination I guess you could call it, they all write them down first and then see how many matches they have once it's over."

"This seems like a lot of work and effort. Do they ever actually hear anything?"

"I mean, they pick up some weird noises and sometimes there are things that sound like human voices. Were the houses haunted by something that I could see? No. But Chivington has me reconsidering my previous conviction that I'm an expert on ghosts. Maybe they really do need to lug in all of this equipment for these investigations. For all I know, there are things out there that I just can't see."

"Well, that's terrifying."

"I thought so, too."

After much arguing about what the noises were supposedly saying, all of which sounded like squeaky doors and people talking in the background where the audio was recorded, and absolutely none of it anything that either I or Jessica had actually said, the group moved on to discussing the upcoming investigation.

Randy took his spot by the overhead projector and slid on a sheet where he'd diagrammed the layout of the single wide trailer. "Okay guys, like Greg said, I scheduled this very small investigation after Chivington on purpose. We keep finding so much great stuff at the Castle investigation and this one won't take a lot of time or manpower, so we'll be able to catch up on all the audio and video we have left. Once we finish, I'm going to dub some VHS tapes of the highlights and send them out to some friends that I've met in an online paranormal chat room. They're eager to look them over and give... well, I guess you could call it a second opinion.

"Overall, we've got some really great stuff here and if I didn't say it before, I really appreciate how professional everyone was. You guys really held it together even when stuff was literally flying off the shelves. I can't tell you how proud you all made me." There was a brief murmur of approval around the room. "But before we get started going over this new investigation, I have one more thing to add. Mr. Browning, the property owner, called me this afternoon requesting our help removing the ghosts from the property."

"Removing them?" Chandra said, throwing her hands up in the air. "What, like we're the GhostBusters now?"

"Do we do that?" Bagel turned to ask Blake.

"Absolutely not," Blake grumbled. "If they want them gone, they're going to need a priest or a medium."

"And that's pretty much what I told him," Randy confirmed.

Pansy raised her hand before remembering that she wasn't in school and didn't need to wait to be called on. "I was under the impression that Mr. Browning wanted the hotel to be haunted? What made him change his mind?"

"He said he'd had a near miss with a chunk of concrete earlier today. If he'd been six inches to the left, it would have hit him directly on the head and he's blaming the ghosts. He said an electrician had fallen from a ladder, a chunk of handrail broke off while someone else was going up the stairs and there were a few other accidents lately, but apparently his brush with death was the final straw after a water line busted and flooded some of the back rooms on the first floor."

"Did you see the concrete incident?" I asked Lee.

"No, it must have happened after I left this morning. I stopped at the police station to check up on things before I headed over to meet you. I saw the water line, though, but it didn't seem like a supernatural event. To me, it just looked like a run-of-the-mill pipe that sprung a leak."

"Do you think the business partner did it? The concrete chunk to the head, I mean. Or maybe the Other? Or did Jessica wait for you to leave before she tried to, like, knock him off or something?"

Lee shrugged. "I'd need more information to have an opinion."

"The water line could have been an accident," I said, thinking out loud, "but that wouldn't do the business partner any good unless he wanted to make an insurance claim."

"They're on top of a hill," Lee said, shaking his head. "I doubt they took out flood insurance."

At the front of the room, Randy had already launched into

his spiel for the upcoming investigation. "So, what we have here is a Mom, Step-dad, and eight-year-old boy living out at the Canyon Run Trailer Park north of town past the cemetery. They've reported hearing strange noises at night, and their son wakes up covered in bruises and scratches and they don't know why. The parents say he doesn't sleepwalk, that no one else is staying there, and both parents sleep in their room on the other end of the trailer. They don't know what else could be happening other than something attacking the kid in his sleep. The plan of attack here is that Greg and I will set up a few cameras in the house and do remote monitoring from the van so that the family can carry on just like they normally would, and we'll be watching to see what happens."

"Do they think it's a poltergeist? Wouldn't the activity extend beyond just the child, though?" Summer asked.

"Yeah, you'd think that objects elsewhere in the home would be thrown, broken, moved, or even the parents themselves attacked, but the activity seems to be centered solely around the child and naturally, they're concerned," Greg answered.

"It wouldn't be the first documented case of a poltergeist or even a demonic entity latching onto a child," Randy said. "This could be really dangerous for him." There were more murmurs of confirmation, and Lee and I looked at one another.

"Omigosh, could there really be another poltergeist type thing running around? Let's go check it out. Curiosity's killing me."

"Did anyone ever tell you that you were too nosey?" Lee asked, one bushy gray eyebrow hiking up as he looked over at me.

"All the time."

"It's my favorite quality about you. Let's go."

Pansy pretended to get a phone call on her cell phone so

that she could walk outside with us while talking to me and not look like a crazy person. Or, at least, a crazier person.

"You can't just get up and go right now," she said as she pushed through the entrance and out into the parking lot. The neon lights of the various beer signs hanging in the windows cast her in a flashing red glow.

"Why not? If there really is something demonic, it's not like I'm going to rush back to tell Randy and Greg about it and ruin the surprise for them. I'll tell you about it, of course, but then you can't tell them anything or they'll start asking how you could know."

"Can I tell Summer?"

"I guess. She already knows about me."

"Whoa, whoa, this Summer person knows you're a ghost? When did this happen?"

I may have forgotten to mention it to him. "Yes, she kind of saw us doing ghost stuff on one of the tapes and Pansy came clean."

"Good grief. Well, tell her we'll fill her in when we get back later tonight. Let's go, kiddo. I want to see a demonic entity at work."

"Gotta go, talk to ya later," I yelled back to Pansy as we floated out of the gravel parking lot. Pansy was still holding the cell phone to her ear, her eyeballs shooting daggers at me. If I was living, I'd worry about her locking me out of the house when I got back home. There was something else to add to the pro column.

11

"One fifty-eight Blue Jay. That's our target."

"I hate to judge a book by its cover," Lee began.

I interrupted him. "Since when?"

"Okay, fine. But one of these things is not like the others."

Bluejay Lane was one of several dirt and gravel lanes laid out in a grid pattern of single and double-wide house trailers. The yards were oversized, and many contained storage sheds, patio tables, and children's swing sets. Flowering annuals planted in galvanized stock tanks seemed to be a popular option, although the occupants of one fifty-eight had other ideas about yard decor.

Instead of a storage shed, the Coopers had opted for what looked like thirty to forty sun damaged Rubbermaid containers of varying sizes partially covered by blue tarps. The tarps were weighted down with a variety of rocks and broken cinder blocks, as well as multiple garbage bags, the big 32-gallon yard kind, which appeared to all be full of empty beer cans.

"Is that a mattress?" Lee asked, pointing to a pile of larger junk items leaning against the rusted exterior of the trailer.

"It absolutely is," I muttered, my attention drawn to a

woman I assumed was Mrs. Cooper sitting in a rickety lawn chair talking on a cordless phone. She was telling someone about the money she planned to make selling the rights to her family's story, never dropping the cigarette that seemed to be super-glued to her lower lip.

"I think we've been bamboozled," Lee muttered.

As we neared the trailer, I heard a child screaming and cursing from inside. The mother gave no indication that she noticed. She shifted her weight in the aluminum framed chair, its nylon straps creaking in alarming ways as she got comfortable.

"Why don't you go check it out just in case? Then you can give a thorough report to your sister when you get home."

"What? You're not going in?"

"I can already tell you that there's nothing in that house that I want to see."

Grumbling to myself about wimpy old men, I floated into the trailer, happy that a full sweep should only take a minute or two. It was easy to find the kid by following the sounds of obscenities screamed at full volume to the end of the trailer. Inside voices must not be a thing in this household. He was in his room playing Mortal Kombat on a Sega game system, jumping, screaming, and kicking his legs into the air along with his character. As I watched, he paused the game long enough to grab a two-liter of Mountain Dew from the TV stand and take a swig like it was a jug of moonshine in a Bugs Bunny cartoon. My mom would have grounded us for a month if we'd tried to drink a whole 2-Liter of anything by ourselves. Judging from the empties strewn all over the room, it wasn't an isolated incident.

If there was a poltergeist living here, I wished it luck with its endeavors and turned to look over the rest of the house. Besides a firmly established colony of German cockroaches in the kitchen, there was nothing interesting of note and I floated back outside.

"No self-respecting ghost would haunt this home," Lee said when he saw me emerge.

"Norman Rockwell, it's not. But yeah, I didn't see another ghost and the only things that were creepy all had six legs."

We floated back out to the street where I felt like I could breathe again. Even though I no longer breathed and I had no sense of smell, which I was also very, very grateful for. "Randy and Greg are going to have to wear hazmat suits in there. Their wives will kill them if they bring back cockroaches in the equipment."

Lee shuddered and looked around the trailer park before floating off without a word. Intrigued, I followed him. We circled around the park, going up and down the rows before he came to a stop in front of a white single wide with a blue stripe. He was silent for a moment, his brow furrowed in that way it did before he started telling a story. "Do you remember me telling you about Thomas?" he finally asked me.

"Yeah, why? Do you think he could be haunting the Cooper family?"

Lee gave a short laugh. "There is no chance he would haunt those people. No, this is where it all happened. Not the same trailer, of course, but this is where I covered that story back in the day."

Lee just paused, waiting for me to ask, "What story?" I wanted to not ask, purely for spite, but the man knew his audience and the curiosity was too much. "Okay, I give. What story?"

"Well, the year was nineteen seventy something, I don't remember exactly, and Bobby, he was Thomas' stepdaddy, Bobby was a drunken good-for-nothing. His second favorite pastime, after drinking, was beating on Thomas and his mother, Annamarie. Unfortunately, that went on for years because back then people firmly believed that what happened inside a family home wasn't anyone else's business. There weren't all these women's shelters and feminism stuff like there is now."

I rolled my eyes so hard he had to have heard them.

"So, one day, Thomas' little sister does... something. I couldn't ever get a straight story, but she made Bobby mad. He, in turn, takes a belt to her. Now, unlike Thomas, she was actually Bobby's kid, and she's young. I'm thinking just four or five years old. Real young. Well, Annamarie steps in to stop him, which just makes him even madder, and he starts wailing on her too. At some point, he must have dropped the belt and started using his fists. I tried to interview her two days after the murders, but he'd broken her jaw and she could barely speak."

"Wait, wait. The murders? Plural?"

"Yeah, I'm gettin' to that. So, Thomas, who was fourteen I believe, and full of righteous anger, goes to the kitchen and grabs the biggest knife he could find. He then proceeds to stab Bobby in the back while he's leaning over Annamarie, who had been on the ground for a while at that point. The knife glanced off a rib—the autopsy showed it took out a considerable chunk of bone before sliding under it, and went straight through his lung."

"Holy crap." I wasn't able to be more articulate.

"But you see, the problem with stabbing someone is that unless you've cut their throat, they generally have enough blood and air to do some major damage to their attacker before they either bleed out or pass out. Thomas didn't move away fast enough after ramming that knife in, and Bobby caught a hold of him. Now, Bobby, while he was a fat lazy slob, had a foot in height and at least a hundred and fifty pounds on the kid. As I understand it from the EMS workers I interviewed, the little girl was sobbing in a corner, Annamarie was passed out from her beating, Thomas was dead with a shattered skull, and Bobby might have made it if anyone had been able to call for the police. But they couldn't. By the time Annamarie came to and called for an ambulance, both Bobby and Thomas were dead."

"That is... awful."

"Yeah, Annamarie and the girl picked up and moved immediately. I interviewed her that morning while she was packing and they were gone by nightfall. She'd mentioned that she had some relatives in New Mexico, so I assume that's where they went. I hope she had a better life, wherever she went, poor woman."

"But you said you interviewed her two days later. Thomas wouldn't have come back until the third day and they would have already been gone. Is that why he's still here? He doesn't know where they went?"

"I can't say that I've ever given the *why* of the matter much consideration. It all seems random to me. I just assumed he wanted to stay here where it was familiar. I mean, you know where your family is, and I know exactly where my wife is, and we're still here." He paused to look at me closer in the yellow-orange glow of the sodium street light. "You have that look in your eye. You can't put him on one of your lists."

"I most certainly can. I never found Christopher's parents, but I did find his body and then the police found his dad. He moved on. Maybe this Thomas just needs to find his mother and sister."

"The police found his father two weeks after he'd already moved on. You're grasping at straws."

"Look, it's an imperfect theory, but it can't hurt to try helping him. Besides, we have the internet now."

"You say that like it's magic."

I mean, I certainly didn't understand how it worked. Who was I to say that it wasn't?

I thought about Thomas as I floated home, wondering what it would be like growing up in that kind of environment. I almost forgot that Pansy was going to be jealous, whether or not she admitted it, that I had gone to investigate something that, in theory, sounded really exciting. It was a little after ten when I floated into our bedroom, but Pansy was still up, scribbling in a notebook.

She looked over her shoulder at me, flung her unbound hair over said shoulder with a sniff, and went back to writing.

"You will be ecstatic to know, A, you missed nothing, and B, you're lucky that I can't bring cockroaches home."

That had her whipping around in her seat. "What?"

"Dude. It was a trash pit. And the mom was on the phone with someone talking about how she was going to convince these ghost hunting people her house was haunted so she could sell her story to the news."

"Oh. So no new poltergeist or things that go bump in the night? Well, that's disappointing." She was quiet for a moment, tapping her pen on the notebook she'd been writing in. "I feel like I should warn Randy and Greg. They're going to waste their time setting up equipment and spend all night away from their families for nothing."

"But you can't warn them without telling them why you know."

"Ugh," she groaned, throwing her pen onto the desk, the little fuzzy top keeping it from rolling too far.

"That's not all." I filled her in on what Lee had told me about Thomas.

"But you've never met the kid?"

"No, Lee said he keeps to himself and hardly ever comes to town."

"What is it with all of these antisocial ghosts?" Pansy grumbled. She picked up her notebook and flashed it up so I could see she'd been making more lists.

"So, after the meeting, Bagel and I had a little conversation with Summer out in the parking lot."

"Did you tell her I went to investigate?"

"Of course. She's going to want an update, by the way. Which, come to think of it, maybe she can think of a way to keep them from wasting their time at the Coopers'. Anyway, what I was going to say was that I asked her about the cemetery. I told her you couldn't get in. She thought that was hilarious because it was one of the first places the PPS had investigated. It was before she moved here, but apparently it was one of the few things that Randy truly believes is haunted."

"I mean, it could be, I guess. Parts of the cemetery are probably older than that fence, so it's possible someone could be trapped in there and can't get out. You'd think they'd come to the edge and talk to the other ghosts that have tried to get in, though."

"Unless it's another antisocial ghost who's happily hanging out with no fear of ever being bothered," Pansy said, standing to stretch. "I'll call Summer tomorrow after Bagel and I get back. Right now, it's bedtime. What do you want to watch, cartoons, MTV, or Springer?"

"Springer," I told her without hesitation. What could I say? I was a sucker for petty, overly dramatic people.

12

By nine o'clock on Sunday morning, we were on the road. Well, Bagel was driving, Pansy was directing him by listening to me, and I floated in the back of the Blazer with Lee, who was the only one who knew where we were actually going. It was awkward, but we made it work. During the long straight stretches, Pansy filled Bagel in on The Secret of the Unfaithful Partners, The Mystery of the Cemetery, The Curious Case of Thomas the Ghost, as well as The Fraudulent Haunting of Cooper Manor. The two-hour drive allowed her time to catch him up to date with everything we'd learned in the last few days.

"Good grief, Pansy, I literally just saw you Wednesday night. How have you two managed to dig up this much drama in just three days?"

"Well, I had surprisingly little to do with it. Lee and Gerri have been working on the Chivington case and are just incredibly nosey."

"Hey, I resemble that remark," I mumbled.

"Okay, but it sounds like they're adding more questions to

the pile and I hear nothing in there that sounds like an answer to how to get rid of a poltergeist."

Unable to deny this, Lee and I kept quiet. Finally, after detouring for a Golden Arches drive-thru, we arrived at a small gravel parking lot halfway up a mountain. The lot was ringed with thick cables strung through knee-high logs planted upright and painted a shiny shade of brown that logs don't sport in nature. The gate was open, but there were no other vehicles in the lot. There was a little covered noticeboard with a map of the trail protected by a thick layer of plexiglass next to the trailhead. What looked like an oversized birdhouse on a pole next to it housed the trail log and Bagel went over to sign in. "We're the first people to sign in for the last two weeks," he said, flipping through the pages. "It looks like this trail doesn't get a lot of traffic. No wonder no one ever found this body."

"But they would have signed in, wouldn't they? Didn't anyone notice when they never signed back out?" Pansy asked. She tossed the paper bag full of empty cheeseburger wrappers into the backseat of the Blazer with all the other garbage before sliding the straps of her bookbag over her shoulders. The bag was filled with bottles of water, an emergency first aid kit, a flashlight, and every other random thing she'd packed this morning, just in case.

"The body is down a deer path that gets pretty steep in places. It's unlikely anyone else would have found him, even if they were looking," Lee said, and I relayed this to Pansy.

The sun had burned off the fog and, with temperatures predicted to be in the high fifties, Pansy and Bagel had both dressed in jeans and sweatshirts. The long sleeves would protect them from briars, although they'd still have to do a thorough check for ticks when we got home. Neither owned hiking boots, so they'd worn old tennis shoes. Bagel also wore his 35 millimeter Nikon camera on a strap around his neck. The camera was a prop for the cover story they'd planned for why they'd leave the trail and just 'happen' to find the body.

The beginning of the trail was wide enough to drive an off-road vehicle down, so the walking was fairly easy. Pine needles littered the trail, keeping the mud to a minimum and making Pansy and Bagel's footsteps nearly silent. Not that the forest was a quiet place. The frogs chirping somewhere downhill were obnoxiously loud and the birds flitting overhead were bois-terous in their discussions over spring nest upgrades.

"Lee said that he figures it's going to take you about an hour and a half to get to the spot," I told Pansy as Bagel stopped to take a picture of a massive spider web. I felt that an hour and a half was optimistic if Bagel kept taking pictures of every random pinecone and variety of mushroom, but kept my opinion to myself for once.

The wide easy trail didn't last for long, as parts had been washed out over the winter or were blocked by trees that had fallen under heavy winter snows. Several parts of the trail had to be hiked uphill and over the obstructions.

"Getting a recovery crew in here is going to be a pain," Bagel grunted as he swung a leg over a fallen log.

"Are you sure we're going the right way?" Pansy asked, wiping sweat off of her forehead with her sleeve after checking her watch. "We're almost at the two-hour mark."

Lee had already flown up ahead to find the best spot for them to leave the trail and access the body, so I told her to take a break while I went to see how much further it was going to be. I took off, zooming straight through the trees, because I could, keeping the trail in my peripheral vision. I didn't have to go far before I spotted Lee and came back down to ground level to meet up with him.

"Hey, they're almost here. How hard will it be to get to it from here?"

"It? It is a dead body, Geraldine. Have some respect."

"Sorry," I mumbled.

"If they follow this deer trail down toward the water, they shouldn't have many problems. It's the least overgrown option that I've found."

I flew back, thankful that while Bagel and Pansy had pulled out bottles of water to drink, they'd hadn't stopped walking. They were only five minutes out from where they needed to turn.

"Tie your scarf to this tree, Pansy," I directed as they drew closer to where Lee waited.

"This is it? This is the path I'm supposed to go down?"

"Yeah, this is the place."

Pansy eyeballed the break in the overgrown brush, a gap approximately four feet in height and maybe a foot and a half in width, and began shaking her head. "I cannot express to you how much I do not want to crawl down something called a 'deer trail' to see a dead body that's been out here for years." She made 'deer trail' sound like we were asking her to jump into the dumpster behind the Chinese takeout place.

"Can't you just tap on Bagel to let him know when to turn left or right?" she asked.

"Oh my god, you are such a wimp," I said at the same time Bagel volunteered to go it alone.

"I can make that work. There's no reason for both of us to go in there. Give me your ribbons and I'll do it."

"Fine," I said. "Tell him I'm going to do a test."

Standing in front of him, I touched his left forearm, right shoulder, and put my hand to his chest without going through it. He called out left arm, right shoulder, chest, as I did them, so I figured we should be able to do this without getting my boy lost in the woods. Pansy handed over the handful of ribbons we'd scrounged out of a drawer that morning. They were covered in rainbows and kittens. We hadn't worn ribbons in our hair since elementary school, so the pickings had been slim.

With that done, Bagel started pushing his way into the claustrophobic tunnel that led through the underbrush.

"I'll just wait here for you," Pansy called as we moved away from her.

Bagel was a full head taller than Pansy, so he had to bend over and squat in some places to get through. He moved confidently down the hill, holding onto smaller trees to keep from slipping in some of the steeper spots. Every so often he'd tie a ribbon to mark his progression, but we only had six ribbons and I hoped we'd arrive at the destination soon.

"Boy, deer are some agile little critters, aren't they? These trails aren't made for two-footed animals," I heard Bagel mutter. By the time we made it to the place where Lee was motioning me towards, the underbrush had cleared and Bagel could move upright.

The sound of rushing water was louder down here, and I could just make out a glint of the creek reflecting through the trees. A few feet ahead, the deer path doubled back on itself, continuing downhill at a gentler angle. Straight ahead was what looked to be a twenty-foot plunge straight into the creek below. The elevation must have kept the body safe from being washed away when the creek flooded.

I tapped Bagel's chest and he stopped walking. A tap on his right arm had him turning, and I tapped his chest again when he was facing the right direction. He just stood there, and I wished Pansy hadn't been such a wuss so she could explain where the body was lying. Lee was pointing to a deadfall covered in honeysuckle vines off to the right of the path. I tapped Bagel on the back, trying to urge him forward, but he made a 180-degree turn. Growling, I gave him a double tap on the back and he turned back around. "Do you want me to go forward?"

"Yes," I yelled at him, giving him a double tap on the right hand, our signal for 'yes'. He started forward, the honeysuckle coming up to his ankles with each cautious step. I had him aligned correctly, and it was only about seven steps before he came to the fallen tree. Five more quick taps on the chest, avoiding his camera so as not to screw up his film. I hoped he would understand my signal to stop, and he got it.

"I think I see it," he said. Bending over, he pulled back a handful of vines that engulfed a prominent lump, uncovering a faded hiking pack.

"Holy crap," he whispered. Pulling back more vines and entangled weeds, he unveiled a hiking boot with a tattered scrap of denim. "Okay, that's good enough." He took a photo of the leg and the bag, framed by vines and half buried in leaf litter. A ribbon with little pink ice cream cones printed on it was quickly secured to the closest tree limb. "You can see the hiking pack now from the deer path. That should be good enough. Okay, let's get out of here. Gerri, if you're still here, I'm fine to make my way back up the hill. Fly back up to Pansy. She's probably freaking out by now."

He was probably right. She wasn't exactly the commune-with-nature type. More like the worry-about-someone-in-a-Jason-mask-popping-out-from-behind-a-tree type.

"Yeah, kid, go let your sister know that your walking breakfast pastry has located and tagged the body. I've got him. If he wanders off in the wrong direction, I'll lead him back to you." I gave Bagel a double tap on the right hand, saluted Lee, and flew back up the hill, debating to myself all the way if bagels counted as pastry. I'd always considered them more in the same category as bread.

I yelled for Pansy as I came up the hill so that I wouldn't scare the crap out of her and found her sitting on a fallen log facing the trail. "So, did he find it?" she asked, jumping up as I came into view.

"Yep, right where Lee said it was. Correction, where HE was. They're coming up the trail now. I just wanted to let you know it's done."

Pansy sat back down and stretched her legs out in front of her. Her sneakers were muddy and had a leaf stuck to the bottom of her sole. She looked like she needed a nap. Step one of our good deed was done, but they were both going to be exhausted by the time we made it home. Bagel's arrival was heralded by loud cursing as he pushed his way up the hill and back onto the hiking trail.

"Are you ready to blow this popsicle stand?" Bagel asked, leaning over and ineffectually brushing at the multitude of triangle shaped stickers attached to his jeans.

"Yeah, we need to get going so we can make the call and get the authorities out here. Hopefully, they don't keep us too long once they get here." She handed Bagel another bottle of water and he drank it all in one long gulp. She tossed the empty back into her bookbag and took her cell phone from an inside pocket, holding it up to see if she had a signal.

Zero bars.

"What's the point in having a cell phone if it never works anywhere you are?" she grumbled, placing it back into the bookbag.

"Duh. That's why there are literally payphones all over the place. You can't rely on a cellular phone," Bagel sneered.

Pansy hauled the bag back onto her shoulders and started back down the trail, but after Bagel described the condition of the body, their conversation became limited. They were busy climbing over brush and negotiating the path, intent on getting back to the parking lot as quickly as possible to begin the next step of the plan. Lee and I floated behind them, completely unbothered by the pace.

"Okay, so what on earth were you doing out here to find that body in the first place?" Lee didn't strike me as the one-with-nature type any more than Pansy did, so the out of the way location could easily have gone a hundred years without being found.

"Well, I was bored, so I was floating around in the woods looking for dead bodies."

"As one does."

"Look, I worked the crime beat in Denver for several years before we moved back to Perth. I've seen things that would curl your hair, and we've got miles and miles of the perfect dumping ground out here. It's just a thing I do when there's nothing going on at the station."

"You know you could just go hang out in a bigger city, right? I'm sure Boulder or Colorado Springs has a lot more crime going on. I bet their stations are hopping all night long."

"Been there, done that. It's just not the same. If I hear a call come in for a domestic disturbance in Perth, I can almost guarantee that I know exactly who it is. I already know their entire backstory. In the big city, it's all too impersonal. It's a crime happening to strangers, and while that can be entertaining for a few weeks, it's just not the same as knowing all the victims and perps. In Perth, I know their parents, their siblings, their children. Now, you've got me off track here. Where was I?"

"You were doing a one man search and rescue."

"Yeah, so, I was going down this trail and spotted a Momma deer and two fawns and I followed them down a path towards the creek because the babies were... well, they were really cute, okay?" He cleared his throat and I held my tongue.

"Now, like I said before, this was about ten years ago and he was propped up against the log then. He hadn't been dead long. He still had skin and hair and the animals hadn't messed with him much at that point." I was suddenly grateful for the disguising vines of honeysuckle that may have hidden any animal activity on the poor man's bones, from my view.

"So, I would come back and check on him every once in a while, but trying to find him in the winter snow is almost impossible. Covered in a three-foot blanket of fluffy ice, he looks just like every other snowy lump by a creek."

Lee kept me entertained with Denver crime stories until we were finally out of the shade of the forest and back into the sunshine of the parking lot. Pansy made a beeline for the payphone and lifted the receiver, smashing the 0 for the operator as soon as she had a dial tone. We were too far from home to call without paying an outrageous amount in quarters, so Pansy pulled the oldest trick in the book, a collect call that we had no intention of being collected upon. I waited next to her as she gave the operator our home number and she shot me a wink as the call was connected. Dad must have answered, because as soon as I heard the prerecorded voice of the automated operator ask if he'd like to accept a collect call, Pansy spit out, "DadWeFoundItWe'reSafe," all at once. She listened for him to respond and hung up the receiver. "Mission accomplished," she told me with a wink before lifting the receiver again and dialing 911.

The 911 operator seemed to have a hard time understanding that the body wasn't recently deceased and that performing CPR would not produce favorable results for anyone involved. After a few minutes of questioning, Pansy finally made her understand where they were and what was going on. After promising to sit tight and wait for the calvary, Pansy hung up and made her way back over to the Bronco. Bagel had the tailgate open, leaning against the back of the seats with his knees dangling from the edge. Pansy jumped up to join him and he offered her a Slim Jim that he'd dug out of his glove box. Lord only knew how long it had been in there, but much to my surprise, she ate it. That double cheeseburger must have worn off a few miles back.

13

About twenty minutes later, a mint green F-150 pulled into the lot, a Colorado Forest Service badge on its side and yellow lights flashing on top to show it was on an important mission. The truck pulled a trailer carrying two four wheelers with large plastic tool boxes on their back racks. Two young guys wearing dark green coveralls got out of the truck and one came over to confirm with Bagel that he and Pansy were the ones that had called in the body. The other guy began futzing with the trailer to offload the Kawasakis.

"There's a couple of places where trees are down and at least two slips in the trail before you get to where we marked the deer trail down to the body," Bagel said, eyeing the machines. Four-wheelers would cut their trip down, but the trees were definitely going to make them go the long way around some of them.

"Yeah, we know," he pointed to the black utility box on the back. "This trail was already listed for repairs, so we packed the chainsaws. The slips we can go around for now, so we're going to go ahead and clear a path for the medical examiner when they send a crew out tomorrow."

"What? They don't work on Sundays?" Pansy asked.

"Not if they can help it. Besides, if its skeletal remains, one more day won't hurt him any. We'll post someone out tonight to keep watch over the site and make sure no one gets too close. We've got a bunch of weirdo looky-loos around here, so we certainly won't leave it alone, but moving it out of there can wait another day. So, how far out are we going and what are we looking for? Did you mark the trail with anything?"

"It took us about two hours to get there on foot and I left my scarf around a tree branch. It's hot pink with little fuzzy balls on the end. You can't miss it."

"Gotcha. So, if you don't mind me asking, why did you leave the trail in the first place? You know that's incredibly dangerous, right?"

Bagel held up the camera, still dangling from the strap around his neck. "I saw some cool shapes in the light and left her on the trail so that I could explore a little. Then I heard water and thought I could get some shots of the creek, but it was too far down. When I turned around to start back up the hill, I saw the bag and went over to check it out."

Bagel was pretty adept at this ad-libbing script thing. If photography didn't work out for him, he may need to enroll in the community theater. He'd brushed his hair out of his eyes and gave the officer a charming smile. No sullen emo kid here. Nope, just a perfectly normal boy and girl out hiking in the woods. Ignore the two ghosts lurking in the background.

A silver Crown Vic with blue and black decals pulled into the lot just as the forestry dudes started down the trail on their four-wheelers. The state patrol guys introduced themselves and the portly older guy that looked like Wilfred Brimley took Bagel's statement while they stood at the back of the Bronco. The younger guy, who looked like he'd actually be able to chase a suspect if needed, had Pansy in the passenger seat of the

Crown Vic asking her questions. Lee and I were floating back and forth to confirm everyone's story stayed the same. As no crime had actually been committed, neither of them were stupid, and it was a pretty simple story, the cops didn't show a single hint of suspicion.

"I'm probably going to hang out with the body, if you don't mind. Once they clear all of the vines and debris away, I want to see what condition his body is in and see if they mention any signs of foul play. I always felt like he probably broke his ankle or something and then froze to death, but maybe that's just the story I made up for myself." Lee was staring out into the forest and I knew his journalist brain would demand that he get the whole scoop.

"Yeah, he's your find. Go babysit him and let us know what all they do tomorrow with the medical examiner. Honestly, that is all stuff I do not want to visualize for eternity, but you can tell me the PG version tomorrow evening, okay?"

"Sure thing, Kiddo. Oh, and tell the kids how much I appreciate this. I'm hoping this brings some closure to a family out there somewhere."

"I hope so too."

Lee disappeared back into the forest and as I was floating back over to the Bronco, I saw a familiar van with a satellite dish mounted on top pulling in with a spray of gravel. Oh, crap. The reporter and cameraman from the other night jumped out and Cameraman Mike was filming in less than thirty seconds. He panned over Bagel and Pansy by the Bronco, the entrance to the trail and the forest service truck with its empty trailer.

The patrolmen, who had been leaning against the hood of their car comparing notes, quickly straightened up and started towards the news van. I assumed they were going to stop the filming. It took me a second to realize that they were elbowing one another out of the way to be the first to be interviewed about a dead body that neither of them had actually laid eyes on.

"It's like they've never been on television before," Pansy said, the disdain evident in her tone.

"Well, not everyone gets interviewed every other month like you do," I told her.

I was telling Pansy about Lee staying the night with the body when the reporter must have looked over and recognized them from the Sanitarium. He hastily finished up his interview with the patrolmen and jogged over to the Bronco.

"Mr. Ventura, Miss Bellafini, am I to understand that you have found yet another body? This is a phenomenal coincidence. Do you mind if I ask you both a few questions?" I didn't like the look in his eye, and I still hadn't forgiven him for the hatchet job interview he'd done at Chivington. Apparently, neither had Pansy.

"Judging by your last interview, it doesn't make any difference what questions you ask me if you go back and dub in entirely different questions before broadcast, does it?" I don't know that I'd ever seen her this mad, or this vocal about being mad. I sincerely hoped that she didn't start to cry and ruin this moment of righteous fury.

Mr. Smith held both hands up in surrender and chuckled. "Now, now, I promise you, I just do the field interviews. What my producers do with that footage afterward, I have no control over."

"If you're not in control, then I guess you're not interviewing us," Bagel said. He was leaning against the open tailgate with his arms crossed, his sullen emo-teen-look firmly back in place.

"Look, I promise I'll work with the editing team and my producer and give only factual news bites on this one? Okay? I swear. I think you both deserve recognition for locating this person, and the family of the deceased will want to see the faces of the people who worked so hard to reunite them with their loved one."

He was smooth, I'd give him that, and Pansy finally capitulated. Before they were done with Mr. Smith, two journalists from rival newspapers showed up one after another and the questioning continued.

"Well, that wasn't as traumatic as I thought it would be," Pansy said forty minutes later as Bagel finally pulled out of the parking lot. She turned the heat on full blast before searching the depths of her bookbag for her Chapstick.

"Lord, I hope they cut our interviews. I expected cops. I didn't think about having to deal with a news crew, again," Bagel grumbled.

"I know! At least I didn't have on a hot pink hat and mittens this time around," Pansy said, brushing her windswept hair out before pulling it back into a ponytail. "You did pretty good, though. With both the cops and the news people. It's like you turned into a whole different person."

"I was just trying to be friendly."

Pansy snorted. "Maybe that was it. You act like you're mad all the time. Friendly isn't a default setting for you."

"Well, it's school. I'm usually mad about something."

"Well, I'm just saying that you handled them really well."

"Thank you. You didn't do too bad yourself. And I was really proud of you for calling out that news guy. The nerve of that guy. But you sounded great in the interview, no stuttering or anything."

"He's right, you did great. Tell him I was super proud of him, too."

"Gerri said she's proud of us."

For the first time in weeks, my boy grinned with genuine happiness. We'd all done our good deeds for the day.

Pansy had showered, eaten half the fridge and then passed out on the couch under a fluffy blanket after returning home. So, when Dad yelled, "You're going to be on TV!" He scared the crap out of her. She surfaced from the depths of exhaustion by sitting straight up and swinging at whatever must be attacking her.

"Sorry, Pumpkin, I didn't mean to scare you. But look," he pointed toward the television which had already moved on to a commercial break. "Well, it's gone now, but they did a little preview of what's coming up next and your face was up there."

Mom grabbed the remote and hit 'record' on the VCR while Pansy jumped up to grab the cordless phone from the coffee table. She called Bagel. His mom answered the phone and I could hear how excited she was from halfway across the room. Pansy hit 'end call' and laid the receiver down before looking over at me. "She already knew."

"Of course she did. Look, it's back on!"

"Welcome back," the lady said, holding her papers up and tapping them on end to straighten them before turning her 100-watt smile to the camera. "Sad news coming out of Costilla County tonight. The remains of what is thought to be a deceased male have been discovered near the Los Fuertes trail on the western edge of the Culebras. Two teenagers, students at Perth High School in Las Animas County, stumbled across the body while out on a hike. One teen, Dario Ventura, an aspiring photographer, had wandered off the trail while taking photos. Here's the interview conducted this afternoon by our own Josh Smith."

"Dario, what made you decide to leave the trail?"

The video showed Bagel swinging his camera up into frame and giving his most charming smile. "Well, I was taking photos, and I thought the light looked really nice, filtering through the trees, you know. So I started down this deer path. I could hear water, so I thought maybe I could get pictures of the creek. I just kind of stumbled across the backpack."

"And you, Miss Bellafini, were you with him when he found the body?"

"Oh, no, I was waiting on the trail. There's been a lot of rain lately and I try not to slide down muddy deer paths as a general rule."

"Well, that's not bad," I said, relieved that they hadn't made her look like a lunatic this time. After a week or two, no one would remember this, right?

The feed switched back to the studio and the angle changed; the newscaster looking straight into the camera now. "While our sources cannot officially confirm the identity of the deceased, they did tell us that a bag near the body, believed to have belonged to the deceased, contained a driver's license indicating that the body may be that of famed musician, Stewart Mays." The screen changed to a photo of a mustached man with a crooked smile wearing a cowboy hat no cowboy would be caught dead in.

"Oh no," Pansy and I exhaled at the same time.

"Now, country music fans will remember that Mays went missing almost a decade ago after a public argument with model girlfriend, Trina Breeze. Again, authorities have not positively identified the body at this time, and won't be able to give us a cause of death until an autopsy is performed later this week. However, it looks like one of the most infamous mysteries of the 1980s may have finally been solved."

My heart sank. Mom and Dad stared at one another, and Pansy had her eyes squeezed tight.

"Now, for you regular viewers at home, if you think these teens look familiar, that's because we interviewed them both just last week. That's right, they're part of the Perth Paranormal Society and we recorded them as they investigated the infamous Chivington Sanitarium, better known as the Castle around these parts."

They played a clip of the interview with Bagel and Pansy in the basement, muted while they talked about it, and then a generic clip of the Castle investigation that they'd filmed as part of their B-roll that night. In it, Randy was pointing at something with an EMF detector while talking to Summer.

"You may also recognize young Pansy Bellafini from her discovery several months ago of the body of young Christopher Fairchild. The discovery helped to solve the forty-two-year-old missing persons case while also uncovering an illegal mining and real estate scheme that was taking place near to where the body was found." The screen changed to a montage of clips from that news interview, video of the body being lifted out of the canyon, and an archive photo of Christopher from days when he'd been a living, breathing little boy.

When the screen changed to a clip of our Cavalier with the guardrail still impaling the passenger side door, the whole family gasped at once. "You may also remember the story of the Bellafini sisters' wreck last November, a tragic motor vehicle accident where only one twin, Pansy, survived."

"Could they make this more sensational?" I whispered. I'd never seen the footage of our crash, just the photos from the police report. No one had ever told me we'd made the news that night.

Pansy had her hand over her mouth, but the newscaster didn't stop there. "Joining us in the studio to discuss this phenomena, everyone's favorite psychic medium, Madame Brousseau."

All four of us gasped again as the camera panned to Madame Brousseau, a self-professed psychic who was a favorite for the local news stations to trot out and entertain their audiences.

"Why are they doing this?" Pansy whispered, more to herself than to the room at large, but I heard her.

"The news guy. He only swore that he would air what you actually said. He didn't promise that they wouldn't still make you look like a human cadaver dog."

The effort required for the Madame to speak in an obviously fake accent, one that varied wildly between French-ish and German-ish, caused the ridiculous purple turban on top of her head to bobble with every word. It was just enough out of sync with the swaying of her third chin to be distracting. "Zome-times ze tragic death of a loved vun, ezpecially vun as close as a twin seester, it opens ze veil between vorlds. It makes vun more susceptible to conversations with ze spirits on ze other side. I can feel zis connection from the young Miss Bellafini. I sense zat she is vun with ze spiritual vorld and zis is vhy ze dead are seeking her out to help locate zem."

"Oh my god," Pansy hissed.

Oh yeah, this was absolutely the worst-case scenario.

14

Pansy stayed home from school the next morning and Mom didn't even bother arguing with her about it. She'd gone back to sleep and was still in bed when I got back from Mrs. Garcia's, so I woke her up and put her to work.

"If you're not going to school, then you've got time to search through the internet for anything that has anything to do with beings that thrive on pulling energy out of humans."

"What, like I can enter that as a search parameter?"

"Just scroll. Make notes on anything interesting, scroll some more. I feel like we've made no progress on this thing.

"And you're sure that it is a thing? It's not just Jessica messing with us?"

"I honestly don't know. My plan was to go hang out at the castle today and ask Jessica about the near death experience Mr. Browning had. I'd like to warn him about his wife and this Dixon dude trying to kill him off, but I can barely make a pencil roll, let alone pick one up and write with it.

"I could write him a letter," Pansy offered.

"Yeah, but what if the wife opens the mail? We need to get him a message that we know he'll see."

"What about email? Do you think he has one? Would he have written it down anywhere?" Pansy gestured to her list of emails and favorite websites that she'd pinned to the corkboard above my desk. I was still mad that she'd put a pushpin right through Brendan Fraser's face when she'd tacked her list up there, covering the photo that I'd ripped out of a magazine a few years back. She could have at least had the decency to put the hole in Pauly Shore.

"Maybe. Email would certainly get to him faster than snail mail or having someone hand deliver it. I'll see what I can find."

I left Pansy scrounging in the kitchen looking for breakfast and headed west to interrogate a ghost. I swung east first, checking in at the Perth Police station to see if Lee had made it back, but there was no sign of him. It hadn't occurred to me to ask him where the body would be taken, so I didn't know if he'd be in Trinidad or since the body belonged to a huge celebrity meant it'd be transported to one of the bigger cities. At least I knew what he was doing, even if I didn't know where he was doing it.

The morning was sunny and looked warm and the columbine and may flowers blooming wild along the roadsides gave the scenery a nice pastel tint hinting at warmer temperatures to come. I was surprised by the lack of noise as I approached the Castle. It was almost ten on a Monday morning and there wasn't a single human being on site. No electric saws, no hammering, no drilling. The extension cords were still strung through the rooms and hallways like multi-colored spaghetti, but they weren't connected to anything.

"Lucy, I'm home!" I yelled in my best Ricky Ricardo voice. After Pansy had cried herself to sleep last night, I'd needed the brainlessness of watching Nik at Nite all evening to let my mind decompress and there'd been an I Love Lucy mini-marathon. A joke, however, was only funny if someone was there to hear it.

Jessica didn't answer and was nowhere to be found. Why did she never answer?

"Jessica!" I yelled again as I floated up and down between floors, waiting for her to pop out of a wall and scare me. Why was no one here? I floated out to the carriage house and began to snoop around the dining room, quickly locating a spiral-bound notebook next to a laptop that was full of what looked like passwords. Near the top of the list was what I assumed was the owner's email address, and I took a few minutes to memorize it. That was hands down the easiest thing we'd done in this entire investigation.

Proud that I'd accomplished something useful, I left the carriage house and spotted Jessica in the back patio area of the hotel, floating next to what looked like some kind of maintenance shed. Rusted metal panels and rotted two by fours that must have originally given it shape appeared to have fallen down about twenty years ago and no one had touched them since. Weeds stood up around the mess like whoever had mown the grass hadn't wanted to get too close, and most of it was wrapped in morning glory vines. All in all, not exactly something scenic to come out and stare at. Jessica hadn't spotted me yet, so I hung back, waiting to see what she was doing.

The silence was broken by something inside the building crashing. Jessica turned at the noise, clearly startled to see me floating there.

"What was that?" I said, forgetting that I was supposed to be sneaking around.

Jessica quickly floated back inside to see what had caused the noise, and I was right on her heels. A scaffolding in one of the first-floor hallways where small offices were being opened up to make larger office spaces had fallen over, dumping three five-gallon buckets of paint into the floor where they'd busted. The top corner of the scaffolding had busted through the drywall of the opposite wall, making quite a mess. I floated away from the spreading pool of paint and looked up to see Jessica pointing down the hallway toward the lobby. There, backlit by the early morning light streaming in through the lobby windows, was a man-shaped shimmer.

It was a distortion, like a heat shimmer on hot blacktop, but as I stared, it moved across the lobby and away from us. "Was that...?"

"So you can see him," she whispered. "It is not just me. He has fed too much in these last few weeks and has become stronger."

"That's probably not good news, right?" her look said it all. "We've been looking for books and searching online for any hint of other ghosts like this one. We haven't had any luck so far, but Pansy's scrolling through the internet today." Her confused look made me pause. "Yeah, don't worry about what that is, but she's doing research today to see if anyone else has experienced anything like this and if they can help us or not. Which reminds me, you said he doesn't talk, but do you mean he doesn't have conversations or really can't make words?"

"I have never heard him speak. That, of course, does not mean he is incapable, but why do you ask?"

"I was hoping he had a name or had said some word or made some sound that could help us narrow down who or what he is."

Her face never changed expression, but she paused for a minute, and I supposed she was thinking back to any clues she may have missed. "I cannot help you with this, but I pray a solution is found before it is too late. No one has been killed as of yet, just weakened, but you can see," she waved her hand toward the end of the hallway where I had, in fact, seen the being in question. "The Other is becoming more like himself.

Soon, he'll have the strength to drain an entire person in one sitting."

"Well, it's a good thing that there's no one here to feed on today. Where is everyone, by the way?"

"They are too afraid to come. There was an incident over the weekend involving Mr. Browning and, I'm afraid, it frightened the workers."

"Yeah, I heard about his close call. That's part of the reason I came today. Did you see it happen?" I didn't want her to immediately think that I was accusing her, although she was certainly a suspect on my list.

"I was actually standing right beside him," she said. "He was screaming at someone while holding something that looked like a black brick, but smaller, to his ear. I was trying to get a better look at it because it seemed to be a kind of telephone device, but there was no cord."

"Yeah, a cell phone. Where did it happen? Did you see if it was one of the workers who dislodged the concrete or if it was the Other?"

She tilted her head to one side, thinking back. "It happened on the west stairs and no, I remember looking up to see if... to see if the Other was there, but the only person above Mr. Browning was his business partner, that Dixon fellow. As I have never seen the man lift a finger to do any kind of labor before, I could not imagine any reason he would have been carrying such debris. It must have been left on a stair tread and perhaps the vibrations from the equipment knocked it off?"

"Uh, huh. Sure. So, did you already know that the business partner has been sleeping with Browning's wife?"

"Well, I may have noticed their indiscretions, but I certainly would not spread such tales." She looked... offended was the only word I could think of to describe her expression.

"They're also planning to kill him, collect the insurance, and run away to Florida."

Jessica showed no signs of being shocked by any of that, her dark brown eyes narrowed as she thought over the ramifications of such a plot. "And then they would leave, correct? They would take their blood money and leave once and for all."

"I mean, that's their plan, but we can't let them kill the man."

"No, no. Of course not." I was not reassured by her words.

It was mid-afternoon when I tired of following Jessica and the Other around. I'd tried to talk to it, but like the loop ghosts, it didn't respond to me. It was too much to hope that it would just stop and give its name and a list of demands. By the time I made it home, Pansy was dressed and in the middle of brushing out her hair.

"Where are you going?"

"To Summer's to watch tapes." I rolled my eyes, but I guess Summer was as social as Pansy was willing to get right now.

"Before you go, write this down before I forget it." I gave her Mr. Browning's email address, and she jotted it down in her notebook.

"I'll send him an email tonight when I get back. Did you talk to Jessica?"

I filled her in on the new tricks the Other was gaining, and let her know that Mr. Dixon was the most likely suspect in the attempted braining of Mr. Browning. "Jessica said that all the workers have run off and no one will come back. It's not looking good for Mr. Browning to get this hotel built even if his wife and partner don't take him out first. Or Jessica."

"Jessica? Why would she want to kill him off?"

"Well, I explained to her the wife's plan to kill him and collect the insurance so that she can sell the place and go back to Florida. And Jessica... I don't know, she just seemed to appreciate the idea a little too much, you know what I mean? It would mean the hotel would be empty again and everyone would be safe. What about you? Did you find anything helpful while you were playing hooky?"

"I don't know about helpful, but I searched for everything from vampires to demons. We should either shoot it with a silver bullet, trap it in a salt circle, or dig up the body and burn the bones. There was also an article from some dude down in Louisiana that involved beheading a chicken that I will absolutely not be discussing."

"We may have to go to the chatrooms and just straight up ask," I said.

"Then the answers would come directly to us, right? That seems like less work," she set her hairbrush down on the dresser and pushed her dark hair back with a headband. "I've got to go. I told Summer I'd be there after her two o'clock class, but we can try it later and maybe get some better results."

At this point, I'd be happy with any results. I felt like, much like the Other, we were running around in circles.

15

Pansy parked in the employee lot behind Wild Harmony as much to avoid the attention of the other students as to avoid any of her teachers from seeing her out and about when she'd claimed to be sick. A bright yellow Geo Tracker was hard to hide in a small town. After exiting the alley onto the sidewalk, she diverted into the Firefly to get a soda. I was checking out the hanging baskets that Summer had hung from her awning when the school bell rang to dismiss.

Somewhere mid-pack, Bagel emerged from the front doors of the school, head down, walking at a pace way slower than everyone else pushing and shoving to make their escape. I recognized the look of barely contained rage on his face and wished that I could whisk him a hundred miles away alá I Dream of Genie. He'd been left to face all the comments by himself today and judging by his trajectory, he planned on drowning his anger in a chocolate peanut butter milkshake. He'd almost crossed Main Street and was two steps from the sidewalk in front of the cafe when Pansy walked out the door.

Oh no.

"Oh, hey. I was just going to Summer's to watch some tapes

if you want..." she paused, finally keying in to his facial expression. "What's wro—oh."

"Yeah. Oh." he said, moving past her and pushing through the front door of The Firefly Cafe. The cheeriness of the overhead bell was misplaced as Pansy turned and followed him back inside.

"Look, I'm sorry. I just couldn't face anyone today."

Bagel continued walking towards the back counter. "You could have called me this morning and given me a head's up. If I'd known I was going to have to face everyone by myself, I would have stayed home, too."

The bell jingled again, but Pansy was looking at her shoes and Bagel was staring straight ahead at the menu board.

"I'm sorry, I just didn't think..."

"About anyone other than yourself?" Bagel interrupted. "Yeah, you seem to be stuck in that rut lately."

Ooh, way harsh, Tai.

"Oh, are the lovebirds having a fight? What's wrong? Are you two upset that your romantic hike in the woods was ruined by some dead guy?" Danielle had laid her books on an empty table and stood with her hands on her hips. Once they'd both turned to look at her, she flipped her waist length blond hair over one shoulder and scanned Pansy and Bagel over like they were a new species of fungus. Andrea, who I'd always thought of as Danielle's sidekick, quickly assumed a similar pose, the effect slightly diminished by her chewing a piece of gum like a cow with its cud.

"You know what you should do? You and your little boyfriend here should go see that new movie about witchcraft. It seems like something that freaks like you would be interested in," she continued.

"Are we having a disagreement? Yes. Is it any of your business? No. And he is not my boyfriend," Pansy snarled.

"Oh, that's right," Danielle smirked. "Bagel Boy here was dating your sister, wasn't he? I mean, you two were identical, so I guess one is just as good as the other?" She turned to Andrea with as much drama as she could muster, the bell sleeves of her babydoll dress fluttering through the air as she held her hand to her heart. "Andrea, please remind me to never hang out with freaks. Obviously their ideas of what's normal get skewed when they associate with Satan."

Several sharp intakes of breath could be heard throughout the room.

"You know, Danielle, we were actually fighting over whether or not you stuff your bra. Pansy seems to think that those giant knockers of yours are real, but me and some of the other guys at school think you've got half your sock drawer in there." Way to deescalate the situation there, Bagel.

Danielle all but growled before pulling her spine straighter, her hands clenched at her sides. Andrea choked on her gum.

"Everyone thinks that you're doing it," she spat out. "Who knows what you two are really up to when you're supposed to be investigating those houses at night." Her eyes narrowed and if I'd been able to sling an insult, I would have warned her about anger causing crow's feet. "Just so you know, Jamie Peterson said he saw you two out in the graveyard. He said that you were both naked." Andrea, who'd never had an original thought in her life, nodded her head in agreement like this was the general consensus around school.

"I am not dating Dario!" Pansy screamed. Every head in the place turned in her direction and I watched in horror as my sister apparently lost her dang mind. "Look at me. Do you honestly think that someone like him is my type?" She waved a hand down the length of her oxford shirt and sweater vest before turning to gesture towards Bagel in his oversized Slayer tee and wallet chain. No, these two things did not go together, but she didn't have to sound so offended. "He doesn't even like girls, for god's sake," she hissed.

In the time it had taken this argument to take place, the room had filled with the after-school crowd and as Pansy made this proclamation, every single one of them, including both Bagel and myself, gasped in shock. She had not just said that.

Bagel's face hardened. Without looking at Pansy, he said, "I know this may come as a shock to you, but have you ever considered that maybe I just don't like you," There was complete silence as he walked past the other tables towards the front door. No one moved a muscle. Even Danielle and Andrea were too stunned to move. The bell jingling as he walked out was like a signal, and everyone started talking at once, the volume suddenly crushing. Pansy, her brain finally catching up to her mouth, ran out the door after him.

I stayed to see how bad the fallout would be. At least fifteen different conversations and debates sprung up around the room, and I tried to catch the gist of each.

"I can't believe she was that rude to him."

"Yeah, just because he was in love with your sister doesn't mean there's something wrong with him when he doesn't want you."

"I don't know. I can kind of see it. He's so freakin' sensitive."

"He's an artist. Have you not seen his paintings? Besides, he and Gerri were like, practically engaged since middle school."

"He doesn't play any sports, you know."

"I cannot believe she would say something like that. I mean, I had a math class with Dario and he has the most beautiful eyelashes."

"Well, you know, I flirted with him a lot in eighth grade and he never even asked me for my number, so I've always wondered."

"As if! Who does she think she is insulting him like that? It's not like she's such a great prize or anything."

It seemed like while Bagel may be scrutinized a little closer for the next few weeks, most of the crowd preferred to believe that Pansy was jealous and trying to be cruel. I was completely fine with that if it meant my best friend was protected. With a sigh of relief, I floated out of the restaurant and quickly caught up to the pair. They were standing in the alley between the row of businesses along Main Street, tears running down both of their faces.

"I am so sorry. I didn't mean it." Pansy tried to grab his arm, but he ripped it back out of her grip.

"Do not touch me," he hissed.

Pansy was ugly crying at this point, but I was still so mad at her I couldn't even bring myself to console her. "Are you trying to get him killed? I told you, in confidence, that I suspected he was gay. He never told me he was, and do you know why? Because his dad already told us that if any kid of his decided to be gay that he'd have to beat it out of them." I didn't want her to feel better, but I also didn't want him to be afraid. "Tell him that almost everyone thinks you were just mad because you were fighting and only said that about him being gay because you were jealous. He's still safe."

"Really? Oh, thank goodness." She relayed this information to Bagel, and he leaned against the brick building, sliding down until he was sitting in the filthy alley.

"Dario, I... I feel terrible."

"Good. You should feel terrible because you are a terrible person. How dare you insult me like that? Did you ever think that you weren't my type? In your little buttoned up shirts and shiny shoes and never a hair out of place. Do you think guys like this kind of preppy look? I know a lot of guys and this," he waved his hand up and down in front of her, "is not what they're looking for. Even if I did like girls, and even I'm not really sure where I stand on that, not that it is any of your business, there is no chance on earth that you would be my type."

"I said I was sorry. I know that I was rude, I know. I was... I don't know. I've never had anyone be mean to me before."

"Of course you haven't. You had a perfect little family in a perfect little house and Mommy and Daddy buy you whatever you've ever wanted and you're so smart that you've never had to study for anything, ever. You and Gerri both. But you know, Gerri was never stuck up about it, and that's all that you've ever been. You have wasted so much of your life concerned every second of the day about what other people think about you. Always trying to be perfect. So, yeah, I'm glad that you finally get to experience people talking about you behind your back and to your face. Welcome to what real life is like, Pans. It's not butterflies and rainbows for the rest of us."

He leaned his head back against the dirty bricks and wiped the tears from his face. "I need to get out of this town and away from these small-minded people. Most of the jerks in our class will bask forever in the glory of their high school popularity and do nothing else with their lives. I need to get out of here."

"Look," Pansy said, wiping her nose on the sleeve of her shirt. "I was going to Summer's to review the last batch of tapes. Come with me? Keep me company, please?"

Bagel didn't respond for a minute and I thought maybe he hadn't heard her until he finally started shaking his head. "No, you've made it clear, repeatedly, that I'm not good enough for you. I'll respect your wishes and get out of here." He pushed to his feet, brushing the dirt from his pants and the back of his shirt. Pansy nodded, wiping at her cheeks as she watched him walk away. At the end of the alley, he turned and gave her one last parting shot that left both of us no doubts how furious he was.

"You know, every single day I wish it was Gerri that had lived in that crash."

Pansy looked like he'd smacked her across the face as he turned and jogged back across the street.

"He's right though," she finally said, her voice barely above a whisper. "I wish it was you, too."

Since I was almost mad enough to agree, I kept my mouth shut.

I fully expected Pansy, who was still clutching her drink, although I was sure most of the ice had melted by now, to get back in her Tracker and go home. Instead, she walked back out to Main Street and turned toward Wild Harmony.

"I figured you'd just go home," I said as she stomped into the store.

"I need to blow my nose," she muttered.

Summer was at the counter talking to Sarah but stopped mid-sentence when she saw Pansy's tear-streaked face. "Pansy, what's wrong? Are you hurt?"

"No, I'm okay. But can I bum a tissue? Or ten?"

"I mean, I certainly don't want them back, but yes, of course. Why don't you come upstairs? You can wash your face off and I'll make us some tea. You look like you could use it."

Pansy nodded and followed Summer up the stairs, careful not to step on Summer's dark green broomstick skirt that trailed three steps behind her. Summer directed Pansy to the bathroom while she went to the kitchen and filled an electric kettle. The kettle was beeping by the time Pansy emerged from the bathroom, face scrubbed and sleeves rolled up to her elbows.

"Lemon verbena or vanilla chamomile?" she asked as Pansy

took a seat at the little two person table that looked like it would barely hold two plates.

"Uh, vanilla? I guess?" Summer chose a tea bag and placed a mismatched cup and saucer in front of Pansy along with a box of Thin Mints she'd pulled from the freezer.

"This looks like it calls for Girl Scout cookies. What's up?"

"I stayed home from school today because of the news and Dario was mad because he had to face it all alone and then I accidentally outed him in front of everyone in the Firefly and now he's never going to speak to me again."

"Okay, so that's a lot," Summer said, pausing to take a sip of her tea from a chipped mug decorated with the faded image of a feather . "Let's start at the beginning. What news? Facing what alone?"

"You know she doesn't watch television," I reminded Pansy.

"Oh, you...you haven't seen the news yet? About the body we found?"

"You found a body? Where? Who was it?"

Pansy quickly explained about Lee finding the body and that they had volunteered to go pretend to find it. "We just thought it was some lost hiker, you know? If I'd known it was someone famous, we would have found some way to let someone know without having the news people trying to hunt me down. I tried to do some research online today, and the phone kept ringing and kicking me off the internet. Our answering machine tape is full of people wanting me to do interviews. This one woman who claims she's a psychic medium left me two separate messages today. Like, take a hint already, lady, I don't want to talk to you."

"Oh, that's not good," Summer whispered. "And you said the local news had already picked this up?"

"Yeah, we were on locally last night. I just couldn't face everyone at school today, so I stayed home. But I didn't call

Dario to tell him and he went and... apparently he took a lot of crap from the other kids all by himself. So, I ran into the Firefly to get a drink and he was there and we started to fight, and then these two girls who think they're like, god's gift or something, started picking on us and I opened my mouth, and..."

"And what?"

"Well, they were saying things about him dating Gerri and now must be doing things with me, and that's just ridiculous. Before I knew what I was doing, I told them he didn't even like girls." She was whispering by the time she got to the end of that sentence, and I made sure she could see me glaring at her.

"Oh, no," Summer said, pushing the sleeve of crisp minty chocolate toward Pansy.

"I'm a terrible person," Pansy spat out before the sobs began again.

"No, you're just young and made a bad decision under stress," Summer told her, reaching for the box of tissues. "Welcome to adulthood."

"So now," Pansy said, blotting her nose with a tissue. "Dario is never going to speak to me again and at the same time, what seems like every news reporter in the country is trying to interview us about locating this missing musician."

"Is it really that big of a story?" Summer walked the few steps from the table to the living room and began rummaging under a stack of paperbacks and half completed cross-stitch projects until she found the television remote. Turning the set on, she quickly turned the channel to CNN where Headline News was playing a piece on tornado damage across the Midwest.

"Maybe it won't be on. Surely, just because the dude was famous won't make it a bigger story than this," Summer muttered. Momentarily distracted by the images of the damage, neither said anything else until a photo of Stewart Mays came up.

"That's him," Pansy said.

The story played—an abbreviated version of the previous evening's broadcast. It left out the parts about my death and Pansy finding Christopher, but it did mention that she was a member of the PPS and used the same footage the local news had used the previous evening.

Summer sat on the couch so abruptly that I turned to make sure she hadn't tripped over the rug or something. Her eyes were wide, her face had gone pale, and she slowly covered her gaping mouth with one hand as she stared at the screen. "I'm on CNN," she whispered. Summer had never struck me as the type who was out for fame, so I was momentarily distracted by her amazement before Pansy started whining again..

"At least you look good. I look homeless in both of my interviews, and now the entire world is going to see me covered in mud."

"You know, not everything is about you," I said before she could start crying again. I was still mad at her and was over the theatrics. "That man gets to be buried by his family. They got answers. It was a good thing to do, even if it mildly inconveniences you for a few weeks. Bagel was right. Once you graduate from high school, you can leave and never see these people again. You're still alive. You have options. Suck it up."

I left her there with Summer and went to check on Bagel who, despite being upset, had pulled himself together and was at Foodarama bagging groceries. I floated there, watching him, but no one was asking him about the body. No one mentioned him being on the news, and no one seemed to notice that his eyes were red and slightly swollen. As he'd told me many times before, no one noticed the bag boy.

16

When there are only two people on earth that you can talk to and you weren't speaking to one and the other was off somewhere adventuring without you, it was easy for loneliness to creep in. I didn't go home that night, choosing instead to hang out at the Police station where Die Hard was playing on loop and the cops on night shift talked smack about those on day shift.

It was around one or two in the morning when Lee floated back through the door.

"What, are you staking out the office waiting for me?"

"Not really. I'm currently avoiding Pansy because I'm mad at her and this is the most interesting place to hang out at night."

"I'm aware, that's why I spend so much time here. So, what's up with you and Pansy?"

I filled him in on the news segment and the resulting fight between Pansy and Bagel.

"Do I need to go haunt this news reporter? I could track him down and follow him home," Lee offered.

"That sounds fun, but unnecessary. If we could just not find any more dead people or do anything that will get her face on the news for a few more weeks, that'd be great. Speaking of, I saw this evening that they'd confirmed the body was that musician dude."

"Yeah, you'd have thought from all the hoopla that they'd found the body of Christ or something. But his driver's license was in the pack and the police in whatever town in California he'd been living in had a copy of his dental records on hand because they'd already had a false alarm once before. They faxed the info over earlier this morning. Or yesterday morning, I guess," he said, looking at the clock to confirm we were firmly into Tuesday now.

"I went to Chivington yesterday to see if I could find Browning's email address and guess what I saw?"

Lee shuddered. "Hopefully it wasn't what I saw while I was there."

I resisted the urge to gag. "No, the Brownings weren't home and the construction crew was gone, so none of that is going on. But I saw the thing, the Other."

"Wait, why is the construction crew gone?"

"Apparently, they're all too scared to show up. Jessica said that the Other has made so many people sick or weak by drawing on their energy that they're all too afraid to come back."

"And you saw him?"

"Yeah, he was just how Jessica described him, a shimmer in the shape of a human."

"So he's drawn enough energy to be seen."

"Jessica said that the stronger he gets, the more damage he can do to a person he's draining. Also, I really hate using the word draining. We need better words for this."

"Words are the least of our problems." Lee waved his hand dismissively as he began to pace, floating in front of Crane's desk. "So Pansy sent the email warning him. Did you go back to see if he got it? Has he read it?"

"Uh… no. She hit send and then we left. Before we'd even made it into Wild Harmony, she was fighting with Bagel. Since then, I've been floating here, watching this stupid movie on repeat and reliving every single time in our entire lives she has made me mad and coming up with better arguments that I should have made."

"Well, that sounds productive." Lee rolled his eyes at me and I would have kicked him in the shin if I'd been able. "I think I'll head back to the Castle to see if this email hit home or if the wife deleted it before he even saw it. You coming?"

"Sure, but it's the middle of the night. Won't they be asleep?"

"Ahh, but will they be asleep in the same house or will someone have been kicked out already?"

With a shrug, I tagged along to see what we could see.

Our first stop was my bedroom where I left Lee outside and went in to wake Pansy up. She was never a fan of being woken up in the middle of the night and even less happy about it after our last conversation.

"What, what's wrong?" she mumbled, turning to face me.

"Did you check your email before you went to bed?"

"What?" she was snuggling back into the covers and I knew I was about to lose her.

"Pansy!" she snorted into an almost upright position, rubbing the sleep from her eyes.

"What?" she hissed.

"Email. Did you check it? Did Mr. Browning respond to the email you sent?"

"No," she whined, flopping back down onto the bed.

"No, you didn't check it or no, he didn't respond?"

"I checked it before bed and it showed that it was still unread."

"Good. Lee and I are heading back to the Castle to see how it goes when he reads the email."

Pansy pulled her purple daisy comforter back over her head and grumbled something about it being a school night, but I was already floating back out to Lee.

"She said she has the read receipt on and he hadn't read it when she checked it before bed."

"Which doesn't mean that he didn't read it after that, but he doesn't strike me as the kind of guy who spends a lot of time on a computer."

We floated directly to the carriage house without stopping in to see Jessica first. Honestly, I was surprised to see both of the Brownings snoring in their bed together, the light from the red LCD numbers on the alarm clock reflecting off of Mr. Browning's bald spot. It was enough to confirm his identity for us, even in the dark.

"Well, looks like he doesn't know yet."

"Did they ever mention how they planned to kill him? Poison him? Smother him in his sleep? Drop a cinderblock on his head?"

"I think their plan only extended to make it look like an accident. If it's obviously murder or if the insurance company suspects that it's suicide, they won't pay out the life insurance. At least they're smart enough not to write anything down." He floated back to the living room and looked over the laptop, which was still powered off and charging for the night. "We have a few hours to kill before this one will be up. Let's go see if I can get a gander at this poltergeist."

"In the dark?" I asked, but he was already halfway across the back lawn.

The place took on extra levels of spooky in the pitch black middle of the night with no living person around. One light was left on in the lobby area, I supposed to deter thieves or to give Mr. Browning a view through the wall of windows as he drove past. Either way, one bulb against the volume of darkness pressing against it was not a battle well fought. The corners all remained in darkness, and I couldn't even see the rocking knitter. I waved, just to be polite. Not that she noticed.

Lee was yelling for Jessica, and I surveyed the lobby, looking for any signs of a glimmer in the gloom. I started humming "Rainbow in the Dark" and Lee gave me a look when I broke out the air guitar.

"Are you done?"

"The question is, are you done? Unless it just happens to have a light behind it, which is the only reason I saw it in the first place, you won't be able to see it. A shimmer in the dark is still just darkness unless you've developed some paranormal sensory perception that I don't know about?"

"What I developed is the ability to turn on lights," he said. The 'duh,' was silent but implied.

"Oh."

"No need for that. Our friend is very regular in his patterns. If you wait for just a moment, you should be able to see him quite clearly." Jessica did that thing where she just popped out of nowhere, scaring the crap out of me once again.

She wasn't wrong, in less than ten minutes of what I would like to call a companionable silence (but couldn't because Jessica was just weird and too composed at all times and did the woman ever just relax?) we were finally treated to approximately seven or eight seconds of a shimmering mass coming down the east stairs and turning down the first floor wing. Lee was over there patting on his pajama pocket, looking for his notepad with what I assumed was a gleam in his eye. I could only assume because it was too dark to see it. After another few minutes, the shimmer appeared coming back out of the east wing and across the lobby to the west wing. Lee followed, leaving me alone with Jessica.

Great.

"So, this looks like the same path he took the other day. Does he ever vary his pattern?" I asked.

"No. During the rare times the building is not occupied, he continues to make his rounds."

"So, you've been watching him either attack people or float around in circles for decades?"

"Even when Chivington changed hands, there was not a long period where it sat empty. There were still workers here, much like now, but the building was only empty for a few weeks, not years. I remember that there was a veritable army of workers and they completed their tasks quickly. They made improvements to the kitchen with new appliances, and updated the electrical wires and plumbing, as they are doing now. Workers painted the walls, expanded the rose garden in the back, removed all the markers from the cemetery, and then added the fountain to the front drive."

"I'm sorry, what? Rewind. They removed the markers from a cemetery? What cemetery? Where was there a cemetery?"

Jessica pointed to the back of the building. "On the hillside beyond the Carriage House. It is where all the TB patients were originally buried. They had individual graves, of course." She seemed lost in thought for a minute. "When the Spanish flu struck the sanitarium, there was no time for individual graves. We were buried en masse to save time and digging. That was easier for the new owners, of course, there weren't any markers to remove. I don't even know if they knew we were there."

I'd heard of the Spanish Flu in history class, but our teacher had skipped the part about mass graves. "Why were you buried here? Didn't your family have their own cemetery somewhere?" I tried to visualize the area she'd indicated as it looked now, overgrown with scrub pines, sumac, and wild roses. There were no signs that anyone had ever been buried there and Blake hadn't found anything about it in his history of the property, or he certainly would have mentioned it.

"My family was notified, but they were also ill. In fact, my father was the only one to survive. Besides, time was of the essence. The dead needed to be buried quickly to remove the disease from the premises." Her voice trailed off like she was remembering to herself more than speaking to me. "We wrapped them in sheets until we ran out of sheets. There were so many... the tunnel to the mortuary was lined with bodies."

"What tunnel to what mortuary?"

"There was a mortuary?" Lee was back, a grin on his face and a spring in his... floating.

"Originally. It was in a building behind the Carriage House. You can still see the foundation stones, but the building itself collapsed years ago. There was once a tunnel that led there from the basement. It was walled off as part of the renovations for the nursing home."

"Jessica said that there was a cemetery on the hillside across from it and that she's buried there in a mass grave. She said when they updated things to make the place a nursing home, they took out all the grave markers."

"I guess a cemetery full of tuberculosis patients didn't jibe with their idea of aesthetics," Lee muttered before turning back to Jessica. "Why didn't you tell us there was a cemetery on the property? Maybe this Other was buried there, too?"

"Maybe he's in an unmarked grave and that's why he's haunting the hotel," I added.

"There were hundreds and hundreds of us buried in unmarked graves. None of them are haunting the hotel," Jessica pointed out.

"Except you," Lee pointed out.

"Except me."

"Can we see the tunnel?" I asked.

"See it? I can show you where it was, but it was filled in. There's nothing there to really see." She looked confused with my curiosity, but floated down to the basement and turned the light on for us. Disguised by multiple layers of paint and graffiti, the doorway was obvious when you were looking for it: a brick patch in a stone wall. I pushed my head through, but there was nothing but darkness on the other side, of course.

"I think I'd like to go check out the cemetery," Lee said after his own quick examination of the brick cover-up. "Nurse Daniels, would you like to give us the tour once the sun comes up?"

"It would truly be a waste of your time. There is nothing there to see but weeds." She was definitely an indoor cat.

"That's okay, we have to get back to watch the Brownings, anyway."

"Thanks for the history lesson. See ya later," I added.

She gave a curt nod and floated upstairs to do whatever it was she did when we weren't making her play twenty questions. Lee turned the light back off and we floated in the direction of the Carriage House.

Birds were waking up and conversing in the trees and the sky was lightening in that weird pre-dawn grayness that happened before the sun finally put in an appearance across the edge of the plains. We naturally floated over to the tumbled stones still marking the outline of the old mortuary, now a depressed pit covered in weeds. I looked back toward the Castle, trying to estimate the straightest line between the two.

"She said the bodies lined the tunnel. I guess I'd never thought about what happens when you have people dying left and right and no way to keep up."

"Especially when the doctors and nurses are also sick," he said absently. He was scanning the hillside and started floating that direction, so I tagged along because that is just what I did when I hung out with Lee.

"I touched the Other," he said with no preamble and I stopped floating after him for a second.

"What do you mean, you touched it? Like, you put your hand through it?"

"No, I reached out like I was going to touch something, a light switch, a piece of paper, and I touched him. I gave him a little push and my hand only went into him about an inch or so but he felt it. He stopped, turned, and looked at me for half a second before continuing on his way."

"Do you feel me when we've floated into each other?" I knew all I felt was like a little extra electrical buzz, but I'd never thought to ask him if he felt something different.

"No. Whatever this thing is, it's not like us."

I absolutely did not have the cojones to go around pushing weird paranormal beings, but decided not to bring that up. "So, he's definitely not threatened by you." I mean, as far as scary ghosts went, Lee was much more Tim Burton than Stephen King.

"I'm not worried about me. It's the living people who are in danger. He's powerful enough in just a few weeks to cause damage. I can't imagine what he'd be like once there are people living in the hotel, again."

As I thought about the potential disaster, I noticed that Lee's random floating was more like a grid pattern and I stopped following him again. "What are we doing? If you're looking for something, why don't you wait an hour or two when the sun is up and you can actually see?"

"I doubt there will be anything to see. I just wanted to know if anything out here was giving off any weird vibes."

"Weird vibes?" I muttered to myself because Lee was halfway up the hill by now. "Wait," I said, floating up after him. "I thought you didn't feel things like hot or cold, or weird vibes."

"Well, I don't, but I also didn't think I'd be able to touch the Other. It was worth a few minutes of my time to check it out, just in case." He pointed behind me. "Besides, I see a light on over at the carriage house."

The coffee pot in the Browning's kitchen sounded like it was in its death throes as we entered the house. I missed the smell of coffee. Browning was in an undershirt and a pair of pajama pants, sitting at the kitchen table with his PowerBook opened and powered on.

"Good news," he said as Mrs. Browning stumbled across the living room. Her hair was still in curlers and I was happy to see she'd at least pulled on a purple sweat suit before coming to get her morning coffee. "One of my investors saw that spot on the news about Chivington being haunted and they want to invest more money."

"More money?" she asked. It was obvious that the gerbil who ran on the wheel powering her brain had just picked up the pace. "That would be nice," she said absently as she spooned sugar into her coffee cup.

"Nice? I don't think you understand how broke we are right now. If we don't get more investors soon, we're going to have to file bankruptcy and sell everything here just to pay off our debts. Even if we sold it all, we'd still be in debt."

"Oh," she scowled into her mug.

"I'm going to have to fly out today to go to Salt Lake and

meet with them, can you drive me to the airport?" Lee had floated over behind Browning and was reading the screen of the PowerBook over the man's shoulder.

"He has Pansy's email pulled up," he said, grinning.

"So, there are no investors?"

"There might be, I can't see the rest of his inbox, but he's definitely plotting his escape from these people. He's a quick thinker, I'll give him that."

I floated behind Mr. Browning to see the screen for myself. Browning waited for his wife to wander into the living room with her mug of coffee before forwarding Pansy's email to someone with the email address of RobertSCarlysleAttorneyAtLaw.

Honestly, I'd expected some kind of denial, some waffling back and forth while he decided if an unsigned email from an account he didn't recognize could possibly contain a grain of truth, but Mr. Browning didn't seem to need time to think about it. Apparently, he had no problems believing that his lovely wife was capable of murder.

17

I was home by ten, leaving Lee behind to follow Mr. Browning and see where he really went, just in case we needed to locate him later. We'd also established a plan to meet at the Perth Police Station every night at midnight to exchange information and catch one another up. It wasn't like my midnights were booked solid or anything.

I landed in my front yard just in time to see our mother repeatedly screaming "Go away," and angrily waving a dish towel at two middle-aged men. One carried a handheld tape recorder, and the other was scribbling in a pocket-sized notebook. Both were beating a hasty retreat to their respective vehicles parked along the curb.

My plan to never speak to Pansy again lasted until she got home from school that afternoon. I absolutely needed to tell her all about how the email had worked and how Mr. Browning was escaping the evil clutches of his wife, and especially about Mom chasing off the reporters. However, all of that had to wait for her to quit crying first. She'd apparently held it in until she reached the safety of our house, but the minute she crossed the threshold she began sobbing. I followed her up the stairs, watching as she threw her book bag onto her desk before flinging herself across her bed.

"So, it went well, then?"

"Shut up," came the muffled reply from the depths of her pillow.

"What happened?" I asked and received a scream into said pillow as a response.

"Pansy, honey, what's wrong?" Mom had finally caught up and was standing in the doorway looking like she was afraid she wouldn't be welcome.

"Nothing, Mom," Pansy said, lifting her tear-streaked face from the pillow this time. "I'm just a freak who talks to ghosts. Or a witch, or a Satan worshiper that talks to the devil. Take your pick. I've heard it all today." She sat up on her bed, reaching for the box of tissues on her nightstand and blowing her nose. "Not that they say anything to me directly, it's all whispered loudly behind my back."

"Tell her about your fight with Bagel," I prompted.

For a second there I thought the sound that came out of her was a growl. "And I got into a fight with Dario yesterday at the Firefly," she finished, almost whispering.

"A fight with Dario? About what?" Mom came in to perch on the edge of the bed.

"He was mad that I skipped school and didn't tell him, because everyone was just as awful to him yesterday as they were to me today."

"Well, that doesn't sound like something he'd stay mad about for very long."

I glared at her. "And..."

"And then Danielle and Andrea came in and started teasing us about being in a lover's spat and I kind of accidentally outed him in the middle of the Firefly."

"Outed? You kicked him out?"

"No, Mom. I was really frustrated with everything going on and I kind of opened my mouth and... it just kind of came out. I told them he didn't even like girls."

"Why would you do that?" now Mom was whispering. I could tell she was having a mom-crisis, suddenly needing to mother someone but unsure which child needed it more. Who knew that this was all we'd needed to do to get her back on track?

"Gerri said they didn't believe me, or at least most of them didn't. But then we had a big fight in the alley, and said things we shouldn't have and, well, he's never going to talk to me again."

"Well, honestly, you were never very kind to him before Gerri died. Which was a shame, but I'd hoped when you two started hanging out that you'd come to be a better friend to him."

"I'm sorry. I tried to apologize today at school, but he held his hand up in front of my face and told me to talk to the hand because the face ain't listening. We were right by my locker in front of everyone in the hallway. They were all laughing at me."

She patted Pansy on the leg and stood up. "Give it time. The other kids will find some other scandal to pick apart and Bagel never could hold a grudge for very long. He's a good boy. After a few days of brooding, I'm sure he'll let you grovel out an apology."

"Don't let her leave," I told Pansy. "You spilled your secret, now it's time for hers. Ask her how her morning went."

"So," she sniffed. "How did your morning go?"

"Oh, you know, same old, same old. Nothing new here." Mom was trying to back out of the room slowly, but I wasn't going to let her get that far.

"She kicked two journalists off the lawn earlier this morning."

"Why were there journalists on the lawn?"

"Crap. I didn't know Gerri was lurking," Mom mumbled.

"You also had at least three messages from self-proclaimed psychics on the answering machine she deleted," I added. Pansy rolled her eyes.

"Why wouldn't you just tell me? I mean, I'm okay with you getting rid of them, but why would you try to hide it?"

"I just know that you're already stressed with the stuff from school, and I didn't want to add to that."

"I appreciate it, but you don't have to treat me like I'm fragile, Mom." The red-rimmed eyes said otherwise, but for once I kept my mouth shut. She blew her eyes again and stood up. "I'm done crying over this stuff. I have a case to solve, and that's what I'm going to do."

Winston Churchill she was not, but Mom seemed satisfied that she wouldn't spend the entire evening crying. "I also spoke to your Aunt Bev this afternoon. She'd called because she and Mom saw you on the news and they were both worried about you. So, just remember, no matter how much you may feel like the world is against you, there are people out there who love you. Got it?"

"Got it," Pansy mumbled.

"Good. I'm making chicken parmigiana for dinner, so don't get too wrapped up in... whatever it is you plan to do to solve your case."

"Okay, Mom." We watched her go, Pansy waited for her to be back downstairs before she shot me a dirty look.

"Don't even start," I interrupted whatever she was about to complain about. I filled her in on the email and Mr. Browning's escape plan.

"I kind of can't believe that worked. But now the whole place is empty?" She had a look on her face that I didn't think I was going to like. "I want to go back to Chivington."

"As there's a giant demon ghost thing on the loose trying to kill living people, I'd call that an incredibly bad idea. Besides, I don't think Mr. Browning is open for tours, yet."

"Which is why I don't plan on asking. I was thinking about this yesterday when I was online looking things up, before… well before everything. I want to sneak in and do a seance, but I'll need more people to help."

"Uh, you'll also like, need to know how to do a seance," I stated. I didn't see a book on how to do that anywhere around.

"I think if we call forth the spirit that's causing these problems, then maybe we can figure out what it is and ask it what it needs to be free. Maybe Jessica can also be free."

"Jessica is perfectly happy taking care of her patients. I don't remember her asking for you to help her move on. She just wants this thing that can hurt living people gone."

"Maybe she can help us get rid of him, and then she can decide if she wants to stay or not."

"I promise you, I can't decide if I want to move on or not, and it didn't look to me like Christopher had any choice in his departure. Besides, it's already visible, it's already there. Well, it's visible to the ghosts, I actually don't know if living people can see it yet or not. But it can hurt the living. How am I supposed to keep you safe? Not to mention whoever else you decide to drag into this construction zone. Even besides the ghost stuff, someone could fall down the stairs or step on a nail. And if everyone has flashlights, there is no way Mr. or Mrs. Browning won't notice that it's crawling with teenagers."

"Well, from what I was reading yesterday, if we call a spirit forth, it has to answer our questions. Ghost can't lie."

I stared at her.

"During a seance, I mean. They can't lie during a seance."

"And you're just going to, what, call him over to you, tell him he can't attack you and that he has to tell you why he's hanging around? What if he doesn't know the answer? What's the internet say about that?"

She seemed intent on ignoring my logic and reasoning, probably because this was the first time for this kind of role reversal.

"I'm going to talk to Anne and Amber at school tomorrow and see if they want to join in. If I can get Dario to talk to me long enough to tell him my plan, I think he'll want to help, and I feel like that's enough people to do a seance properly." Pansy went to her desk and pulled out a fresh clean notebook from the drawer. She found a wide Sharpie and wrote, 'Research' across the top. Vague enough to not draw Mom's attention because she'd ground Pansy for life if she thought we were going to do a seance.

Settling herself in front of the computer, she turned it on and waited for the boot screens and the Windows 95 logo to appear. While we waited, I filled her in on her email, Mr. Browning's possible lie about investors to keep his wife from killing him while he plotted an escape, and that Lee had touched the Other.

"Touched it? Like, it was a physical object?"

"That's what he said."

I was filling her in on the Chivington Cemetery that we hadn't known existed when the AOL home screen finally appeared, giving us the option to join various chat rooms sorted by subject. Pansy hovered the mouse over Ghost/Hauntings.

"Do it. We'll make up a story about who we are. No one can see us, right? They're not going to know how old we are," I urged.

"Wait. One of the guys at school said he set up a few different accounts so that he'd have different screen names to use. Maybe we should set up a new one so that it can't be traced back to me." With a few clicks of the mouse, Pansy was set up with a new account and waffling over what she could use for her new screen name. "Okay, I want to pretend to be a dude, then they'll take me more seriously."

"An ADULT dude," I said, nodding my head. She could be a ghost authority with a few keystrokes. This was great.

It turned out that everything we tried with the word ghost or spirit in it was already taken as a screen name. Apparently, no one was going to use their real names here, and we finally settled on Inspector_Unknown, which we thought sounded like we had some experience and people would believe us when we asked questions. Although, we probably had more experience with the whole ghost situation than everyone else in this chat room, combined, so we had that going for us. Pansy wrote down her username and password, as well as the name of this particular chat room in her notebook. We were making progress.

"Okay, first question," Pansy said. "Hello, all. I'm starting an investigation of a hotel... like, it's going to be a hotel, right? So I'm not lying," Pansy paused in her typing to confirm her moral code with me. I shrugged, and she went on. "I have experience with hauntings and ghosts, also not a lie, but this is the first time I've encountered a malevolent spirit which I believe to be a poltergeist. Am unsure how to handle or dispose of—I like that word, dispose, what do you think? And am requesting any advice." She turned back to me. "Okay. Does that sound like a grown man wrote it?"

"I mean, it's typewritten words, so it's hard to tell, but you didn't use any slang or other teenagerisms, I guess. As long as you don't turn your letters hot pink, I think it should be okay."

Pansy hit 'enter' and sat back to wait. I guess we both expected people to instantly jump on here with answers, but after five minutes, there was still no response. Just as we were about to give up, we finally heard a notification ding and did a little dance.

"A slash S slash L. What the heck does that mean?" Pansy asked, wrinkling her nose in confusion.

"I don't know. Read other people's posts and see if any of them have it." It took us a few posts to find one and realized it meant age, sex, location. "Gross."

"Fine, I am forty-two, male, and Colorado. There, Mr. Sexy-GhostMan, eat my shorts."

We scrolled through the rest of the posts, looking for questions previously asked that may help us or at least point us in the direction of other questions we should be asking. There was a whole thread about someone who swore a poltergeist had sex with her. We'd noticed a trend in weirdos who wanted to have sex with ghosts, and Pansy put her finger in her mouth, made some vomit sounds, and kept scrolling. We noticed there were several other people who had posted about having paranormal activity in their homes. Some mentioned the word poltergeist specifically, but none of the answers actually included any helpful ways to dispel said entity.

We took a break for dinner, or, at least, Pansy took a break for dinner, and then logged back on to continue the search. We were on, like, page 30 of previous posts when we ran across one that made Pansy stop scrolling.

"Haunted sanatorium in Colorado, Perth Paranormal Society investigates." The headline was attributed to PPS_Prez, and we both said, "Oh my god, it's Randy," at the same time. She clicked the post and read Randy's post, asking for anyone with professional credentials to review the tapes for authenticity. "Wait, how long ago was this?" We hadn't really been looking for time stamps, but this post, this far back, had only been posted on Saturday, four days ago.

"Well, either your question will be lost in this mess or we'll have a whole bunch of answers in another day or two. It could go either way."

"Look, there's a search button up here." Pansy clicked on it and typed in the word *poltergeist*, bringing up all the posts that mentioned the word. There were 5,652 results.

"Nothing like a little light reading before bed," I grumbled. We spent the next several hours reading through poltergeist posts, not even searching the topic of seances, which was the entire reason we'd gotten online in the first place. Mom must have gotten up to go to the bathroom or something because she heard Pansy typing and came in.

"It is almost midnight, young lady, and on a school night. I know you've had a bad day, but if you can't go to bed at a reasonable hour, then we'll just have to take this thing out of your room, won't we?"

"Yes, Mom. I got pulled into this research project and lost track of time." Pansy shut the computer down and quickly crawled into bed. She lay there in silence for a while, staring at the ceiling.

"What?" I finally asked. I needed to go meet Lee but I needed to know what was worrying her more.

"What if I can't get rid of it? What if they finish remodeling the hotel and people move in there and then that thing starts sucking the energy out of people just like he used to do with the patients? What if they all end up just doing things on a loop because there isn't enough of them left to move on?"

"What if it's not your job to solve this problem?" I countered. "Sure, you know that this is a problem that exists, but that doesn't mean that you're the only person in the world that can fix it. You're still just a kid, Pans."

"But what if I can? What if... what if it's, like, my destiny or something?"

"Then I'd say you've been watching too many movies. You are one person, you can't save everyone all by yourself.

"We didn't look up directions for how to perform a seance."

"There's a book on it at the library. We'll remember to look online tomorrow and if we don't find directions, we can always stop there. Stop worrying and go to sleep, Pansy. We have time."

"Do we? I feel like something bad is going to happen and I need to find answers faster."

"The Other has been there for almost eighty years. Another week or two won't make a difference."

I hoped.

18

Pansy looked beat down after School on Thursday, but better than Wednesday and certainly better than Tuesday. Perhaps the novelty of making fun of her and Bagel was wearing off, or the hyenas had found fresh meat to laugh at. I'd suggested a paper chain to count down the days until graduation and she'd looked at me like I'd lost my mind. I was serious, but whatever.

I was waiting at The Firefly and watched as Pansy walked out the front door of the school and walked across the street without even looking both ways. Not that there was a lot of traffic in our town. The students who drove to school left out the back way and I guess she figured she'd hear a school bus before it took her out, but I was definitely frowning as she approached.

"Summer isn't home, so you guys aren't finishing up tapes tonight."

That pulled her brain out of whatever hole she'd climbed down in. "That's weird. She didn't call me."

"I went to do yoga this morning and the store is closed, the Bug is gone."

Pansy paused before entering The Firefly and it hurt that one of our favorite places was now tainted by the ugliness of that fight. I watched her mentally brace herself and open the door, and luckily Chandra was out front rearranging flower vases on the tables.

"Hey, girl, how's it going?" Chandra asked, pushing a strand of cranberry hair behind her ear as she straightened from one of the four-tops.

"It's going," Pansy mumbled. "I was supposed to watch tapes with Summer today. We were going to finish up the stack, but Ger… but the store is closed."

"Oh, yeah. Sorry, she didn't mention you were coming, but she ran in to tell me this morning that she had a family emergency and had to go out of town for a few weeks. She said she was dropping off all the tapes with Randy on her way out of town."

"Oh."

"Yeah, oh," I echoed. If I'd had a heart, it would have stopped. Maybe she just forgot to give him that tape of Pansy talking to me in the basement. Or maybe she'd managed to delete that part. Or left a note for Randy to start the tape after a certain time. Surely she would have tried to protect Pansy, but there were a lot of ways that could still go wrong.

"I've still got three audio tapes to go through if you want one of them to listen to?" Chandra asked. "It would definitely help me and Shawn out."

"Oh, yeah, sure. Absolutely."

Chandra went to the back to get the tape out of her purse and Pansy stood at the plate-glass window in the front, looking over all the students getting onto school buses or walking home. A few came into The Firefly, but none were Danielle or her crew and they didn't even look Pansy's way.

"If Randy sees the tape where you're talking to me…"

"I know," she whispered. "I think I'm too numb to process it at this point. What's that saying Grandma used to say, don't go borrowing trouble?"

Chandra gave her the tape and some last-minute directions about recording any events onto a new tape to be played all as one thing and we left the cafe without Pansy even buying a milkshake or some onion rings to go. A sure sign she was distracted.

"Hey, let's head over to the library and see if that book about how to do a seance is still there," I offered as a way to get her out of her funk. At this point she had funk piled on funk

"Yeah, that's fine. We've got time now."

"So, Lee followed Browning to a roadside motel in Cuchara," I said, referring to a small town northwest of the Castle. He hadn't run far, just enough to hide from his wife.

"That's cool, but I can't stop thinking about how much we don't know about Summer."

"I know. I wonder what her family emergency was? Have you ever heard her talk about her family? I know that she moved here like, what? Five years ago? But from where? She doesn't talk about growing up or her old schools or anything, does she?" I asked.

"Yeah, I was just thinking that I'd been thinking of her as a friend, because she literally knows everything about me, and not once have I ever asked her anything about herself. What kind of friend does that make me? I've been so worried about myself that I didn't even notice that I don't really know her at all."

"Well, you know she comes across as an open book, but I guess only for the first few pages, if that makes any sense."

Pansy nodded, and we continued down the sidewalk towards the library. Bagel drove past in his Bronco as we neared the door, pulling into the parking lot for the

Foodarama. He must have to work tonight. "Has he spoken to you yet?"

"Nope. Cold shoulder every time he sees me."

"Maybe I could try to talk to him."

"Good luck. And I mean that, not like, sarcastically," she said.

We entered the cool, dark confines of the library, the industrial strength carpeting muffling Pansy's footsteps, the beige metal shelves crammed with books on every subject. Luckily, we already knew exactly where the one lone book on seances should be because it lived on the same shelf as the books about ghosts. We'd never read it because I was literally already here. No need to call me forth.

"I hope you have a pen and paper in that book bag of yours. If you check out a book about seances, Mrs. Williams will call Mom and tell her about it." As well as everyone else in town, I thought, but didn't say that part out loud.

"Yeah, I've got that covered."

We found the single thin volume about the history of the seance, crammed between the Guinness World Records and a book on Ghosts of the Midwest which was somehow shelved as nonfiction even though we one hundred percent doubted any of the stories in it were real.

The paperback was old and the cover was held on with scotch tape, so Pansy carried it over to the nearest table, all of which were empty because we were the only two people in the library, other than the librarian.

"Okay, let's see what we need," Pansy said, taking out her math notebook and pulling a few sheets free from the spiral binding.

I read over her shoulder, much to her annoyance, but we finally compiled a list of things to take with us, as well as what to do once we got there. I was excited and nervous, but Pansy seemed determined to do something to further the investigation, even if that meant calling spirits like you were paging them to the principal's office.

It took us less than half an hour, and by us, I mean the person who could take notes, which wasn't me, to make a plan of action. "I really want Dario to be there. He's been involved in all of this, I don't want to do it without him," Pansy said as she shelved the book. She sighed and hung her head. "I don't know how I'm supposed to apologize if he won't even let me get near him."

"Give him time. He's mad. Maybe he'll decide he has other things to do in life than avoid you. Maybe he'll decide to never speak to you again, I don't know. What I do know is that right now, at this moment, he doesn't want to talk to you, so just leave him alone for another week or two, okay?"

"It's just, well, I'd started to think of him as being the George to my Nancy Drew. I kind of miss him."

I figured it was probably best if I didn't tell Bagel he was now playing the part of Nancy Drew's best friend, Georgia Fayne, in this scenario. Although, as I briefly pictured him with a brown bob and wearing a smart pantsuit with kitten heels, I didn't imagine that sharing that information would help anything.

"Let me try to talk to him. I'll see if I can get him alone in the parking lot."

"While I'm here, I might as well see if I can find some articles on the murder of that Thomas kid." Lee had remembered the year, and that it was summer, but couldn't remember the last name of the family. It was a shot in the dark, but still worth searching for in case something in the article could point us toward the next clue. Nancy Drew, indeed. I turned to leave when Pansy spoke again. "Don't be late tonight, it's ER night," she whispered from the corner of her mouth before heading over to the librarian on duty to request some microfiche.

The library sort of shared a parking lot with the grocery store, and the bank, and the Loaf 'N Jug, and a few smaller businesses. It was basically a huge wash of blacktop surrounded by multiple buildings, their individual lots divided by a confusing labyrinth of concrete curbs holding overgrown hedges and weeds. I spotted the Bronco sitting in the employee lot of Foodarama.

Before I even made it into the store, I spotted my boy pushing a shopping cart out for an old lady. I waited for him to load everything into her trunk before approaching him with the five taps on his shoulder.

"Gerri?"

Two more taps for yes. "No," he said, shrugging his shoulders as if to throw me off. "I'm not doing this right now, I'm working," he muttered under his breath. I gave him three more taps.

"I'm not apologizing to her. I don't even want to be in the same room as her."

Honestly, I couldn't blame him. This was going to be really difficult to have a conversation though with just the two of us. I gave him five more taps, just to show I was aggravated by this method of speaking. He gathered another shopping cart that had been left in the parking lot and started pushing them toward the door, the sound of the hard wheels over the rough and patched parking lot masking the sound of him speaking.

"Fine, I'll tell you what. I bought a ouija board to talk to you. Meet me after school tomorrow at home and you can try to tell me whatever it is, then."

Two taps for yes and our plan was set. He'd bought a ouija board for me? I wanted to give him a hug, but figured that would freak him out. He went back into the grocery store and I left him alone. It was a date.

I made it home about an hour before Pansy did, and the first task I assigned her was to look up Randy in the phone book. We didn't know where he lived, and we were disappointed to see he was unlisted. His exterminator business was listed with a number, but no address. We knew where he'd be Saturday night though, he'd be in a van on Blue Jay Lane. As long as he didn't watch Summer's tapes before then I could sneak in and erase it or something. Maybe I could knock it into the trash. Either way, we had a few days to work out a plan.

Since we still had time before ER started at eight o'clock, Pansy jumped online and checked our chatroom question. We'd been checking every night but other than some junk responses wanting to know if we were available for a private chat, we hadn't had any luck with a real answer to the problem.

"This guy says that we have to make a salt circle around the building," Pansy read.

"What? That would be, like, an all day project. How many containers of Morton's finest do you think that would take? A hundred? Two?" I was trying to estimate how far you could make a line with a single container to extrapolate how many that would actually take, when Pansy pulled her notebook out of her bookbag and waved a sheet of paper at me.

"Don't even bother doing the math, we're not doing that. Next issue."

"Did you find it?"

"Of course I did. But, like, only by luck. Lee was off by a year. The third issue I looked through had a little paragraph about the one year anniversary of the deaths, which made it easy to find the original article. Their last name was Grayson." She searched for both Annamarie and Bethany Grayson, but neither Web Crawler nor Yahoo returned any results. The article didn't mention a maiden name or the names of any relatives, and if Annamarie was smart, she would have changed their names after the murders. She'd also have paid extra to remain unlisted in the local phone book, just like Randy. Neither would make our search easier, finding a living link was going to be nearly impossible.

We tried searching for Thomas' name, the words 'Perth double murder,' and then 'Perth child abuse' which brought up some results, but all were recent and there was nothing from the summer of 1974. Our hope to find something online had been a long shot, there was almost nothing online from that far back, but at least we could mark it off the list. I made a mental note to ask Lee what he thought our next step should be.

We settled in to watch our favorite drama, Pansy sprawled on the couch with her giant Tupperware bowl full of popcorn, and me floating on the couch pretending that I was really sitting there. As we argued over who was cuter, Noah Wyle or George Clooney, I took a moment to appreciate the normality of the evening. It was almost like I was alive again. Almost. Which reminded me, I should probably go sit in a power line somewhere to get charged up enough to push that little triangle thing around for Bagel, tomorrow. My thoughts were interrupted when I heard Dr. Benton say that he needed to make his rounds.

"He's making his rounds," I said out loud.

"What?" Pansy asked, looking over at me like I'd lost my mind.

"Rounds. When Jessica mentioned the Other was making his rounds, what if she didn't mean that he was just making a loop? What if the pattern he makes is to make his 'rounds' like when he was a doctor?"

It didn't take her long to be on the same page as my brain. "And what if she knows that because she knew him?"

"You need to know the spirit's name, right? That helps to call it forth, according to the book?"

"Yes."

"So, maybe call Jessica first. If she has to tell you the truth, then she'll have to tell us who he is if she knows him."

"Plus, you can actually see her, so we'll know if it's really working."

"Two birds and all that. I like it."

"We'll have to plan it for next Friday. Tomorrow isn't enough time to prepare and Amber is going to Red Rock tomorrow night for a concert."

"Are you sure they'll do it?" I asked.

"Yeah, I already talked to them about it yesterday at school. We can all tell our moms that we're spending the night at the other girls' houses and they'll never know."

"What if Bagel won't agree? Who can we get as a fourth?"

"I don't know. Not Rachel. Her parents are really strict. If we get caught, they'd send her to one of those survival boot camp places like you see on Oprah."

"Yep," I agreed, thinking through our options for assistance. "And Jenny would be crying before you even got into the building. Chrissy might do it."

"She might do it, but she'd tell everyone and their brother about it before we ever got there. She can't keep a secret to save her life."

"I guess I'll just have to work on Bagel Boy then, won't I?"

I mean, no problem, right?

19

Everyone needed to have that one story of wild youth to tell their grandchildren one day, didn't they? Surely breaking into a haunted sanitarium to perform a seance and call forth the ghost of a nurse counted as 'wild,' wouldn't it? I was thinking about all the steps we'd need to take for this seance while hanging around outside our house, floating in the power lines and hoping that I wasn't driving up anyone's electric bill. If Bagel had a ouija board, I wanted to be able to push the little triangle thingy around and just hanging out inside the television and house lamps wasn't giving me enough of a boost. I didn't want to wait years and years to accumulate energy. I was impatient, so sue me.

I gave Bagel time to get home before I invaded his space, floating out to the dirt road just north of our neighborhood where Bagel's family lived. The houses in this development were smaller, but the yards were bigger and the properties had more individuality. Bagel's house was a split level that was brick on the bottom half and vertical wood plank siding painted baby blue along the top half. I could hear the thump of the bass coming from his stereo system clear out in the front yard, which usually wasn't a good sign.

Mrs. Ventura was in the kitchen singing along to the radio while she made dinner, and I floated past her up the stairs that I'd run up so many times before. Bagel was sitting on his bedroom floor with the ouija board already set up in front of him. He'd cleared a space for it amongst the piles of dirty laundry and art supplies. His easel was currently empty, and I spotted the portrait of me he'd started after I'd died hanging on his wall, the canvas listing crookedly on a nail he'd driven into the faux wood paneling. My face was now covering up two-thirds of a Lamborghini poster that had been taped to the wall since he was in second grade. I was momentarily distracted by feeling honored, but also wanting to straighten the canvas to hang correctly.

Bagel was reading the little pamphlet of directions when I gave him three taps on his shoulder and he jumped like he'd been electrocuted.

"Gerri?" he asked, one hand over his chest, holding his heart in.

Two taps on his right hand.

"Holy heart attacks, Batman, you scared the crap out of me. I'd uh, offer you a seat, but... well," he gestured to the cardboard and paper game board in front of him and leaned over to turn his stereo down. "I don't know how well this will work, but I saw it at Wild Harmony last week and thought it would be worth a shot."

Pansy and I had also seen them for sale at Wild Harmony but knew that Mom would burn the house down if she found a ouija board in our room. Although, maybe that was just us projecting how she used to feel about all of this spiritual stuff. I mean, Pansy now communicated with a spirit every day, so how upset could she really be? We should probably start her off with those little refrigerator magnets shaped like letters or even Scrabble tiles first, though.

I managed to move it to "Hello," with a little effort. Was the energy I'd absorbed a finite resource? Would I run out of gas halfway through this? Is that why Jessica had to constantly pull more energy from batteries when she was putting on a show?

"This is going to be a slow process, isn't it? Maybe that's why they always have a living person moving the planchette around. How about I just move it and then you can tap my hand when I'm at the letter you want?"

That sounded like a much better idea to me, so I gave him a double tap.

"Okay, here goes," he leaned over the board, two fingers on the planchet and started at the letter A. I was instantly distracted because I could hear a ringing in the distance and it took me a second to realize it was the phone in the kitchen. The handset on Bagel's nightstand lit up, but remained silent.

"Just ignore it. I turned my ringer off because these journalists won't quit calling, but Mom won't let me unplug them all." He started back over at the letter A and when he was close to the letter O, I tapped his hand. We followed that up with a K.

"Are you asking me if I'm okay?"

Double tap.

He snorted, leaning back against his unmade bed and staring at the ceiling for a minute before answering. "I don't think I'm going to be okay until I get out of this town, honestly." He sighed, reaching for a can of Jolt he'd left on his nightstand and taking a swig. "But yeah, I'm not like, suicidal or anything, if that's what you're asking. The news people are driving me nuts, but this one guy from Greeley that showed up on my doorstep asking for an interview was actually pretty cool and we started talking about photography. I showed him some of my work and he said he thought he could get me some work this summer at the Tribune."

I tapped him on the arm about five times to show my excitement and that got a smile out of him. Moving the planchet toward the S, Bagel got back in the groove, moving slowly through the letters with me. I continued tapping his hand until we spelled out SEANCE.

"Seance? What? Who's doing a seance?" I tried to move the planchette again, concentrating hard to not let my fingers push right through it. I was thinking maybe we'd be better off learning Morse code, but Bagel got with the program and helped me. All I needed to spell was PA, and he took it from there. "Pansy? Pansy is going to have a seance? Does she even know how to perform a seance?" I gave him a double tap for yes followed by a single tap for no, because really, what did we know other than what we'd read in a book?

NEEDU

"No. Absolutely not. She can figure that one out without me. She's made it abundantly clear that she has zero respect for me." He took another sip of his Jolt before putting his fingers back on the planchette. "When is she planning this craziness?"

CASTLEFRIDAY

"Has she lost her mind? And Mr. Browning is just going to let her do this at the Castle?" I gave him a single tap.

"No? No, what? She hasn't lost her mind or Mr. Browning isn't letting her... oh my God. Is she sneaking in?"

Double tap for that one. Yes and no questions were a much easier way to communicate.

"She's going to get in trouble."

I put my hand back on his and held it there until he went back to the board.

SUMMERGONE

"Summer? Oh yeah, actually Blake called me and asked me

if I wanted to help him go through tapes since Summer was going to be gone for a while. I'm supposed to meet him tonight around six after he gets off work. Did you know he has a full darkroom in his house? He develops all the camera film himself —said he doesn't trust the developing machines in drugstores. He said they're all run by sixteen-year-old morons."

Fascinating, Bagel, but you're missing the point.

RHASTAPE

"Rha's tape? Rha? Isn't that like, the Egyptian god dude?" Single tap. I wanted to smack him but refrained.

"Rha stape. Rhast ape," I was getting ready to spell out Randy when he finally got it. "R has tape. Is R for Randy?" Double tap. "What ta... ooooh. Oh, no."

Yeah, that was the reaction I was going for.

Bagel jumped up and began pacing back and forth in the small space. "Maybe he won't see it. Summer would have left it queued up past where Pansy was talking to you, so like, there's no reason he'd back it up to the beginning, right?" He sounded like he was trying to convince himself, but wasn't sure he believed it.

"Crap." He checked his watch and looked around his room like he was going to find answers buried in his discarded laundry piles.

"Okay, I need to eat something and get ready to go." He stood silent for a minute and I could see him arguing with himself. Finally, he seemed to come to a decision and chugged the rest of the can of Jolt. "Okay, tell her I'll do it. I'm not ready to forgive her yet, but if we're going to be infamous either way, then I want in on the seance."

I moved the planchette to Goodbye and left him there with his hands buried in his hair, most likely questioning his life decisions.

20

Pansy was so embarrassed to show her face in town that she wouldn't even stop at Blockbuster on the way home from school. Instead, she'd spent her exciting Friday night listening to the audiotapes she'd gotten from Chandra until bedtime, recording every random noise she heard. I'd met with Lee at midnight and we arranged to meet later at Canyon Run Trailer Park because he didn't want to miss out on an opportunity to spy on someone. I still hadn't come up with a good plan for how to get rid of the incriminating tape, but maybe between the two of us, we'd figure something out.

Pansy was asleep by the time I returned from my midnight meeting, so I spent the next few hours watching a mini-marathon of My Husband Slept with My Mother episodes on Springer. I was only slightly shocked at this point that there were enough of these stories to make a whole mini-marathon. That was something else I could add to the pro column for being dead—my family couldn't do anything to embarrass me.

I thought about what Jessica had said about checking in on her family after she'd died. About how Thomas didn't even know where his family was to check on them. Lee's parents and wife had died before him and he had no living family to watch over after he'd passed. In another hundred years, no one I knew would still be alive. Pansy would be long gone, and I'd no longer have a link to the living. Without the ability to communicate, I wouldn't be able to help anyone. I also wouldn't have anyone to leave the TV on for me, or whatever people used for entertainment in the future.

Maybe in a hundred years televisions would be replaced with something new, like the CD player was replacing the tape deck, and tape decks had replaced the 8-track players. Pansy had read an article in Dad's Newsweek a few weeks ago that said they were working on some new-fangled machine that would allow you to watch a movie on a CD and that everyone would have to get rid of their VCRs and switch over. How many times over the course of the next hundred years would I have to learn all new technology and wouldn't have a live person to talk about it with? Would Lee still be around?

Can you call it an existential crisis if you don't actually exist? But I did exist, didn't I? I was here. Pansy could see me. Chandra and Bagel could feel me. I existed, just not in the normal way.

I was jarred from pondering the meaning of the universe when I heard Billy Mays telling me to, "Wait, there's more." We'd obviously moved onto the Infomercial level of Dante's Inferno and I figured I could sit here and make myself crazy, or start my morning by checking on Mrs. Garcia before Pansy woke up.

I was impatient to make progress on our case, and being forced to wait around all day made me twitchy. That, in turn, made Pansy twitchy, because I spent the day following her around. We'd killed a few hours playing with some of the game software that had come with the computer, learning nothing but having a good time, all the same. By the time I left for the trailer park that evening, she was busy copying a chain email to everyone she knew to avoid seven years of bad luck.

Since we weren't interested in the actual investigation, Lee and I had planned to get there around eleven that evening, hoping Randy and Greg would not continue to 'investigate' until three or four in the morning. As we approached the trailer park, we saw the blue and red strobing lights flashing through the night sky and Lee shot me a glance before putting on the speed. I was hot on his heels.

There were two Las Animas County Sheriff's Deputies parked in front of the trailer at one-fifty-eight Blue Jay. Greg and two of the cops were leaning against the side of the van, watching Randy and Mr. Cooper yell at one another, while a third officer held a teenage boy by the arm. The boy was dressed in a black sweat suit and wearing black gloves with black paint smeared all over his face. For a minute, I thought Randy and Greg had caught a cat burglar in the act.

"Are we pressing charges here or not?" the deputy holding the boy asked the two men squaring up in the front yard.

"Absolutely not. He had no right to call the cops!" Mr. Cooper spat, shaking a finger in Randy's direction.

"I'm going to press charges against you for wasting our time," Randy snarled back.

"That's not actually a thing you can..." the deputy began to say.

"Fraud!" Randy yelled, interrupting him.

"What in the Sam Hill is going on here?" Lee asked me. I was just as clueless as he was.

"This brat," Mr. Cooper pointed towards the kid. "Wasn't supposed to get caught. I want my money back, you idiotic little twerp." He started toward the kid and the deputy took a step forward, placing himself between the two and pointing his flashlight right in Mr. Cooper's face. Temporarily blinded,

Cooper stopped in his tracks and threw his hands up to block the light.

"He's the idiot?" Randy was still yelling, his face taking on an unhealthy sheen. It was too dark to see what particular shade of red he was turning, but it probably wasn't good. "You're the idiot! Do you not understand how infrared cameras work? Dressing this kid up in all black doesn't make him invisible, you moron!"

"Ohhh," Lee and I said at the same time. I hadn't put any real thought into how the Coopers planned to pretend that their house was haunted, but this was certainly not the way I would have gone about it. On the bright side, we wouldn't have to wait for hours while the PPS wasted their time investigating.

After a few more minutes of discussion, the cops sent the kid, who lived two doors down, home with a stern warning. Then they had to go inside to gather the PPS film equipment since the Coopers wouldn't let Greg or Randy back into the trailer to retrieve it. Since they didn't have a warrant, there was some discussion about what they could do about the marijuana joints sitting in the kitchen ashtray. In the end, they didn't want to do any extra paperwork and told the Coopers to clean up their act. And their house. And their yard.

Lee and I followed the van out of the trailer park.

Randy drove south down Main St, through downtown Perth, and over the East Bridge. Just past the turnoff for the Buffalo Chip, he turned left onto a dirt road and drove for about two miles down the rough and irregular surface to Greg's house. Greg lived in a really nice double-wide with a huge front deck and white work van in the driveway that had Abernathy Plumbing & HVAC painted on the side.

After making a three-point turn, Randy headed back out to Main St, which was actually County Road 8.8 this far out of town, and continued east for another mile or two until he turned down a driveway between two fenced fields that seemed to stretch on forever. There was an old farmhouse at the end, surrounded by several outbuildings, barns, and overgrown fields that looked like they hadn't seen a cow in forty years. Randy got out of the van, grumbling to himself under his breath, and seemed undecided on whether he should unpack the van. As we watched, he opened the back doors, stood there for a minute, and then snarled at the equipment before shaking his head. He slammed the doors shut again. Apparently, unpacking the equipment could wait until tomorrow.

Lee and I headed into the house in search of Randy's office or wherever he watched tapes. We floated through the kitchen, the light over the stove left on to light our way. In every other room, we were guided by the electric candles that Randy's wife had sat on every windowsill. Upstairs, we found two little boys in a bunk bed and a little girl by herself in a second bedroom. We passed his wife, Angie, in the hallway on her way down-stairs to the living room. She was coming from the bedroom at the end of the upstairs hall and I could see that the bedside lamp was on, a book facedown on the quilt. She was probably surprised to hear her husband pulling in so early on an investigation night.

We floated back down to the living room, where the VCR was surrounded by a mountain of Disney movies. I turned to tell Lee that I didn't see our stack of tapes anywhere, but he was already half sunk through the kitchen floor. With a sigh, I followed, praying there was a basement and not just a bunch of dirt.

"I saw the door to the basement steps in the kitchen," he said by way of explanation. There was a faint light coming in from the two tiny windows near the ceiling, the illumination provided by the dusk to dawn light in the backyard. I could see an old recliner, several televisions and multiple VCRs set up on a work table against one wall, but couldn't make out any of the titles.

"I can't see anything," I said with maybe just a hint of whining.

"Geez, Louise, kiddo. Give them a minute to go to bed and I'll turn the light on."

We floated back up to wait them out, but Randy had decided that he needed a midnight sandwich after his exciting evening. His wife was sitting at the kitchen table in her night-gown and robe, listening as he told the tale. His sandwich making was slowed by his need to wave his hands around as he spoke, but I could have sworn he ate the sandwich in four bites once he'd actually assembled it. I was practically tapping my foot by the time he'd finished the story, answered Angie's questions, and calmed down enough to go to bed. We gave them ten minutes after the last light had been turned off before we began our search through the basement.

I floated to the lamp on the workbench and turned it on all by myself, receiving a soundless golf clap from Lee for my efforts. The basement was only about the size of the kitchen above, and I assumed it had probably started off life as a root cellar. It was mostly finished and not as creepy as I'd thought it would be. Instead of open studs and visible insulation, there was actual drywall that had been painted white. Framed Ghostbuster movie posters were hung like fine art, and a massive rag rug covered most of the polished concrete floor. None of the tables or shelves were made of the same type of wood and the chairs didn't match, but it looked like Randy spent a lot of time down here and had tried to make it cozy. Paranormal magazines were strewn across the coffee table and a brass reading lamp set next to the lumpy loveseat. The VCRs were hooked up to allow tapes to be dubbed, and there was a computer set up in the corner, a list of paranormal websites tacked to the corkboard nearby. There wasn't a cobweb to be seen.

"How did this guy find a wife?" Lee asked, unimpressed with Randy's hobby/obsession.

"Hey, he's a nice guy, he's not on drugs, and he has all of his teeth. Have you seen the options around here?"

Lee shrugged and we honed in on the stack of tapes sitting in a crumpled Wild Harmony bag on the workbench.

"These are the ones Summer had," I confirmed. "Here, this is the first tape from the western side of the basement. This is the one we need."

"The garbage can is clear on the other side of the room," Lee observed. There was no way he could carry it that far.

"And knocking it behind the table won't do any good because there's no back to it. He'd just see it laying there on the floor."

"Can you wave a hand in there and erase it?"

"I mean, I could, but I might take out the tapes on either side of it, too. Let me see what this one—crap. He's got the tape from the lobby, the one with the best footage of the Other going crazy stacked right on top of it. I definitely don't want to erase that one."

I moved out of the way and let Lee give it a shot. He nudged the corner of the top tape, careful not to put his hand through it, sliding it over until he could see the twin viewer windows of the tape below. "I can see that it's already forwarded about half an hour into the tape. Maybe Summer left it cued up right where they needed to play some other tidbit? But if you want me to, I can erase the whole thing."

I thought back, trying to remember what had been going on after the fun and games in the lobby. "No, I think what happened next was Randy and Blake getting EVPs and the

Other made a folding chair fall off a table. They'll want to see that."

"Okay, so just the part that's already been wound to this side?"

"Yeah. Just do it." Lee gently swirled a finger through the first part of the tape, and I hoped that small action would be all we'd need to do to keep Pansy's secret safe. Somewhere, at some point in my life, I'd read that the only way to keep a secret was to be the only one that knew the secret. At the rate we were going, we were going to have to start a club and get matching T-shirts.

21

For once, we had an uneventful week. I'd spent a lot of time stalking Randy, but spring seemed to be a busy time for an exterminator and he barely finished watching the fifth floor tapes before the weekend. At no point did he indicate that he'd noticed anything amiss with the basement tapes. Summer was still MIA and so Pansy listened to another of Chandra's tapes, finishing the last of the audio for the Chivington investigation. Bagel had spent his after school hours either working at Foodarama or helping Blake finish up his share of the videos.

Bagel still wasn't talking to Pansy, but she'd written the plan for Friday night, using code words in case it was intercepted. She told me she'd folded it into a paper football and slid it through the vent of his locker. He'd slipped a note back into hers later that day with just the word, 'ok.' It promised to be a super fun evening with him still refusing to speak to her.

They were both still being snubbed at school, but most gossip had moved from speculating about their love lives to arguing over how Stacy Venoy had really broken her leg. She'd fallen off, or been pushed, depending on who was telling the story, from the bleachers while in a fistfight at a baseball game. At least Pansy hadn't come home in tears this week.

By Friday, we were ready to break into Chivington, and by we, I meant the living. I'd already been there several times that week while Randy was at work, watching over the Other. Creepy haunted hotel won hands down over watching Randy pull snakes out from underneath someone's house. Browning had finally found another investor, and either hired a new construction crew or had somehow sweet-talked the first one into returning. Either way, work was moving along with only a few minor accidents. The Other, it seemed, was pacing himself with this new crew of hard hat hors d'oeuvres.

The weather had been warmer, but the cold still seeped up from the ground and the wind was vicious, so when most of the Scooby crew arrived at Sycamore Plaza, they were bundled up. Pansy had left her highly reflective silver coat at home for once, opting for one of Robbie's dark blue hooded sweatshirts over her own sweatshirt and tee. She was hoping the multiple layers would keep her warm.

Anne, who was short and very curvy, had gone all black— black jeans, black tennis shoes, and an inside-out black sweatshirt over a black tee. Her thick brown curls had been pulled out of her face and into matching French-braided pigtails, mostly hidden by a black beanie. She looked like she was trying to channel Joe Pesci in Home Alone. Amber wore black Converse sneakers, ripped jeans, and what I thought at first was a black and white Christmas sweater until I noticed it actually said KISS across her chest. Because of course it did.

Bagel pulled in at the very last minute wearing a Smashing Pumpkins tee shirt and a normal pair of blue jeans he must have borrowed from his dad. He'd left his JNCO jeans at home since they would have been nearly impossible to run or climb a fence in. Pansy offered him the use of Robbie's sweatshirt, but he claimed to be perfectly comfortable and not a wimp like some people.

The entire crew loaded into Pansy's Tracker in a flurry of bookbags and nervous giggles. They'd brought flashlights, candles, and Amber had stolen a bottle of sage from her mom's spice cabinet. "I read somewhere that burning sage will ward off spirits."

"We're doing a seance," Bagel said, turning to look back at her from the passenger seat. "Don't we want to attract the spirits, not get rid of them?" He hadn't really wanted to sit next to Pansy, but the girls had insisted that he take the seat with the most leg room. The side eye and giggling they were doing also told me they were trying to get Pansy and Bagel back 'together' or to at least be friends again.

"Well, duh. We won't use it before the seance. But once we're done, you don't want them just lingering around, do you? It can't hurt," Amber said, flipping her waist length blond ponytail over one shoulder.

"Except we'll all smell like Thanksgiving stuffing," Anne commented.

"I'm actually good with that," Bagel said, turning back around in his seat. "The whole place smells like mildew, sawdust, and paint right now. Anything we burn could only improve the aroma."

It took a little less than an hour to drive there from town and as dusk fell, they sang along to a Walkman CD player that Amber had rigged up to the radio with a cassette adapter. It did my heart good to see Pansy relaxed and having a good time with her friends. Were they on their way to a misdemeanor? Possibly. But as long as she was taken to jail with her friends, did it really matter in the long run?

"Pull over here," I told Pansy from my place in the backseat between the two girls. "Lee said Browning had a security company install a video camera at the gate earlier this week. He wanted to see who was coming and going from the property."

Pansy pulled over, the crunch of gravel under the tires loud even over the sounds of TLC warning us about the dangers of chasing waterfalls. The Castle loomed somewhere overhead with nothing but a rusted wire fence and a hillside full of Ponderosa pine and mountain laurel separating us. Pansy shut off the engine and the music fell silent. Everyone seemed to take a deep breath, bracing themselves for what was to come. The clock on the dash read 9:26. The sun had long since disappeared.

"The owner put a security camera up at the gate, so we'll have to cross the fence and go up from here to keep from being seen," she explained to the group.

The wall at the gate, the part that visitors saw, was an impressive ten foot tall structure made of stacked field stone flanking a wrought-iron gate original to the building. It was mostly decorative. While the gate did function to keep cars from driving up to the building at night, the wall only extended for about twenty or thirty feet into the pine forest on either side. After that, the rest of the property was surrounded by a much cheaper system of stainless steel posts and wire that did little in the way of deterring teenagers.

The four-foot tall fence was wobbly and hard for them to climb, but eventually everyone made it over. The only problem occurred when the strap of Anne's bag caught the top of one of the steel posts, yanking her off balance and onto her butt. Unharmed, she was quickly back up on her feet and ready to hike. As the crew trudged up the hill, flashlights on so they wouldn't trip over tree roots or step in a hole, I flew ahead to make sure no one was lurking above. Lee was pacing in front of the fountain under a dusk to dawn light that had been mounted to a temporary pole.

"There you are. Everything is good to go, kiddo. The last worker left around four and no one else has been in or out since. Jessica is waiting inside and seems pretty excited about having some good entertainment."

"That's because she doesn't know that she's part of the entertainment yet."

"Did you tell Pansy to be careful? Now that Browning can monitor who's coming through the gate, he's moved back into the carriage house. They can't make any loud noises or do anything to draw attention to themselves."

"I know, I know. She already covered all the do's and don'ts on the way over. We're ready to get this show on the road." I flew back down to Pansy to let her know the coast was clear, and she nodded, unwilling to say anything out loud and that would give away her secret to Amber and Anne. I figured that there was an eighty percent chance the two would figure out something was off before the end of the evening and she'd have to come clean. Pansy was convinced that she wouldn't slip up.

The four finally crested the top of the hill and broke free of the wood line, making their way through the high grass and weeds to the asphalt loop.

"Wow, this place is truly creepy," Anne said. The stone practically glowed in the moonlight and everyone looked up at the looming exterior wall, much like we'd all done the night of the investigation. It was a little overwhelming, I'd give her that.

"So, what's the plan?" Amber asked, bending over to brush the scraps of dew-soaked foliage from her legs. "Are we breaking a window, or do you know a way in?"

"I unlocked the door over here on the side," Lee said, pointing to a fire door about midway down the east wing.

"This way," Pansy told the crew after I'd relayed the message. The door was unlocked as promised, and both Pansy and Bagel were impressed with the improvements that had been made since they'd last been there. The four padded quietly down the freshly painted hallway towards the lobby, the glow of their flashlights magnified as the light bounced off all the shiny white paint.

"Wow," Amber said about five times once she'd entered the lobby's open space. The reception desk was finished, as well as most of the tile work on the walls. The original marble floors were still covered in heavy paper to protect them, but the elaborate chandeliers evenly spaced across the ceiling of the lobby looked ready to use.

"Where should we do the seance, do you think?" I asked Lee. He shrugged and swept his hand around, indicating that anywhere would probably be fine.

"You need a room where the windows cannot be seen by those horrid people, and a door that closes fully to protect your candles from any drafts," Jessica said, floating up through the floor and scaring me once again. Apparently, the fight-or-flight response did not go away after there was nothing to fight or flee from. "You brought candles, did you not?"

"Of course we did," I said, like we did this kind of thing every day of the week and twice on Tuesdays. I shouted for Pansy to follow me and she gathered her troops. We went back down the east wing and chose the empty office across the hall from the fire door. It would give us a quick escape route if we needed it later. The brand new door and knob opened without a single squeak of its fresh hinges, and although there was no furniture in the room, it had clean white walls and freshly laid linoleum tiles. The floor had been swept clean and was free of any construction debris, so no one had to worry if they were up on their tetanus shots. There were two windows in the room that looked out over the overgrown mess of a rose garden, but if we couldn't see the carriage house from this angle, they couldn't see us either.

"This looks like a good spot. There's nothing to catch on fire and there's less chance that anyone will see us back here," Pansy explained to the group.

"And if the Other comes through and takes one of you as a snack, we're close to an exit," I told her. I watched her struggle to not respond to me.

Once the candles were set out and lit, creating a circle around the group, Pansy sat down on the floor and Bagel maneuvered to sit across from her so that he wouldn't have to hold her hand. The other girls joined them on the floor, making a circle, or a square, really, as they were all kneecap to kneecap. I felt it was probably not normal to have four living people and three ghosts taking part in a seance, but maybe it would give us the extra amperage we'd need to contact this thing that wasn't really a ghost after we picked Jessica's brain. I was totally willing to give it a go.

"It has been many years since I have witnessed one of these," Jessica said.

"You've been to a seance before? When you were alive, or... after?"

"Oh, spiritualism was a great pastime for women of a certain social standing in my day. It was all the rage to commune with the spirits. After the war, there was a resurgence. People tried to contact lost loved ones, but there were so many charlatans trying to take money from the widows that it eventually fell out of favor."

"By certain social standing she means rich white women," Lee told me, rolling his eyes.

Jessica gave him some severe side eye before continuing. "Do not be foolish. Men were also obsessed with knowing what came next once this mortal coil had served its purpose. There was much interest in obtaining a description of the Kingdom of Heaven. Attempting to contact spirits, especially the spirit of those good souls guaranteed to have entered heaven, and then extracting a description of such a wondrous place, was the goal of many seances.”

“Because all of those rich white… people,” Lee sneered, “were also Christians. Of course, they considered their ideal of heaven as the only possible option for those spirits. Assuming, of course, that they even spoke to a spirit and weren’t just making it all up to begin with.”

“I’m glad to see that your reporter’s sense of skepticism is still alive and well, even if you aren’t, Lee.” I laughed at the expression of disgust he shot me.

Once everyone was settled, a few more white candles were lit and placed in the center of the circle in the cheap candle holders Pansy had borrowed from our kitchen junk drawer. She pulled a tee shirt from her bag and gently unwrapped the only bell we owned. It was a ceramic elf on an upside down tulip that our grandmother had given us when we were young. The elf’s cap was chipped, but the book had only said that we needed a bell, not that it had to be in perfect condition. Pansy placed the instructions she’d scribbled in her notebook in front of her and reread the first few steps. “Okay, first I hold my right palm up and ring a bell to attract the spirits, and then we all hold hands.”

I hadn’t considered what would actually happen if this worked, but the thought of that poltergeist, Other, crazy evil thing, entering my sister made me uneasy. What if he possessed her and we couldn’t get him back out? What if we accidentally pulled something demonic out of the ether? Something worse than what was already here? What if I’d just watched too many scary movies in my life?

Despite my misgivings, when she rang the bell, I couldn’t resist cracking a joke. “Oh, I’m super attracted? How about you, Lee?”

"I don't know. I've always been partial to the dinner bell myself."

Pansy shot me a dirty look across the circle to where I was floating behind Bagel.

"Spirits, we call upon you and ask that you lift the veil between worlds and speak with us tonight. Our circle is protected by goodness and light, and we ask that no harm should fall upon those within the protected circle. Tonight, we call upon the spirit of Nurse Jessica Daniels," Pansy's voice was surprisingly confident, her tone a little deeper than normal. I was getting nervous, almost afraid that this would work, but also afraid it wouldn't because we needed answers. We'd been floundering for weeks, making no progress while this thing was getting stronger. "We've come here this evening to speak to the spirit of Nurse Jessica Daniels, who died in 1919. You worked here at the Chivington Sanitarium at the turn of the century. Please come forward and speak with us."

Jessica, for the first time since I'd met her, wore an expression that could not be called serene.

"What is this? I thought we were contacting the Other, not myself?"

"We need to see if it really works," I lied.

Anne was fidgeting, ready to bolt. I saw Bagel squeeze her hand tighter, and she took a few calming breaths. Amber looked like she'd be happy to sit there all night. "Do you feel anything?" I asked Pansy.

"I sense no change in temperature or atmosphere," Pansy answered without breaking character. "Nurse Daniels, I command you to come forward and speak the truth." Pansy had her eyes closed, but the others were looking at one another, and when every candle suddenly dipped and flickered, almost going out before flaring back to life, she didn't realize it until we all gasped. "What?" she asked, looking around the room for danger.

"The candles," Bagel said.

Much to my surprise, Jessica took on a slightly luminescent shimmer and Pansy's eyes widened. "I can see her," she whispered.

"I can't imagine why you would choose to call my spirit forth when the entire point of this evening was to find a method to exorcize the Other."

After twisting around to see what Pansy was staring at, the girls and Bagel turned back to face Pansy. Clearly, she was the only one that could see Jessica floating behind Anne.

"I apologize for the surprise, Nurse Daniels, but I needed a test subject before we moved on to bigger game. I have some questions that I've prepared for you."

"Ask them then. There was no need to go through all of this trouble when your sister speaks to me with far less effort."

"Who was this spirit that you refer to as the Other when they were alive? What was their name?"

"Why would I...I don't..." she struggled, the words gaining no traction. She gripped her throat with both hands as if she were determined to pull the words out.

"A spirit that has been called forth cannot lie, Nurse Daniels. That's why I didn't just have Gerri ask you. She already did, and you lied about it."

There were audible gasps from Anne and Amber, and their heads swiveled back and forth between Pansy and Bagel. Bagel sighed and looked consigned to the game of twenty questions they'd be playing on the trip home. It looked like we were adding two more to the club.

"We'll explain later," Bagel whispered to the two girls. "Don't let go, don't break the circle."

"What was his name? I demand the truth."

Pansy's eyebrows were drawn together, and she looked so serious that I had to suppress the urge to respond, "You can't handle the truth." For once, I kept my mouth shut.

"You demand?" Jessica was furious now, but she didn't seem to have control over her own spirit. Her mouth opened and sound poured out, even though her tongue and lips did not form the words. "Doctor Herbert Welling."

As soon as the words were out, Jessica slumped as though the information had been physically removed from her body.

"How did you know him?"

She stiffened again, her spine and limbs straightening unnaturally, and though she seemed to be paralyzed, her jaw dropped open and words sounded once more. "He was a doctor at the Sanitorium when I began here." She slumped forward as she finished and wrapped her arms around herself.

"Ask her how he died," I said to Pansy.

"No," Jessica yelled, holding her hands up in front of her as if to ward off an attack. "Please, spare me this indignity. Do not ask," she implored Pansy. "I will tell you my shameful secret." As Pansy waited, Jessica drew herself back into her normal ramrod straight posture, hands clasped at her waist, her eyes turned toward the ceiling as she gathered her thoughts. "Dr. Welling exists as this savage entity because of me. I caused this when I murdered him."

"His name is Doctor Herbert Welling, and she murdered him," Pansy told the others.

"He was not a good man." Jessica's composure cracked, her head hanging in shame as she resigned herself to the telling. "Welling took advantage of the power he wielded here. He…he did unspeakable things to the female patients, things that he referred to as treatments, though all knew they held no medical merit. He was especially fond of torturing the younger girls. Everyone knew. Everyone had known for years and none of them had done anything to stop it. He was fearsome, always raging and screaming at the nurses. When I was transferred here, I was appalled at his actions, disgusted with his behavior." She fisted her hands by her side and looked Pansy in the eye. "I was angry that no one else had put a stop to it. So I... I slipped strychnine into the flask of grain alcohol he kept in his office. He began every evening shift with a stiff drink. It was surprisingly simple."

"She poisoned him," Pansy whispered to the others.

"Why didn't you just tell us?" I asked.

"I was ashamed. Even then, the guilt ate at me night and day. I had sworn an oath to help people, to do my very best to keep them alive, and I had broken that vow. My family looked at me as a sort of hero—I had gone to school, had a career, and traveled the world. But I was a fraud. Knowingly and with forethought, I had taken a human life, planning it out so that no one else would see. I had even gone so far as to dig the hole I would bury him in over the previous few nights. I hid this secret from my friends and coworkers, even as they searched for him. Never once did I ask forgiveness from a priest. Worst of all? He came back. I did not know, of course, while I was still living, but there were so many signs, so many more deaths. Equipment would be broken with no explanation. People who were regaining their health suddenly died with no warning. A short four months after his murder, I succumbed to the flu. When I returned in this form, I realized what terrible consequences my sin had wrought."

"It sounds like being dead didn't make him less of an awful person," Lee muttered.

"Do you swear this story you've told is true in its entirety?" Pansy asked, and I was proud of her for not just taking the ghost at her word.

Jessica's whole body straightened out like a rubber band

pulled tight. Again, her lower jaw dropped and words spewed forth with no effort on her part. "Yes, everything I have spoken regarding the murder of Doctor Herbert Welling has been truthful."

"Then it sounds like death didn't come for him soon enough," Pansy muttered, looking down at her notes. "Umm, okay, so... Nurse Daniels, I release you. Let's see if that works."

The pulsing glow surrounding Jessica slowly faded, and she crumbled with exhaustion.

"Thank you, Nurse Daniels, for trusting us with your secret," Lee said.

"Yes, with his name and history, we have a much better chance of figuring out how to exorcize him," I added.

"I am sorry," she whispered, her eyes still downcast and her entire body hanging in the air like a limp dishrag. I was so distracted by feeling sorry for her I almost missed her next words. "By trying to protect my secret, I have caused more pain. My only goal was to help people. Even in this, I have once again failed. I hope this information assists you in removing this demon's spirit from this plane. I am sincerely sorry."

I hadn't even opened my mouth to reply when there was a blinding flash of light and she was gone.

"I can't see or hear her anymore, so I'm guessing my releasing her worked?"

"Uh, yeah," I confirmed, "You could say that." Lee and I stared at one another while Pansy filled the group in on everything she'd said.

"Umm, okay, but are we just going to skip the part where you told her you didn't have Gerri ask her because she'd already lied? Like, I'm sorry, but whatchu talkin' 'bout, Willis?" Anne asked.

"Yeah, soooo... a few days after Gerri died, her ghost came

back to me. I can see and hear her just like I can see and hear you guys. Bagel already knows."

Anne was muttering to herself, clutching her throat and Amber was staring back and forth between Bagel and Pansy like they'd both grown two heads.

"I have a bazillion questions and don't even know where to start," she finally said.

Pansy started to say something, but the sound of shattering glass coming from the direction of the lobby made everyone freeze. The sound was followed by giggles and several voices hushing one another.

"What the heck?" I muttered, immediately going to investigate. In the main lobby, there was a group of teenagers that I didn't recognize entering through one of the floor to ceiling windows. They'd apparently broken out the glass with the baseball bat the boy in the lead held.

"Where are we going?" one asked. There were three boys and two girls, and they were carrying flashlights and cans of spray paint. This was going to go over well.

"The news showed a bunch of rooms upstairs. We can leave them a little surprise."

I floated back to the office where all four of our seance participants were now huddled behind the door, vying for space to peek out. Not that any of them could see anything from this wing. "You need to go. There's a group of teenagers from another school who saw this place on the news and they're here to break things and spray paint some new artwork."

"Good grief," Pansy mumbled before bending over to snuff out candles. "We've got to go. Gerri said we've got company and, with our luck, they'll have parked in front of the gate where the security camera is."

"Should I go entertain our guests?" Lee asked. "I can't do as much damage as Jessica could, but I can probably scare them off before they do too much damage."

"I think that's an excellent idea. But give us five minutes to get away." I told him. "I'd hate to have a traffic jam with everyone trying to run away at the same time. Don't overdo it, though."

"Don't overdo it and come fill you in on all the details when it's done," he qualified.

"Exactly that," I confirmed.

"I cannot go to jail," Anne was whispering as she shoved candles into her bag.

"No one has ever gone to jail for doing a seance. We didn't even break anything, we just entered," Amber assured her.

They finished cleaning up while I floated ahead to make sure no one was going to see our escape.

"The coast is clear," I told Pansy and they tiptoed across the hall to the fire door. We'd cleared the front yard and were halfway down the hill before we heard sirens.

"Flashlights off!" Pansy hissed. They stood motionless in the dark, hidden behind a giant clump of mountain laurel covering the slope under a canopy of pine limbs.

I floated ahead to make sure they were heading in the right direction to intersect with Pansy's Tracker, and by the time I came back to direct Pansy on the corrections she needed to make, we could see red and blue lights reflecting on the tops of the trees as the cruisers gathered around the fountain. Slipping and sliding on the thick layer of pine needles, our group tumbled through the underbrush with no flashlights, but we were far enough down that hill that they wouldn't be heard. After making sure there weren't any cops staking out the Tracker, I gave Pansy the signal and everyone climbed over the fence and ran for the Tracker.

Anne stopped next to the passenger door, brushing the dirt

from her pants. "Oh my God, I'm covered in mud and pine needles, I can't…"

"Just get in the car!" Pansy screeched, turning the key in the ignition. Bagel all but shoved Anne into the backseat next to Amber and was still closing the door when Pansy hit the gas. She made a U-turn and then proceeded to drive exactly the speed limit the rest of the way home to Perth. Nothing to see here, folks, just a leisurely evening drive.

"Oh my God, I cannot wait to read the police blotter and see who they are," Amber said.

"They're probably juveniles, so they won't give their names. But I wonder if it will say what school they go to," Bagel asked.

"I bet they're going to feel like dummies," Anne grumbled, brushing at the sticky briers attached to her sweatshirt and pants.

"Well, that was a lot of fun and hands down the most excitement I've had in a long time," Amber said once they were on the road.

"You have a warped sense of a good time," Pansy replied with a laugh.

"I really do. Maybe I should join this ghost group you guys are in. If you hang out in creepy places like this, I'm in."

"Not all of them are this creepy," Bagel answered.

"Or that haunted," Pansy muttered.

Pansy and Bagel filled the next hour with a running commentary, explaining to the two girls everything that had happened since my death. By the time Pansy was pulling into Sycamore Plaza, they'd been thoroughly caught up to date, including a play-by-play of everything that Jessica had said during the seance. I still hadn't told Pansy the news that Jessica had poofed—she looked like she was running on pure adrenaline and was going to crash at any moment.

"You could have told us, you know," Anne said as she turned

her key in the lock of her car door. "I understand why you didn't, but we're your friends. We wouldn't treat you differently just because you have this cool new party trick."

"Yeah man," Amber concurred. "We've all been friends since kindergarten. That includes you, too, Bagel Boy. I know you were always Gerri's BFF, but you're totally part of our little tribe. Goonies never say die."

Bagel blushed and thanked them both, quickly heading for his Bronco before Pansy could get him alone and talk about apologizing.

Pansy told the parents that she'd changed her mind about staying overnight, and they didn't even notice that her bookbag was clanking with candleholders. While we'd told them about a lot of our adventures, this was definitely a never, ever, not even under threat of torture, tell the parents event. She'd already showered, brushed her teeth, and was snoring softly by the time Lee bellowed for me downstairs.

"It wasn't nearly as exciting as it could have been," Lee said as soon as I joined him in the kitchen. "The cops got there too quickly. I only managed to knock over one construction light before the sirens scared the crap out of those kids. They all took off running in different directions and one of them hid in the stairwell to the basement. His friends did a good job of not ratting him out, but then he must have heard the cops talk about towing the car and he realized that once they left, he would be stranded there all alone and miles from civilization."

"If I was alive, I think I'd rather go to jail than have to be there all alone."

"You have a point. Anyway, they called the kids' parents to come and retrieve them and let me tell you, they were not happy about it. Browning came out of the carriage house to yell at them all. He told them he'd installed cameras all over the property, so they shouldn't even think about coming back."

"Cameras, plural?"

"That's what he said, but I think he's bluffing. I've only ever seen the feed for the front gate on the little monitor the security company set up in their bedroom. I think they're too cheap or too broke to pay for more than one, but you have to admit, telling the kids that there are more was good advertising to warn off other teenage vandals."

"Maybe he's not as dumb as he looks."

"Maybe. Also, I thought you'd be interested to know that I saw neither hide nor hair from Jessica again after that bright light. Is that what happened to Christopher?"

"Yep, exactly the same. One minute he was there, then bright light and poof, no more Christopher."

"Do you think it was Pansy releasing her, or her confession that did it?"

"I don't know," I shrugged. "I mean, they say that confession is good for the soul."

"But what a way to go," Lee muttered.

22

I arrived at the PPS meeting a little after six the next evening and even Blake had beaten me there. The lights had already been dimmed and Randy was standing at the front of the room, already speaking to the group. The TV was on a blue screen and the VCR was already hooked up and he was waving a tape around. Pansy was sitting by herself since Summer still hadn't returned, and I wondered if we were going to have to put Summer on our list of Weirdness to Check Out. I made a mental note to have Pansy ask Chandra if she'd heard from Summer or knew when she'd be back.

It wasn't until I heard Randy say Pansy's name that I paid attention to what he was actually saying.

"Okay, so, since we've only got a few tapes left to look at, we're going to start at the bottom and work our way up. Summer had a Post It on it that said it starts with Pansy and Bagel's interview with Channel 3. The camera caught the hangers falling off the filing cabinet behind them while they were being interviewed. If you've seen the original piece that aired, you can hear them fall, but this camera actually caught them sliding off the filing cabinet." He pushed the tape into the VCR and hit play.

"This is awesome, you're the one!" Mr. Smith was heard on the tape. Pansy was facing to the side. The newsman and camera lackey were off screen from this angle. Bagel was on the other side of Pansy, furthest from the camera. A minute or two later, we could see the pile of hangers move from the middle of the filing cabinet, sliding off the front edge and onto the floor. And it wasn't a slow creep. One second they were safe, the next they were tumbling through the air. Both Pansy and Bagel could be seen jumping forward and turning to look behind them at the mess.

"Wait," Chandra said. "I didn't see the original news interview. Rewind it so I can see how our girl handled that reporter."

Oh no.

"Oh, that's okay, I mumbled and sounded like an idiot. Trust me, you don't want to watch that."

"Oh, sure we do," Randy laughed, hitting the rewind button on the remote. "The soundbites they showed on the news were obviously edited together. Badly. Anyone with any video experience could see that the questions he was asking didn't go with the answers they had played. Plus, the sound mixing was terrible." Randy hit the play button on the remote, but the video kept rewinding.

Oh no.

He smacked the remote with his other hand and hit play again, the tape finally jolting to a stop before flashing a glitchy, pixelated image up on the screen. You could see what I knew was Pansy's elbow in the corner, but there were three of them stacked diagonally across the screen and they were jumping all over the place. Obviously, our attempt to erase the film had been unsuccessful.

Oh no.

The elbow disappeared from the frame. "She's asking the other ghost how long she's been here," Pansy whispered. Parts of the sound were distorted, but for the most part, there was no question that it was Pansy speaking.

Then we heard, "Gerri's telling her that it's now 1996 and that she's been dead for over eighty years." A pause, and then Pansy's voice again, louder, and the triple elbow was back. "Oh, she's a nurse?" Whispering again. "She's nodding, yes."

There was a long pause on the tape while I'd talked to Jessica. Real-life-Pansy had both hands over her face, but I was sure her cheeks were going to be flaming red once the lights came back on. Every eye in the room was riveted to the screen. Blake's mouth could only be described as 'agape.'

"Ask her if she's haunting the hotel," Pansy's voice was at a normal level on the tape again, her elbow now taking up most of the screen and punctuated with random pink and green rectangles. Randy seemed to shake himself out of a trance, hitting pause. He stood there for a full minute, staring at the image of Pansy's elbow before turning around to face her. Everyone else in the room had also turned to stare at her.

"Pansy..." he trailed off, turned back to the screen to stare for another few seconds, and then turned back to face the room. "Honey, is there something you'd like to tell us?"

Pansy gave a long, ugly sigh that clearly turned into an, "ugh," at the end. "I mean, no, I would prefer to never talk about it. Ever. But it seems it may be too late for that." Her voice was muffled because she still had her hands over her face. Her forehead was lying on the table in front of her and she was talking directly into the gaping neck of her sweater.

"Yeah," Greg croaked. He cleared his throat before trying again. "Yeah, I think it's safe to say that that train has done left the station."

"Pansy, this is amazing," this from Chandra, who moved across the aisle to squat next to her before wrapping one arm over her back. "This is... I don't know. I don't even have words for this." She gave Pansy a squeeze, and I watched my sister melt into her, tears flowing freely.

"Don't cry, sweetie."

"Everyone is going to think I'm a freak." I heard her muffled sob.

"No... Well, okay, a lot of people might, but it's just us, Pansy. Let's face it, everyone already thinks that we're all freaks. But you're one of us. You're a part of our little freak family that we've got going here. Don't be embarrassed, sweetie."

Randy looked like he was doing advanced calculus up at the front of the room, and Blake still hadn't picked up his jaw from the floor.

"This is so freaking cool!" Blake finally yelled from behind her. He punched Bagel in the shoulder. "And you knew about this the whole time, you little twerp? You guys have to tell us everything!"

Greg strode to the back of the room, his long legs getting him there in five steps, and flicked the rest of the lights on. "Please, Pansy. Start from the beginning."

Randy looked like he didn't know what to do first, but he finally stopped the tape and put it back in its protective cardboard wrapper before carefully rolling the TV cart off to the side. "Okay, Pansy. Please. You know we won't judge you, but we have to know everything. I have been searching for paranormal phenomena for over thirty years and I've never seen anything like this. And then you...and I... I don't even know what to think. Kid, you've just short-circuited my brain. Please. Tell us everything."

Chandra pulled one arm away from Pansy to point at her purse hanging by its strap from the back of her chair. Shawn nodded, understanding exactly what she wanted. He rummaged through the purse until he pulled out the travel packet of tissues she kept there, pulling one free before handing them over. Chandra sat Pansy upright and passed her a tissue before moving into the chair that Summer normally sat in.

"Summer knew, didn't she?" Chandra asked her. "She had to have seen the tape when she was reviewing it."

Pansy nodded, pulling another tissue out and blowing her nose. "I didn't realize the camera was already on when we were down there. After Gerri had found the other ghosts that just did the same things over and over, we were really excited to find one that could talk."

Randy's eyebrows couldn't get higher on his forehead, and Greg's beard was twitching. "Wait, there's more than one ghost?" Randy asked.

"There's more than one kind of ghost?" Greg asked.

"Okay," Pansy sighed, wiping her eyes with the sleeve of her sweater. "You all have to promise me you won't tell anyone else. I can't deal with more reporters making things up about me. The kids at school already think I'm a total weirdo."

There was an immediate uproar as everyone promised at once.

"Well, from the beginning," she said, blowing her nose again. "Three days after Gerri died, she came back." She'd told this story so many times by now that I figured she had it memorized.

It took a good hour for her to tell the story of how and why we joined the PPS, how we'd found the ghost of Christopher hiding out at Mrs. Garcia's house, how we'd discovered who was really trying to scare her into selling her house, and how she'd found Christopher's body. She'd also filled them in on Lee and how he'd helped their investigation, including how it had been Lee who originally found the body of Stewart Mays. Food was delivered by the Buffalo Chip servers and ignored—everyone was too fascinated to look away from Pansy. When she'd finally finished the backstory, but before she delved into the Mystery of the Haunted Hotel, she got up to grab a soda, gulping it down.

"So," Blake interrupted, "that time you came into Mrs. Garcia's bedroom and flipped the mattress over, when we found the...the box thing..."

"The signal generator," Shawn supplied.

"Yeah, that. You knew where to look because you already knew that it was there?"

"Yeah. Christopher told Gerri about the men breaking in and planting it while she was out at the grocery store. He didn't know what it was, but he knew it wasn't something that should be there."

"And Christopher led you to his own body?" Chandra asked, obviously struggling to wrap her mind around this new development.

"Well, he led Gerri to his cave so we could hide, and I followed her. I couldn't see him. And he didn't know that his body was there. He hadn't left the house since he'd come back as a ghost because he was naked."

"Naked?" Greg asked. "Are all the ghosts naked?"

"No, they look like they did when they died, just, thankfully, with no signs of trauma. Like, Gerri is wearing her Green Day shirt and ripped jeans, Lee is in his pajamas and a bathrobe. Christopher's mother, well...best we can figure is she didn't want her husband to get custody. The last thing he remembered was getting ready to take a bath. Did she drown him? Drug him? We don't know."

"Where is he now? Is he still in the house? Can we talk to him through you and Gerri?" Shawn asked.

"No, he, uh, disappeared. Gerri says he went poof. I don't

know, I could never see or hear him, but like, she said that he got really bright and then just," she made a little exploding motion with her hands, "gone."

"So, in the last few months, there was only one ghost?" Shawn asked.

Pansy nodded.

Randy had pulled a chair over in front of Pansy's table and was straddling it, his arms folded across the back of the chair, his chin resting on top of his arms as he'd listened to her talk. "So, hundreds of hours spent watching and listening to tapes. So many arguments over bug versus dust orb versus spirit and we've just been wasting our time?"

"Not necessarily. There's a thing at the Castle that even Gerri and Lee couldn't see until it grew strong enough."

"This is amazing. I don't even know what to say," Chandra had one hand on her forehead and a slightly dazed look on her face.

"Uh, by the way, Jessica's gone too."

Pansy whipped her head around to look at me. "What do you mean she's gone, too?"

"Well, I thought you had a lot to process last night, so I didn't want to tell you. But since Lee and I were at the Castle all day, I haven't had time to tell you. She poofed."

"When?" Pansy demanded. When she stood up and faced me over Chandra's head, everyone's eyes grew three sizes larger.

"Is Gerri here now?" Blake leaned over to ask Bagel. Bagel nodded.

"Right after you released her. She went supernova just like Christopher did and then...poof." I made the same exploding motion with my fingers that she'd just shown the group.

Pansy sat back down. "Apparently Jessica has also poofed."

"What?" Bagel exclaimed.

Pansy turned around in her seat to face him. "Gerri said that she poofed last night right after I released her spirit when we were doing the seance."

"The what?" Chandra screeched.

And so followed another half hour or so as Pansy described everything we knew about the Castle, including the seance, and the information we learned from Jessica before she'd poofed out of existence. Finally, everyone was silent, lost in their own thoughts.

"I'll be honest, Pansy," Randy looked antsy, like he didn't know what to do first. "I'd love to write all of this down and publish a book about it. This is incredible. We need to tell everyone." He paused as the look of panic grew on her face. "I mean, we don't have to use your name. We could, like, give you a fake name for the story."

"Even if you used a fake name, it wouldn't take anyone in this town longer than five minutes to figure out who you're talking about," Shawn interrupted. "How many teenage twins live here? The Bellafini girls, that's it."

"I mean, if you ever decide to go public, we'll, like, have to call Unsolved Mysteries. I guarantee that they'd love to interview you!" Greg said. He'd pulled up a chair next to Randy as everyone had crowded around her.

"I don't think that's ever going to happen," Pansy mumbled.

"Well, eventually I'm going to have a couple hundred more questions for you, Pansy. I just can't think straight right now. But let me circle back to this Dr. Welling character that you're calling the Other?"

"Well, Jessica was the one that was calling him Other," she said.

"And you can't see it or Jessica?"

"No. Well, that's not entirely true, I could see her last night when I called her forth in the seance, but normally I can only see and hear Gerri. I can't see or hear Lee. And Dario can't see or hear either of them, but he can feel them. He gets a cold chill every time they touch him." She turned to face Chandra. "You do, too."

"I do, too, what?" Chandra asked.

"You can feel them. Every time you walk through Gerri, you think it's a draft. Gerri," she pointed at me, and everyone turned to look at the empty space. "Give Chandra a tap on the shoulder, please. If that's okay with you?" she asked Chandra.

"Oh, yes, of course."

I tapped Chandra twice on the shoulder and she started laughing, "Oh my gosh, I cannot believe this. Yes, I can feel that." I did it again, and she squealed, "She did it again!"

"Yep."

"Wait, is Chandra the only one that can feel her?" Shawn asked, leaning across the aisle.

"She tested you all at that very first PPS meeting that I attended. Chandra was the only one sensitive."

"This is incredible," Chandra mumbled to herself. I placed my hand on her shoulder and held it there.

"Okay, okay. Parlor tricks aside, how do we get rid of this Other? It sounds like a walking nightmare," Randy said.

"We don't know. We hoped that by knowing its name we could call it forth in a seance, just like we did with Jessica. Maybe then we can ask it what it wants or force it to move on," Pansy told him.

"I don't know, kid," Randy said. His eyebrows, furry on a good day, were smashed together in one lumpy caterpillar. "If this thing is as bad as you say it is, and getting stronger with every person it hurts, I wouldn't be comfortable with you putting yourself out there like that. I understand you seem to have some kind of aptitude for this, but it sounds like he could be really dangerous. It's already hurt so many people and let's not forget, it almost took out Browning with that chunk of concrete."

"Oh. Yeah, no," Pansy said, shaking her head. "That was actually the business partner."

"The what?" came five voices at once.

23

Pansy and I were sitting in the parking lot of the Buffalo Chip, engine running, arguing over whether we needed some Alanis or Shakespeare's Sister to scream-sing on the way home when Bagel tapped on the passenger side window.

Pansy leaned over the passenger seat to flip the door lock and Bagel pulled it open, thrusting a red to-go cup towards her.

"I come bearing gifts."

"Uh, thank you?" She took the cup, fumbling the straw and dropping it into the black hole that existed between the seat and the center console.

"It's Dr. Pepper because I know that's your favorite. Can I, uh...?" he gestured to the empty seat.

"Oh, yeah, of course. Get in."

Bagel climbed in, closed the door, and leaned his head back against the headrest. "I just wanted to tell you that I'm proud of you. Never in a million years would I have predicted that you'd come clean to everyone at once. I know you didn't exactly have a choice, but I think you handled it really well."

"Well, it wasn't like I told the world," she mumbled with

her hand shoved between the seat and console, searching for the straw. "It was just the PPS." The straw would never be seen again.

"Still, you could have lied. Honestly, I fully expected you to bolt. I thought, 'she's going to run away and never come back.'"

"I wanted to."

"But you didn't."

Pansy slid Jagged Little Pill into the tape deck and the two sat for a moment as the music played.

"Are you going to let me apologize now?"

"I guess," he chuckled. "But you'd better make it good."

Pansy let out a big breath of air as she decided where to start. "Well, first off, I didn't expect to miss you as much as I did."

Bagel shifted in his seat to face her and arched one brow. "So far, this is the opposite of good."

"Just hear me out. I realized that I've been jealous of you for years. I mean, not you, personally." His brow arched higher. "But the bond you and Gerri had together. You two were always so close, so in sync with one another that you could speak across a room without using words and finish each other's sentences... I don't know, I just always felt like you were closer to her than I was. She was my sister, my twin, and I had this idea in my head that I should be her best friend." She paused to pop the plastic top off of the cup and take a drink of soda.

"I think a big part of the problem is that I decided I didn't like you in elementary school, because she liked you better than me. And then I never examined those feelings again. It was just this thing that existed in my head, a fact of life. Seeing you grieve over Gerri when she died, it made me irrationally angry. I know that. Logically, I knew you had every right to grieve for her, but my heart said 'No, Pansy. You're the one that killed her, no one else is allowed to miss her as much as you do.'"

"For the last freakin' time…"

"It's not your fault," Bagel said, unknowingly interrupting me. He laid his hand on her arm. "And let me apologize for telling you I wished it were you. I didn't mean that."

"I mean, you probably did a little bit, but I'm not mad. I understand."

Bagel kept his mouth shut.

"But Gerri isn't here, and she wants us to be friends, and I hate that her death is what had to happen to make me even entertain that idea. And then it took me ruining your life to make me realize that there was absolutely no reason for me to have ever disliked you other than my own issues. I'm finally noticing what a selfish friend I am. I really enjoy our adventures and you're a lot of fun to hang out with. You have a great sense of humor, and you are soooo creative." She took another drink. "Anyway, all of that to say, I'm sorry I ruined your life and if you never want to speak to me again, I understand and I don't blame you." She played with the lid and refused to look him in the eyes until she heard him sigh.

He leaned his head back and closed his eyes. "My life isn't ruined. I don't have any gym classes this semester, so it's not like I have to deal with locker room talk from any of the other guys, and I've actually had three girls slip me their phone numbers in the last two weeks. Whose names will remain anonymous," he turned and pointed a finger at her. Pansy's mouth was open, clearly ready to ask for the names. "But you're fun, too. You've gotten sassier, and I don't remember you ever being as, I don't know, take charge as you are now. You were always so quiet and so…perfect all the time. It was honestly nauseating. But you've changed. I mean, personality wise. You're standing up for yourself, you're showing people that you have a weird side, and I like it. I mean, I'm never going to get behind this whole prep look you've got going, and we are never, ever going to agree on music, but... I've missed you."

Pansy flung her arms around him, squeezing him tight, and he patted her awkwardly on the back. "Oh my god, get off of me or we're going to have five new rumors started about us before first period on Monday." Pansy settled back behind the wheel, and Bagel chuckled. "I almost called you twice earlier today because duuuude, I still cannot get over the fact that your hair-brained seance scheme actually worked," he said.

"Honestly, me neither. I was just hoping that Jessica would just believe me when I told her she couldn't lie, you know, like a power of suggestion thing. It never even occurred to me I'd actually be able to see her."

"I feel like that's not normal. Like, how many years has Madame Brousseau been on television? And I have never in my life thought, even for a second, that she was a real psychic. How many times has she done a seance or a tarot reading for the local news stations? It's always looked so fake. Do you think she experiences what you did? Or like, maybe the news is right, which is a sentence I never imagined myself saying, but maybe your connection with Gerri really gives you an extra boost?"

"I don't know. We could have you try to summon Gerri or Lee, I guess. Test it out and see if the same thing happens to you."

"Oh no, you're not. You released Jessica, and she poofed," I told her.

"Gerri wants her complaint noted, for the record, that when I released Jessica, she poofed. Which reminds me, why didn't you tell me last night? What happened? Was it like Christopher?"

"Yeah. So, when you called her and told her to show herself, she took on this freaky glow for me and Lee. And then when you released her, she faded back to looking like a normal living person. Then she apologized for not telling us sooner. She said she was trying to protect herself and in the process, other people were hurt and she was sorry. Then she lit up, flashed, and was gone."

"Okay, but then that means she poofed after she apologized, not after I released her."

"I mean, that's a matter of sixty seconds. There could be some kind of delay between you saying your magic words and her being fully released to...well, to wherever we go from here. Released into the cosmos for all I know."

Pansy relayed this information to Bagel, and he thought it over. "It sounds to me like her admitting to killing this dude, and then apologizing for it is really what made her poof, not anything Pansy did. On the other hand, I don't want to risk it. Unless you're like, ready to move on, Gerri?"

"Smack him for me."

"Ouch, what was that for?" Bagel asked while rubbing his arm.

"She said to smack you. I'm just doing what I was told," Pansy said with a shrug and took another slurp of soda.

"So, what's the next step?" Bagel asked. "We now have the complete cooperation of the PPS behind us. If anyone can figure out a way to get rid of this thing, it's Randy and Greg."

"Yeah, Randy wants me to meet him for lunch tomorrow at the Firefly. He said he needed time to come up with a list of questions. I'd really appreciate it if you went with me, but like, if you don't want to be seen in public with me, I totally understand."

"Whatever. Honestly, the entire school can think we're dating for all I care. It's none of their business and it might shut them up and make them move on to pick on someone else. I mean," he looked over at her and held his hands up like he was fending off an attack. "I don't actually want to date you or anything, so like, don't get the wrong idea."

"Umm, duh. I know."

"Okay, I just wanted to be clear. But yeah, I can meet you there tomorrow. I've got to work two to close, though. I'm sure Randy is going to grill you for hours, so I may not be able to stay the whole time."

"That would still make me feel better, to, you know, have you there with me."

"Tell him about the business partner," I told her while I wracked my brain trying to remember what else he needed to know to get him back up to speed. Pansy told him about the email, the fake investors, Mr. Browning hiding out in the motel, and the security camera that we suspected was installed to keep tabs on the business partner instead of vandals.

"Well, at least Browning knows that the game is afoot," Bagel said. "It sounds like you two have covered that problem as much as you can."

"Yeah, that's one we can mark off the list. Let's see, what else did we learn…oh, there was once a tunnel that led from the basement to a mortuary out behind the carriage house. And there was an entire cemetery on the hillside next to it. Well, I guess, not was, still is, but when the nursing home took over, they removed all the gravestones. And before you ask, yes, Jessica told Gerri and Lee that she was buried out there in one of the mass graves they used for the Spanish flu pandemic. But don't, like, be thinking that she came back because she was in an unmarked grave. She was one of hundreds in that unmarked grave and she was the only one that didn't move on."

"So, the cemetery is a cool little bit of history, but completely irrelevant to any of the mysteries that we have left to solve."

"Pretty much."

"And what about the other ghosts, the ones on loops? When Jessica poofed, did they all go away, too?"

"What? They're freaking ghosts. It's not like werewolves, or vampires, or something, and she was their master. Jessica moving on had nothing to do with the others. Tell him they're all still there. But, also, tell him that Lee and I can see the Other now and Lee actually touched it. Like, it has substance, touched it. It's gotten a lot stronger."

"And I quote..." Pansy said before updating Bagel on the status of the ghosts at Chivington.

"Okay, okay. Fine, ghosts don't have masters. Got it. But like, let me just tell you, it's a lot easier to have a conversation with Pansy around than trying to use the ouija board." He was quiet for a moment, thinking it over.

"This thing being stronger worries me. And Lee and Gerri, they can't actually touch one another, right? It's not like pushing on a physical object that exists in the world?" Pansy nodded. "So then, what is this dude? What's juiced up Casper made out and how can we get rid of it? Do you honestly think we can get rid of it with another seance? What if you're not strong enough to fight it? What if it, like, I don't know, turns the tables and drains you dead after you summon it?"

"I don't know. I don't know what I'm doing. I didn't even know that I could summon a ghost. Like, what else can I do? How do I even test it?"

"We'll ask Randy tomorrow. Maybe if we have the full presence of the PPS there, we can, like, I don't know, lend you our strength or something. Even if that's not a thing, I feel like Randy is the one to ask. He'll have a connection somewhere. But whatever we do, one thing is for sure, we're not asking Madame Brousseau for help."

"Oh, my god. As if. Can you even imagine?"

24

We'd just finished breakfast Sunday morning when there was a knock at the door and both Pansy, Mom, and Dad all looked at each for a second, silently asking if anyone was expecting company. When everyone shook their head, Dad set his coffee cup down and went to answer it while Mom muttered something about reporters under her breath. I was hovering right behind him as he opened the door to a little old lady who looked like she was on her way home from church. I doubted she was even five feet tall, and her very obviously dyed black hair was worn in a pixie cut. She wore an ankle-length floral dress with a fitted cardigan and low-heeled pumps in a matching shade of lilac. Either she was broken down and needed to borrow a phone, or she was the most colorful Jehovah's Witness that had ever stopped by.

"Mr. Bellafini? Good morning to you. And you too, Gerri." I froze. She smiled at me and I noticed she had a bit of hot pink lipstick on her teeth.

She held out one perfectly manicured hand to my stunned father, who seemed incapable of words. "I'm Christine Hermance, professional medium. If you don't mind, I'd like to have a brief chat with your other daughter, Pansy." Her smile never wavered as my dad tried to make words.

"Pansy," I yelled over my shoulder.

"Thank you, Gerri," she said. Was I in an episode of the Twilight Zone and just didn't know it? What was going on here?

"I'm sorry to just show up on your doorstep like this, but I left several messages on the machine." Our father still had his mouth open but wasn't making words. "I'm sure you have plenty of questions. May I come in?"

I'd seen the movie the Lost Boys entirely too many times to ever invite someone into the house. Either they followed me in or they didn't. Dad, however, wasn't as hip to pop culture. Pansy was just entering the front hall when Dad stepped out of the way and motioned for the stranger to enter.

"Oh, you were identical twins, weren't you?" she said, looking between us. Now it was Pansy's turn to be speechless.

"Honey, who is it?" Mom was right behind Pansy and everyone stopped to stare at our guest.

"Perhaps, I should explain. I left several messages on your answering machine, but I assume you may have received entirely too many messages to have actually listened to them all, haven't you? Don't worry, I'm not offended. Anyway, I thought I would stop by and introduce myself. As I mentioned to your husband, I'm what some people refer to as a psychic, although I consider myself to be a spiritualist or a medium, if you will. Before you ask, no, I cannot read minds or predict the future which, yes, is a skill one normally attributes to psychics, but I do see and speak with the deceased who linger here with the living."

You could have knocked all four of us over with a feather. My mother was the first to recover. I guess if you have a child die and then come back as a ghost, your brain is then preconditioned to accept other weirdness as it comes at you. Or she had given up trying to understand the natural order of things and just went with the crazy. I wasn't sure which.

"Come on in. Uh, we were just finishing breakfast. There's still some pancakes left, if you're hungry."

To his credit, Dad didn't lag too far behind. "Can I get you coffee, orange juice, chocolate milk?"

"Oh, no, I've already eaten. Thank you for the hospitality, though." She followed my parents to the living room where they all took a seat. Pansy followed behind slowly, not sure what was going on, and I brought up the rear after popping out of the house to see if there was anyone else with her. No one was hiding in the bushes or in the backseat of her gigantic eighties car that stretched for what seemed to be the entire length of our yard while parked at the curb.

"She's alone as far as I see," I whispered to Pansy since apparently our guest had no problem hearing me.

Once everyone was settled on our gigantic sectional couch, Dad asked, "So, what brings you to Perth, Ms. Hermance?"

Like we all didn't already know that it was the news report with Pansy. The question was really, which news report had brought her here, and why?

She looked around at each of us before answering. "I live in a little town called Clayton in New Mexico. It's about an hour and a half southeast of here, and I saw your daughter on the news. Now, you didn't show up on film," she pointed one hot pink nail in my direction which thoroughly freaked me out, "but I assumed that there had to be some sort of spiritual guide for Pansy here to have found multiple long-dead bodies in such a short span of time. I called the local library and the clerk there was more than happy to pull the newspaper stories from both events, as well as the first time you were in the paper, when Gerri was killed." She rearranged her skirt, avoiding eye contact while mentioning that unpleasantness.

"I must say, joining a paranormal investigation group was a fantastic use of your new skills, but tell me, have you girls found any other paranormal entities?"

"Do you mean ghosts?" Pansy asked. When Ms. Hermance nodded, she spilled all of the beans. "Yes, Gerri met the ghost of a little boy, the boy whose body we later found, and then there's Lee who's been a lot of help. He used to be an investigative reporter, and he's the one that originally found the body of Stewart Mays. He just needed help to alert the police."

"Don't forget Jessica," I said.

"I was just getting there, thank you."

"And can you see and talk to these ghosts like you can Gerri?"

"No, Ms. Hermance. She talks to them and then relays whatever they say to me."

"Call me Christine, dear. Oh, well, that's disappointing, but everyone's gifts are different. I'm currently searching for an assistant to train and I had hoped that I'd finally found someone who matched my...unique skill set."

"Have you ever seen a poltergeist?" I asked, floating a little closer.

"A poltergeist? Yes, unfortunately I have some experience with them. Why? Are you girls holding out on me?" Now she was leaning forward.

"A what?" Mom yelled, standing up and staring down at Pansy. "You haven't told me anything about a poltergeist."

Oops. My bad.

Pansy glared at me and tried to soothe Mom. "We don't even know if that's what it really is, that's why we haven't said anything. Relax, Mom."

"Tell me everything," Christine said, digging through her giant straw handbag and pulling out a tape recorder. "This is just for my personal notes. I promise no one else will hear it," she assured Pansy when she looked at it suspiciously.

Mom sat back down and crossed her arms. "Yes, Pansy, do tell us everything."

"Well, Jessica, she was the ghost of a nurse who watched over the other ghosts at Chivington. She asked us to help her get rid of this poltergeist thing."

"She didn't call it that, that's what we called it," I interrupted her. "She called it the Other." It was nice having someone else that could hear me and not have everything I said filtered through Pansy's Reader's Digest version of what I was trying to say.

"Okay, but I think what she actually called it was a physical manifestation of rage and revenge. It turns out, whatever it is, it started off as a doctor that was, well, let's just say he was a really bad dude, and we just found out that she, Jessica, I mean, was the one that killed him. But like, he didn't come back as a better dude and now he's a human-sized electrical storm that sucks the life source out of the living."

"I'm sorry, he does what?" Mom stood again. Dad did that slow-blink thing he did when he was trying to process too much information at once.

"So yeah, there's that. Apparently, he'd gotten really weak because no one had been there for like a decade, but when there used to be patients and especially when it was a nursing home back in the olden days, Jessica said that he would hover over people and drain them. It was how he, I guess, fed, for lack of a better word. It's what kept him strong."

"But he's just become visible, or at least, visible to Lee and me, in the last few weeks. He's been feeding on the construction workers that are trying to remodel the hotel," I added. The parents didn't need to know that part.

"Right, so Jessica was trying to scare the owners away by

knocking stuff over and making it look haunted, but that's actually what this Fruit Loop that owns the hotel wanted. He thinks he can charge people more money for the experience of staying in a haunted hotel."

"Oh, one of those?" Christine said, scribbling something into her notebook. "Now, you mentioned this Jessica was protecting other ghosts? Did you get their stories, too?"

"No, they're... Well, Gerri said they don't see her. They don't interact."

"They just do the same thing over and over. They don't seem to hear me or acknowledge me in any way when I try to talk to them," I added.

"Ah, a true shade. In my experience, these entities are generally created when the body's soul leaves before the physical body gives out. You see it often in nursing homes and hospitals when patients are kept on life support. It's as if the energy is left with no direction once the brain dies."

"Is there a way to save them?" Pansy asked.

"There's nothing to save them from, child. Despite the worries of your nurse friend, they are nothing but residual energy. The soul, the part that makes you you, that's already long gone."

"So they won't poof?"

"I'm sorry, poof?"

"We don't know what to call it," Pansy explained. "When we found Christopher's body, Gerri said he became a big ball of light and then just, you know, poofed out of existence. He moved on, we assumed."

"And this happened after you found his body? And you haven't seen him since then? I only ask because I've known several ghosts and most knew where their bodies were located. Usually when a ghost moves on, in this ball of light, just like

Gerri here has described to you, it's because they absolve themselves of some kind of guilt."

I thought about the relief that had crossed his face right before he'd exploded into a ball of light. "The baseball card. He'd spent forty-three years looking for that Willie Mays card. He was so afraid that his dad was going to be mad because he'd lost it. It was in the lunchbox in the cave and when you threw the lunchbox at that dude trying to shoot you," I turned to Christine and pointed my finger at her, "You hear none of this, got it?"

She nodded.

"But when the lunchbox opened, and he picked the card up, that's when he poofed. He looked so relieved when he found it."

"Yes, in my experience with the ghosts I've helped move on, it has always been guilt that held them here."

"Helped?" Mom asked. "You're not planning on helping Gerri like that, are you?" My five-foot-three mother looked ready to launch herself across the coffee table at this woman.

"Oh no, don't worry yourself," she waved one hand through the air, "I mean, if Gerri wants to move on and can't find her own way there, then of course I'll help in any way I can, but for right now she seems to be enjoying herself. Would I be correct in assuming that you're not quite ready, dear?"

"Absolutely not. We've barely made a dent in the list of things we need to do and people we can help."

"As I thought, she has better things to do with her time than to just move on."

I'd never thought about it like that, but yes, I had projects that needed to be finished. Questions that needed answers, mysteries to solve. I didn't have time to go deal with my afterlife just yet.

"But you said that they stay because of guilt? What could Gerri possibly feel guilty about?" Dad asked.

"I don't. Tell him I don't feel guilty about anything. I'm fine." The sound of Pansy ugly crying and screaming my name until she was hoarse flashed through my mind. I quickly shrugged it off and concentrated on random song lyrics, instead.

Pansy relayed this message but Christine stared at me with pursed lips and gave a noncommittal "Hmph." I gave her my best, *what could I possibly feel guilty about?* look. Besides, if resolving any feelings of guilt that I may have would poof me, then I considered this the perfect reason to not delve too deeply into my own feelings. Better not to chance it.

25

Christine sat with my family for another two hours, finally agreeing to a cup of coffee. She was determined to learn everything we knew about Chivington, including any research that Pansy and Bagel may have found in the library. Pansy even drew a map of the Castle for her.

"I think I'll call this Browning character this evening and introduce myself, offer my services," she said before setting her coffee cup on the table. "Hopefully he'll let me look around this hotel of his tomorrow and see what I can see."

"But tomorrow is Monday," Pansy said. "I'll be in school."

Christine pulled her massive straw handbag into her lap and began packing her tape recorder, notebook, and Pansy's map into it. "That's okay, Gerri can go with me. I'll call the house as soon as I confirm with Browning. If there isn't a living person home to answer, I'll just leave a message on the machine."

I was shocked to suddenly find myself useful to someone. I liked it. My parents stood, offering Christine their thanks for assisting us, and Pansy offered to walk her to the door. I had one more tidbit to tell her, but we needed the parental units out of earshot.

"I can't tell you how much we appreciate any help or insight that you can bring to this," Pansy was saying as she led the way to the front door.

"I also need to tell you that Jessica poofed after we did a seance Friday night," I said, bringing up the rear.

Christine whipped around, her pencil line eyebrows raised. "You did what?"

"Uh, yeah outside," Pansy muttered, holding the front door open. Christine hustled out, her handbag slapping against her hip as she hurried down the sidewalk toward her car.

"Tell me everything, right now, step-by-step."

We did.

"Ordinarily it would be difficult to discern how much damage you may have done, but in this case you have the advantage of having someone that can see any lingering spirits you may have attracted," she nodded towards me as we all huddled around the trunk of her car. "Tell me, did anything else respond to the call?"

"Not that I saw," I said. "Lee and I were both there, and we saw Jessica. She took on like, this extra glow when Pansy summoned her, and then when Pansy released her, she looked normal again. She apologized for not telling us about murdering the doctor dude sooner and then she poofed. Then we were interrupted by another group of teenagers breaking in, so we had to get out of there before they got us all caught."

"Did you close the door?" she asked, staring Pansy down.

Pansy nodded. "Yeah, Lee had unlocked a fire door for us. It closed by itself after we left."

"Not a physical door." Her eye roll spoke volumes. "The seance, tell me, after you released her, what happened next?"

Between the two of us, we pieced together a replay of Pansy

answering questions from the other participants and Lee and I wondering what had caused Jessica to poof. Christine's glare became more pronounced as we finished.

"You just ended it there, with the door to the spirit realm wide open for any old thing to walk through?"

"Maybe..." Pansy answered. "I had made some notes about some sort of closing prayer we could do, but we didn't have time to do that part."

"Didn't have time to do that part..." Christine looked like she was developing a migraine.

Had we left a door to the spirit realm open? "What would it look like if we had?" I asked. "Is it something we could see? Not Pansy and the others, of course, but something Lee and I could have seen? We didn't feel or see anything that was different or out of place."

"It's not like a bright red door pops up, no," Christine said, digging through her purse to pull out a pack of cigarettes. She offered the pack to Pansy, who declined, before placing one between her pink stained lips and going back in for her lighter. Once the Virginia Slim was lit to her satisfaction, she took two long puffs before turning back to Pansy, elbow bent and cigarette held between her nicotine-stained fingers at shoulder level. "If I had to describe it, I'd say it's more of a glimmer in the air that the living can't see. And the glimmer doesn't necessarily occur right next to where you're holding the seance, it could be anywhere nearby."

Oops. We'd been in a hurry. In a panic, to be honest. I hadn't noticed anything weird like that when Lee and I had been hanging out there yesterday, but we'd spent most of our time in the lobby watching him wander by on his rounds through the empty building. We hadn't gone inside every single room.

"Just in the building, or could it be outside? Is there... I don't know, a range? Like, if we consider the spot that we did the seance the focus, how far would the radius extend?" Leave it to Pansy to set up ghost math like a geometry problem.

"It depends on the strength of the medium. Normally, I'd consider an untested teenage girl to be low on the scale of medium power, but..." she waved her empty hand in Pansy's direction while she took another drag. She exhaled, blowing the smoke from one corner of her mouth, away from us. "I guess I'll have to see for myself. I can't imagine that your power extended outside the building. It's actually surprising that you could even see the ghost you were speaking with." She chuckled and took another puff. "It's rare that you succeeded at all with nothing but a library book to guide you. You may turn out to be an untapped well, but testing you will have to wait until later."

Christine took another drag, tapping her foot while she thought. "You didn't try calling any other spirits, just Jessica?"

"Well, we knew she was there and that Gerri and Lee could see her. We also assumed that she was hiding something, and I'd read online that ghosts can't lie once summoned. She seemed like a good test subject. We didn't want any other ghosts or spirits to appear. It's not like we were trying to add to the ghost population."

"Well, that's cute, but not how a seance works. Which is why you shouldn't use magic you know nothing about."

"Magic?" My only experience with magic was a clown pulling coins from behind my ear at a county fair as a little kid. This seemed to be in a different category.

"It makes the world go round, girlie." She put the cigarette to her lips again and seemed to suck every last bit of nicotine from it, the paper tube burning down to nothing before she threw it on the sidewalk and ground it out under one lilac heel. "From what you've said, it won't be hard for me to sweet talk this Browning guy into holding my own seance there. He should be positively honored that I'd even want to visit his pile of rocks. You," she pointed at me. "Take your fellow ghost friend and go search for that portal. You opened it, you can save me a few hours of work by finding it."

"Yes, ma'am." Lee was going to love her.

"Isn't that dangerous, though?" Pansy asked. "If it's a portal between the living and the dead, what happens if Gerri or Lee accidentally walk into it? What happens if one of the construction workers walks into it?"

"It won't affect the living, but as for our deceased friends... probably nothing. Even if they enter, it's open, they can still come back through. In theory." I was picturing myself stepping out of a door and into a world of sand dunes and giant black-and-white striped worms. No, thank you. "But I can't say for sure. My advice would be, pay attention and try to avoid walking into it."

Fantastic.

Christine walked around the car and hauled open the driver's side door, the hinges squealing in protest. "I'll call you as soon as I talk to Browning. And Geraldine, I expect a report on the location of the portal before we get there."

"Yes, ma'am," we said in unison.

She pulled away from the curb, her exhaust rattling and what sounded like some kind of belt under her hood squealing in protest. Being a medium was obviously not a glamorous life of fame and riches.

"I'll go talk to Lee and let him know that we've been assigned homework," I told her.

"And leave me to fend off the parents by myself? They're going to want to know what we were out here talking about."

"Absolutely," I said, laughing. She'd figure it out. With that, I did my best Supergirl impression and took off through the sky and over the neighborhood towards the police station.

26

Lee and I were torn between our need to search for the needle in the haunted haystack and our desire to eavesdrop on Pansy's conversation with Randy. Since The Firefly was closer, we decided it wouldn't hurt to pop in and see what Randy had to say before we took off for the Castle. After all, we still had plenty of daylight to search for this doorway that may or may not exist.

Pansy was in a booth talking to Randy when she saw us float into the restaurant. Her eyes narrowed. "I'm sorry, Randy, hold that thought." She glanced at me and hissed. "There is no way that you've already found it," Randy froze, looking around the table like he was afraid to make any sudden movements.

"Dude, we haven't even left town yet. We wanted to hear what Randy knows about this Christine chick first."

Pansy looked back at Randy. "Sorry, Gerri and Lee are supposed to be looking for something at the Castle, but they've stopped in for a chat before they go."

"Both Gerri and her friend are here?" he asked, eyes wide.

"Had he heard of her?" I asked.

"I don't know," she gestured to the yellow legal pad full of chicken scratch on the table in front of Randy. "Randy had some questions. I haven't told him about our visitor yet."

Randy was practically vibrating with curiosity. "You know what? The questions can wait. What visitor?"

"Well, this woman stopped by the house this morning. She said she'd seen me on the news and she suspected I had some kind of spirit guide situation going on." Pansy paused to wave a hand in my direction. "She can see and hear ghosts, like, all the ghosts, not just one like me. Anyway, we told her about the seance we did Friday night and she thinks there's a good chance that I opened a door to the other side and then, um...well, didn't close it before we left."

Randy blinked twice. "You didn't...do you mean you didn't actually finish the seance?"

"Well, yeah. Those other teenagers broke in, so we grabbed our stuff and ran."

"Okay." He scrubbed his hand over his face. "Okay, so, you not only successfully performed a seance on your first attempt, commanded a ghost to appear and it did, but then you grabbed your stuff and ran without actually finishing the ritual or closing the door to the spirit realm?"

"Well, when you say it like that...but yeah."

"Holy crap," he muttered, lowering his face into both hands while he thought it over. "Okay, so there could be even more entities there now."

"In theory. Assuming I actually opened a doorway, which maybe I didn't. It's not like Jessica had to come through it. She was already there in front of me," Pansy said. "But that's what they're going to go check on. Is there a portal? Is it open? How bad is the damage?"

"Wouldn't this portal be where you were doing the seance?" Randy asked.

"No, she said that it could be anywhere in the building, or maybe even outside."

"Okay, so, if there is a door and it's open, what was this woman's solution?"

"She's going to call Browning and convince him to let her do her own seance there so that she can close the portal and get rid of Welling. Two birds, one stone. She wants to have the PPS there to participate because I guess the more people present, the more energy she can draw from."

"And this random Christine woman that showed up on your doorstep thinks she can do all of this?"

"Yeah. Ms. Hermance seemed pretty convinced she can pull it off as long as she can get access to the building."

'I can't wait to meet this woman," Lee told me.

"Wait. Christine Hermance is the random woman that tracked you down? Holy crap, kid, do you have any idea who she is?"

"Well, I spent about two hours with her this morning, so I've got a basic idea, yeah. Why? Is she famous or something?"

"Famous or something. Yes. She's like...I...wow. Okay, she's only like, you know, the most famous medium alive today. There've been entire books written about her and you actually met her? And she's here in Perth?"

"Yep. I don't know if you guys can arrange your work schedules or..."

"Are you kidding me? Like I would miss this? This is a once in a lifetime opportunity you're talking about here. We're gonna need cameras. We're going to need the whole crew. I'll call everyone. Greg will not believe this. Chandra!" he said, waving his arm in the air to catch her attention.

Pansy turned to me as Randy was explaining to Chandra what was happening and why everyone would need to be ready to take off work.

"Gerri, you and Lee need to go find this door while there's still enough daylight to see it," Pansy said. "If Christine can actually shove this thing through a portal, we'll have a better idea of how to make a plan once we know where in the hotel it is. For all we know, it's out in the woods, or in the old cemetery."

"What old cemetery?" Randy asked, catching the end of her instructions.

I waved goodbye to my sister as she launched into the tale of the gravestone removal for Randy and Chandra.

We found the Other making his rounds on the center wing of the third floor.

"Hey, Welling," Lee taunted. The shape paused for a moment, although with no face, it was hard to tell if it could see us or not. "Your time here is about to come to an end, buddy. You should probably pack your bags, tie up any loose ends." It definitely noticed us, but I still couldn't tell if it understood what Lee was saying.

"You know what I can't do, Lee? I can't search for a rip in the time-space continuum if I'm running for my afterlife when you make this thing mad."

Lee sneered at the entity. It resumed its rounds.

"Start inside? Outside? Top? Bottom?" I asked.

"Let's start at the top, work our way down. Then, we can look outside and around the grounds if we don't find it here."

Assuming one really opened in the first place, I thought. We started on the east wing of the fifth floor, Lee covering the rooms on one side of the hall, and I took the other. We moved quickly, checking the fifth, fourth, and third floors off the list. I finally spotted it on the second floor in the west wing. I noticed dust motes floating in a sunbeam that seemed to be rippling more than just floating aimlessly through the air.

"Lee! I think I've found it."

Lee floated through the wall, entering a bare foot away from the shimmer. "Stop!"

I pointed and Lee looked over, shifting another two feet before continuing into the room.

"Do you see it?" I asked.

Lee leaned closer, examining the portion of air and space that was not like the rest. Upon closer inspection, I could see that it was shaped like an ellipse, a scant twelve inches across at its widest point and about three-feet long, it started a good foot and a half from the floor. "It looks like a special effect in a B-rated horror film," I said. But a B movie would have added a sound effect for it—a humming or a swishing sound, something to give it an air of magic and mysticism. There were no sparkles, no thrumming, just silence.

"It looks harmless enough," Lee mused, his nose inches away from it.

"Famous last words. Get away from there before something reaches out to touch someone and drags you back through." Lee turned his attention away from the shimmer in the air and surveyed the room. It had new drywall and the concrete floors appeared ready for tile, judging by the marks on the floor. A new drop ceiling grid had been installed.

"It's going to be a cramped space to hold a seance," he observed.

I looked around, trying to decide if the entire PPS plus Christine, and Browning, who I was sure wouldn't miss it for the world, would fit into the room. It'd be tight. "We'll let Christine figure out the logistics. At least we found it and I don't see anything else strange wandering around."

Lee had his nose inches from the shimmer, again. "I'm kind of tempted to stick my head in there and see what I can see."

"Please don't. I feel like we're going to need your help getting rid of this thing. I'd hate for you to be sucked up and spat out on the other side. Who knows if you could come back from that?"

This was like telling a reptile enthusiast not to pet the crocodile. Finally, he shrugged. I hoped that meant he'd agreed not to risk it.

"I'm going home to report the location of the shimmer to Pansy. Are you staying or going?"

"I'm going to stick around, keep an eye on the door and the Other."

"What are you going to do if anything actually comes through it? Wrestle it back in? It could be dangerous."

"But at least we'll know it's here and needs to be dealt with."

"And knowing is half the battle. Okay, so I should be back with Christine tomorrow unless she can't get Browning to talk to her. I'll come back to let you know either way. Until then, keep doing your Sam Spade stake out thing."

"Sam Spade? How do you know about *The Maltese Falcon*?"

I didn't appreciate his shock. "Well, believe it or not, there's more on cable television than *The Real World*. I like watching the Turner Classic Movies channel, thank you very much."

"Classics," he snorted. "Well then, here's lookin' at you, kid." He tipped an imaginary hat.

"That's not even the right movie."

"I know, but work with me here. What are the odds that I'll ever get to use that line again?" He had to have heard my eyes rolling as I took off to update the living on our current situation.

27

Christine called Sunday night and spoke to Dad, letting him know to tell me to meet her at the Castle at ten the next morning. I was anxious all night, floating back and forth across the room, torn between watching over Pansy and going to make sure that Lee was alright. I imagined him fighting the Other, or fighting demonic things that came through the veil. Even worse, I imagined his curiosity getting the better of him and him going through the portal just to see what was on the other side.

"I want you to know that I am insanely jealous," Pansy said as I floated back into our bedroom after my morning visit to Mrs. Garcia.

"Because you don't get to watch Andy Griffith reruns every morning?" I was being purposely obtuse.

"Ha. Ha. I can't believe I opened a door to the other side and I'm not even the one that gets to go see it."

"I can't open doors on any side, metaphysical or otherwise, so just keep that in mind," I advised.

She finished braiding her hair, fixing the end with a light

blue scrunchie that matched her blue and white striped bell bottoms.

"Besides," I paused as one platform mule came flying out of our closet. She was still digging around for the other one as I continued. "If all goes well, you'll get to come to the big show. We're not doing anything today but giving Christine the grand tour."

"That still sounds like more fun than a chemistry quiz," I heard her grumble from the depths of our closet floor.

"Well, have fun with chemistry. I'm going to head out and let Lee know what the plan for the day is going to be. Hopefully, Christine convinces Browning to let her do her seance as soon as possible and we can get this over and done with."

"Fine, but even if I'm still in school, come find me and tell me what's going on and I'll let Dario know."

"Deal."

I flew to the Castle on autopilot. What seemed like the bazillionth trip had caused some of the wonder I'd originally felt when flying over the mountain to wear thin. The scenery was amazing and all, but even floating took too long when you were nervous. There were so many things that could go wrong, so many more dangerous things in the world than I'd ever dreamed could exist. If someone had told me a year ago that I'd die and come back as a ghost, make a few ghost friends, solve some mysteries, and now be on my way to meet with a world famous medium about a wormhole through the fabric of this plane, specifically to shove an evil spirit back through it and then throw away the key? I'd have been calling the people in the white coats.

The sun was just breaking through the peaks and high-lighting the five stories of granite in a rose gold glow, or at least the parts that had been pressure washed. The black mildew covering the top two floors could not be described as rosy or golden, but at least most of the building was showing off its potential. Lee was still pacing back and forth in the room with the shimmer when I got there.

"It's a good thing you're a ghost or you would have worn a path in the concrete," I said.

He jumped. "Did you take lessons in sneaking from Jessica before she left?"

"As if. So, how did guard duty go? Did the Creature from the Black Lagoon sneak in or anything?"

"No. It's strangely quiet. No noises, no voices, no humming. Nothing has come in or out. I'm actually beginning to suspect that it's dormant. Nothing happens when you go through it, at least from this side."

I was going to pretend I didn't hear that. "Has Welling shown any interest in it?"

"I don't know. He comes in, he pauses, but I can't tell if it's because of the portal or because I'm here."

"Not having an actual face does make it more difficult to tell what he's thinking. Christine will be here at ten, so we'll see what she says about this thing."

Welling showed up a few minutes later, pushing through the doorway and running right into me. He didn't go through me. I bounced off of him and was inches from the portal before I stopped my forward momentum. Welling seemed confused by the interaction.

"Dr. Welling." I spoke loudly in case his lack of ears made it harder for him to hear me. "Are you able to speak with us for a moment?"

"Gerri, I've already tried this. Talking to him just seems to confuse him."

"Does the good boy want a cookie? It's in there." I pointed to the portal. "All the cookies you could want, you've just got to go through this little hole over here." I leaned forward and clapped my hands on my thighs like I was calling for a dog.

Lee floated in the corner with his arms crossed. "Okay, I didn't try it exactly like that, but I'll give you credit. This is the longest that I've ever seen him stay in one place."

Welling floated in the middle of the room, hovering there like he wasn't sure which direction he should go. I whistled and clapped my hands to my thighs again. "Here boy."

He moved so quickly that I hadn't even straightened up before he was across the room and one arm like appendage was flying out in a backhand, throwing me into the next room.

"Well, that's new," Lee said as he floated through the wall, presumably to make sure I was okay. The contact didn't cause me any pain, but it had been so long since I'd encountered anything solid that I was twitterpated over the experience.

I expected Welling to follow him, but we floated out to the hallway in time to see him floating on to the next room and continuing his rounds.

"You okay, kiddo?"

"Yeah, just surprised. I guess that answers whether or not he can hear us."

"Maybe he just doesn't like cookies."

"I'll tell Christine to bring some whisky next time."

The construction crew showed up a short time later. Scaffolding was moved on the outside of the building to continue cleaning, and drywall work began on the fourth floor. Plumbing and electrical fought for space on the fifth floor and the entire building was soon alive with saws, generators, and the whine of drills.

"What's it take, like half an hour for him to make a full circuit?" I asked. Keeping track of time wasn't a high priority as a ghost, but there were times when a watch would still have been handy.

"About that," Lee agreed. "Unless he stops for a snack."

"Ugh. I hope not. We don't have time for that today."

I left Lee at the door and I went to float through the hotel, checking out the work progress, seeing what people were going to be doing today. Not that I knew anything at all about construction, but there were a lot of things that I knew nothing about, and I now had all the time in the world to learn.

I was mesmerized by the dude on the scaffolding pressure washing the exterior of the east wing when I heard the obnoxious growl of a rusting muffler and the squeal of a deteriorating belt coming up the hill. Christine's land yacht came into view a moment later and she paused by the fountain, taking in the impressive front entrance, no doubt. She continued around the western side on the gravel road that led back to the carriage house.

I followed, catching up to her as she knocked on the Brownings' door. Christine was dressed in fuchsia polyester today, the material clinging in unflattering ways, and the legs of the pants so long they barely revealed the toes of her white flats. Memorial Day was still two weeks away. My mother would die if we'd left the house in white shoes before Memorial Day. The door was immediately opened by Browning, who was wearing what I had already determined was his only good suit. He had egg yolk on his tie and a hard hat in each hand.

"Ms. Hermance, I presume?" he said, shoving one hat under his armpit to free up one hand to shake. "I saw you coming on the security camera."

"Mr. Browning? It's so nice to finally meet you." She shook his hand and smiled sweetly.

I muttered, "Welcome to my parlor, said the spider to the fly," under my breath, but Christine heard me and squinted one eye in my direction. I interpreted that to mean I should keep my trap closed.

"We're so flattered that you've come all this way to see our cozy little hotel," he schmoozed. She was a medium, not blind. Who did he think he was kidding?

"I can't wait to see inside," she said. "I've already heard so much from the Perth Paranormal Society. Their findings here have been most extraordinary."

He held one bright yellow hat out to her. "Well, this is an active construction site, so I'll need you to have this on when we're inside. I'm sorry to have to make you wear it, but we've already had so many accidents here. I'd hate to have to do more paperwork," he said before launching into the fakest laugh I'd ever heard. I could see Christine grit her teeth.

"The portal is on the second floor, west wing, Room 206," I told her as they started across the gravel lane towards the rose garden.

"Mr. Browning, would we be able to begin our tour on the second floor today?" She asked. "I feel strongly attracted to this area right though here," she pointed up towards the second floor.

"I... are you sure? The lobby isn't completely finished yet, but you can still see how grand it will be when it's done. It will be the shining jewel of our little hotel."

So help me, if he referred to this monstrosity as a little hotel one more time, I was going to try my hardest to kick him in the shin.

"We can take a peek at it later. My goal right now is to locate this source of negative energy I'm sensing. It's very strong and could be dangerous. You alluded to other accidents that have taken place on the premises?"

Browning blushed, the top of his little bald head turning pink. "Well, I don't know that we've had more than any other remodel of this size and scope, but there have been a few accidents, yes."

"I sense several different energies here. There are obviously multiple ghosts on the premises," she said.

I was getting an eye-roll-workout in today.

Christine perched the yellow hardhat on top of her head as Browning opened the rear fire door into the west wing. The two started up the back stairway.

"Here," Christine said in a mysterious voice as she neared Room 206. "This is the source of the negative energy that I've been sensing." She flung the door open dramatically. I saw Lee jump on the other side.

"This must be Christine," Lee said, one hand still clutched to his chest like he was calming his nonexistent heart.

"Yes," Christine said with a nod in his direction. "This is the source. I can see the portal here."

"The portal?" Browning asked, leaning forward with his head in the room but his feet still firmly planted in the hall.

"There is an open portal through the veil in this very room. This is the source of all the bad things that have befallen you lately. Have you experienced any personal losses, Mr. Browning? Financial matters? Love?"

"I, uh, may have umm...what does any of this have to do with a portal?"

"It allows all of the demons through, of course. Those curious little imps that love nothing more than messing up your life."

"Imps?" Browning whispered.

"Is she for real or just straight up lying to him?" Lee asked me.

"Results!" Christine said in an authoritative voice, one finger waving in the air as she made this pronouncement. "What we need are results. I would suggest a seance as soon as possible to purge your adorable little hotel of this curse."

"And this seance?" Browning asked, arms crossed and

looking suspicious. "How much would that kind of thing cost me?"

"One can't put a price on the removal of negative influences in one's life, can they, Mr. Browning? Unless, of course, you're happy with the status quo. Or maybe I should discuss this with your partner, Mr. Dixon." One pencil thin eyebrow raised as she looked at him, still hiding in the hallway.

She was good. I began to wonder if the crappy car was part of the con.

"No, no. There's no need to involve him in any of this. And there has definitely been some unpleasantness lately. Is there any guarantee that if I agree to this seance, my luck will turn around?"

"I never make a guarantee, Mr. Browning. The universe is too fickle. However, I've never had an unsatisfied customer. As a bonus, the Perth Paranormal Society is willing to participate and even film the event. Think of it as a marketing expense."

"Fine. We can do it tomorrow if that's enough time for you to gather whatever you need. Where do I sign?"

Lee looked over at me with raised brows as the two left the room.

"Is she going to make him sign the contract in blood?" he asked.

"At this point, nothing would surprise me."

28

"Did you bring an extra pair of gloves? I think I forgot to pack mine this morning."

"There might be a pair in there." Randy pointed toward the glove box as he parked the equipment van by the rear fire door of the west wing.

"The electricity kept going out last night and I didn't get any sleep," Greg said, capping the thermos of coffee I'd watched him drain on the way to Chivington.

"Yeah, it was weird. Mine started flickering around midnight. I assumed someone hit a pole, but I didn't hear anything on the scanner."

Oops, my bad. I hadn't meant to disturb anyone's sleep, but a few hours spent hovering in the lines of the power substation had given me the extra boost I needed to feel prepared for today.

I heard Nirvana playing, so I floated away as Greg began rummaging through the glove box. Pansy's Tracker pulled in with her and Bagel inside. They'd both skipped school to attend what would be possibly the most educational day of their young lives.

The construction crews had been told to stay away for filming purposes, but Browning hadn't filled them in on what, exactly, was being filmed. Shawn pulled in next to Ms. Hermance's beast of a car with Chandra and Blake, and it reminded me of that car ride home with Bagel, Blake, and Pansy crammed into the back seat of the car after our first night here. Had it only been a month since we'd investigated this abandoned monument to philanthropy? We'd been so fascinated with the unknown, the different kinds of ghosts, the creepy environment. The novelty had definitely worn off.

I watched as everyone introduced themselves to Ms. Hermance. I'd expected her to be wearing something more 'psychic' today—a mumu, a caftan, maybe even a turban. Instead, she wore a vivid red and green Hawaiian shirt tucked into pleated beige dress pants, a strand of pearls at her throat. As everyone gathered in the gravel lane between the hotel and the carriage house, she never stopped chain smoking, even as she shook hands with the crew. Mr. and Mrs. Browning stood together, not shaking hands with anyone. The pair had dressed in matching navy blue track suits with a red pin stripe running down the sides of the arms and legs. Apparently, Mr. Dixon had not received an invitation at all.

"Miss Hermance," Randy said, striding over to the smaller woman and offering his hand out to shake. His meaty paw completely encompassed her hand as he pumped it enthusiastically. "I'm Randy Martinez. We spoke on the phone last night? It's so nice to meet you in person." He acted like he was meeting a celebrity. Greg was right behind with the handshaking and obvious adoration.

"If they stay here any longer, they're going to drop to their knees and start with the 'we're not worthy'," I told my sister.

I had no breath to control, but I was nervous and felt like some sun salutations were necessary to center me as I watched while Randy, Greg, Shawn, and Blake carried several long pieces of iron rebar up the stairs to where the shimmer hovered, still and silent. I followed them up to the room to check on Lee.

"Anything come through the portal?" I asked.

"Not a thing. It's been a really quiet night. Welling has just been doing his normal laps. I figure you have another twenty minutes or so until his next trip through."

Blake and Randy came in with the final pieces of rebar and set to work, lining them up around the outside edges of the room before tying the ends together with wire. It was important that the bars remained touching the entire time. Blake set a shorter piece in front of the door, leaving a two-inch gap between it and the next bar in line. I'd have to slide that piece into position when the time came, essentially locking Welling into the room. Easy peasy.

"Are you sure this is going to work?" Blake asked, dusting his hands off against the thighs of his blue jeans.

"Yeah," Randy said. "We tested it out on Gerri last night. She got the idea from the San Isidro cemetery. Once we'd formed a square and all the pieces were touching, she couldn't get back out." We could safely mark that off my list of things I never wanted to try again. But moving the final bit of rebar by myself had been hard and even though I'd have Lee here to help me, I'd decided that amping myself up with some extra juice would be a good idea. Wasn't, "Be Prepared," the Girl Scout motto? Maybe it was the Boy Scouts, it was definitely someone's.

After a few minutes of discussion, Christine decided to hold the seance in the hallway. There wasn't enough room to fit all the people, all the candles, and the video cameras into the hotel room if we wanted to film anything other than the back of someone's head. Two video cameras would film the seance from different ends of the hallway, and two other cameras would be set up in Room 206 along with a tape recorder. I was watching Pansy, Bagel, and Chandra carry up the camera equipment from the van when we heard some kind of disturbance outside. When multiple car doors slammed shut, everyone on the second floor paused in what they were doing, listening to see who had pulled in. Everyone that was supposed to be here was already here. Browning started down the lobby stairs and his voice carried as he confronted the newcomers.

"What do you think you're doing?" There was some muffled speech that we couldn't make out and I volunteered myself to go check it out.

"Gerri's going to go see what's going on," I heard Pansy tell the group.

There were three men entering the lobby dressed in what seemed like a uniform of blue polo shirts and khaki pants. One had a clipboard, one had a briefcase, and the other had a handheld camcorder much like the ones we were using upstairs. There was a logo embroidered above the left breast pocket of their shirts, and I floated closer to see what it said.

"Oh. Fantastic," I muttered before heading back up to the second floor.

"It's the dudes from MTV," I told Pansy.

"MTV?" Christine said, her pencil thin eyebrows raising.

"MTV?" Mrs. Browning repeated with a squeal. She lost no time whipping a compact and a tube of lipstick from the kangaroo pouch of her tracksuit.

"Yeah," Pansy said as she finished securing a camcorder to a tripod. "Browning has been writing to them, trying to convince them that the hotel would be the perfect place to film one of their reality shows."

"And how would you know what my husband has or has not been doing?" Mrs. Browning snarled midway through her lipstick reapplication.

"Ghosts, Mrs. Browning. The ghosts know everything that goes on here. And I do mean everything," Pansy said, hands on her hips as she stared the other woman down.

Mrs. Browning had the good grace to blush when the implication finally struck home.

Randy paused in his duties of lighting candles all around the room. "They're here? Now? We just decided to do this yesterday. How did they get here so fast?"

"I think Browning is just as surprised as we are," I said. "He seemed to have a mild panic attack when he realized who they were."

Pansy was passing my comment on to the group when the newcomers crested the second floor landing with Mr. Browning leading the way.

"As you can see, we're still remodeling, but we're hoping to have everything completed and ready for guests in about five months."

The three men wore identical expressions of distaste as they took in their surroundings. The cheerful striped wallpaper that had only been applied to one wall and the random drink cups and candy wrappers the construction crew had left crumpled on the bare concrete floors did not seem to impress them.

Christine was pulling more candles out of a canvas tote bag that said Support Your Local Library and squinting at the newcomers with some suspicion.

"Are you observing or participating?" she asked as they approached the rest of the group.

"Observing or participating in what?" Clipboard Dude asked.

"The seance. We need to get started."

"Right now?" Camcorder Dude asked.

"Yeah, either get over here and stand in with us in a circle or stand over there and don't block the camera," she directed. "Got it?"

The camcorders were on and the candles were arranged on the floor, creating more of a long rectangle than a circle around the group. Welling appeared on the second floor landing.

"They're heeeeeeere," I said in a high-pitched voice.

Pansy snorted and Christine glared at both of us. "Geraldine, can the witty commentary. Doctor Welling has arrived," she said to the group.

Welling floated into the first room to his right, either unaware or uncaring that a crowd had gathered at the other end of the hall.

"Who's Doctor Welling?" I heard the guys from MTV whispering to themselves. Camcorder Dude had his camera up and filming.

"Come on..." I whispered. I needed Welling to ignore the crowd and continue on his rounds, to just keep floating through every room until he got to 206. I clenched my fists as I watched him cross the hall and disappear inside. So far, so good. There were just eight more rooms for him to zigzag his way through until he was finally where I needed him to be.

Two more rooms down.

"Come on. Keep coming, big boy," I mumbled to myself. Once he was inside 206, Lee and I would move the bar into place and our part would be done.

Four more rooms. We were so close.

Welling stopped.

"He's leaving," Lee said. Sure enough, the figure was heading the wrong way down the hallway.

"Doctor Jerkface!" I yelled. He stopped moving.

"Can you force him through the portal from here?" I heard Lee asking Christine behind me.

"Maybe. But he's old and strong and I'd feel better about everyone's safety if he was secured before we started."

"Wait, what about our safety?" Clipboard Dude asked. Everyone ignored him.

"Who's a big, bad, scary ghost?" I said, clapping my hands against my thighs again. "Yes, you are. Yes, you are." I slowly floated backwards, hoping he would chase me, prepared this time for any sudden movements. I just had to get him into the room. We were so close. The featureless head shape swiveled from me to Pansy and back again. If his backhanding me yesterday had left any doubt, I was sure he could see. And I already knew he could hear me.

"Get ready," I said to Lee.

"What are you going to do?" Lee asked.

"Everyone, hold hands and form a circle, please." I heard a bell ring behind me and knew that Christine was starting the show. A rushing sound filled the air as she began her prayers, like water moving swiftly in a creek or stream. Through the open doorway, I could see the portal, the tear through time and space coming alive. The shimmer was more intense, distorting the walls behind it in undulating waves. The sound grew louder.

"The door is awake, or something." I reported.

"I can hear it," Pansy whispered. Christine heard her and cocked an eyebrow at her.

"Can anyone else hear the doorway opening?" Christine asked.

It was quickly established that besides Christine and Pansy, Lee and I were the only ones who could hear it. Christine nodded her head. Maybe she was checking things off of a list of her own over there. Welling, perhaps curious about our gathering, was slowly floating closer. The shimmering figure looked over at the trio of men quaking against the wall.

"Is it colder? I feel like it dropped ten degrees," one of them asked.

"I'm going to make him mad," I told Lee. Grating and obnoxious was a specialty of mine. I raised my voice a few decibels. "Don't run away, Welling. I thought you were the big bad ghost, not a scaredy cat. I bet you were a smug jerk who thought this place was his own little kingdom. That's probably why you're still here. You could have gone anywhere, done anything, after you died, but this castle is yours, isn't it? Years with no one to absorb their energy and you could have left, but no. What if they turn it back into a hospital again? That's some sweet low hanging fruit that you just couldn't pass up. People like you always want to put forth the least amount of effort, don't you? Is that your problem? Are you just lazy? That's it, lazy and incompetent. I bet you killed people left and right with your lousy doctoring skills."

Welling moved closer.

"Gerri," Lee warned.

"What do you think, Lee? How many patients did Nurse Daniels have to step in and save to keep Doctor High and Mighty here from killing them off with his incompetence?" Honestly, the man could have been the most skilled doctor in three states, but at the turn of the century, I felt I was safe assuming he was mediocre at best. "I mean, how could you possibly concentrate on medicine when there were so many potential victims for you to abuse? Talk about low-hanging fruit. What did you do to those women, Weller? All of those girls. Jessica told us how you liked the little girls best, didn't you? The younger the better."

The candles fluttered along the edge of the circle about half a second before he rushed at me, but I was ready this time. I floated backward into Room 206 with him hot on my proverbial heels. I stopped in the room, ready to pivot and head toward the rebar by the doorway, when he grabbed me by the throat. Luckily I couldn't feel pain, but he was pushing me towards the outer wall. We'd be out in the rose garden in just a few seconds.

"Close it, Lee," I yelled, gritting my teeth to exert as much force as I could to remain in between the rectangle of rebar we'd erected. I wasn't winning, but I wasn't losing as fast as I had been.

"But you're still in there."

We didn't have time for indecision.

"Just do it!"

Lee slid the bar home and the second the iron touched, all three of us were rocked by the force. Lee was blown backward away from the doorway and Welling and I were violently tossed into the center of the room. His grip on my throat broke, but I was disoriented for a second.

"Gerri?" I heard Pansy yell for me from the other room.

"Do it now!"

"But..."

Thank goodness Christine could also hear me, I didn't need to wait for the delay between Pansy to stop worrying and start translating.

"Doctor Herbert Welling, I command you to appear before me and speak only the truth." Almost instantly, Welling took on a curious glow. The candles by the doorway guttered before flaring back to life.

"It's working," I yelled. Christine repeated her command and the Other began to straighten, its shimmering illusion of limbs stretching out in the same way Jessica's had.

"Doctor Welling, come forth and speak to your crimes. Why do you persist in this place?"

Welling's form was drawn to the doorway, floating with arms outstretched, the shimmer of his legs pulled down and out into a vee. The words issuing from his form sounded like they were being pulled from the bottom of a well. The sound was rough and wet, not even remotely human.

"The body isssss...tied to thisssss place," he struggled against the metaphysical bonds that held him, one hand slowly inching toward Christine.

"He's fighting it," I reported.

"How did you die?" she asked.

"Treachery," it hissed.

"Herbert Welling, I command you to speak the truth. Confess to your crimes."

Something that could have been a laugh burst from his form, rough and shattered. "No crimessss. Power."

This was getting us nowhere and he'd managed to move one leg closer to center. We didn't have time for truth or dare. "Just get rid of him. He's pulling free of your hold. You don't have much time," I yelled.

"Everyone, Doctor Welling seems to be power hungry and unpleasant, even in death. We can only hope that he receives the afterlife he deserves. Gerri tells me he's pulling out of the hold I currently have on him, so we'll need to skip the Q&A and expel him sooner than planned. I need everyone to repeat after me." The gasps and murmurs from the group in the hallway were quickly drowned out by the sound from the portal.

Christine began to command the good doctor to leave this plane and the other voices were soon chanting along with her. Over and over. I caught a few words, but the rushing sound was almost deafening. The glow that surrounded Welling intensified and his struggles became more desperate, his form writhing and straining against the hold Christine held him in. I had just enough time to think that she was way better at this than Pansy had been when my first clue that something was about to go wrong slid across the floor. A crumpled Snickers wrapper, torn and dirty, was being sucked from the hall into the room toward the portal. It was followed by a discarded plastic drink straw, rolling across the floor.

I realized I was also being pulled backward into the portal.

"Lee!"

"Stop! Stop! Gerri's being pulled in too!"

"No, don't stop," I yelled to be heard over the rushing sound, "we have to get rid of him. If I go too, it's fine. He cannot stay here." I didn't want to go, I didn't want to leave my family, but this thing, this Other, it wasn't safe to leave it here amongst the living. I was already dead and if I had to go with it to save others, well, that was just one more adventure. Surely Pansy would be fine without me. Besides, the plan was working. Welling was now halfway across the room, inching closer and closer. I pulled against the flow, the effort reminding me of the times we'd gone rafting and had to fight against a river current. While I fought to remain in the same spot, Welling had almost drawn up even to me.

"Pansy!" I heard Christine yell. There was something about crossing her arms and maintaining the circle, but the rest of the group was still chanting and I was still slowly losing ground. Suddenly, Pansy was in front of me and I reached out, grabbing ahold of her hand. I'd spent my evening absorbing power so that I'd be able to grip a piece of rebar—I'd never imagined that I'd have to hold on to my own sister.

"Where is it? I can hear it, but I don't see it," she said.

"It's about two feet behind me," I said. There wasn't enough yoga in the world to calm my mind at this point. Pansy placed her body between the portal and me, and I turned to face her. Welling slid past me.

"Tell them he's almost there," I said between gritted teeth, every part of me concentrating on keeping my grip on Pansy. She bent her knees slightly to take the force I was exerting on her and yelled an update to Christine.

As Welling moved past me, still struggling, his arm broke free of Christine's hold and he grabbed my upper arm. His touch was numbing and the unfamiliar sensation freaked me out more than a little.

"He's holding on to me," I told Pansy.

"I've got you. I'm not letting go of you." Her letting go wasn't what I was worried about. I was worried that my charge would run out before Welling was gone and I'd have nothing left to fight with.

The chanting continued, demanding Welling depart this plane. He struggled, trying to push himself away from the portal, shoving me towards it instead. Crap, crap, crap. My hold slipped and I was halfway through Pansy before I pulled myself back together. She took a step backward and braced to hold me again. We could not lose ground.

"Doctor Herbert Welling, I command you to leave this earthly plane and to cease your existence here," Pansy joined in the chanting, staring me in the eye. Hers were full of tears and I rethought my earlier assessment that she'd be okay without me. I certainly didn't want to be without her. I joined in the chanting. Face to face, our foreheads pressed together, hands gripping the other's forearms, we held our ground. I noticed the pressure of Wellings grip beginning to weaken.

"He's breaking apart," I heard Lee yell from the other side of the doorway.

An unholy sound was wrung from Welling as small pieces of his shimmering form sheared off and went flying backward into the rippling portal.

"Keep going, keep going!" Lee yelled again.

I imagined my chakras aligned, imagined my lungs expanding with an indrawn breath, my stomach pulled against my spine. I stared into Pansy's eyes and she gave me a slight nod. We were not going anywhere. With a final scream that I knew would haunt me, Welling broke into a thousand pieces of shimmering dust and was instantly sucked into the portal.

"Close the door. Close the door!" Lee, my unflappable companion, screamed. I was so startled by his panic that I almost lost my grip on Pansy's arms.

Christine's brass bell was still ringing when the portal disappeared, the shimmer shrinking into a pinpoint of bright light before flashing out of existence. With nothing pulling me forward, I suddenly went floating backward across the room. Pansy dropped to her knees and began sobbing in earnest. Christine rushed in, kicking the rebar across the doorway and breaking the hold of the iron's magic. Lee came barreling in towards me.

"Oh my God, Kiddo, don't ever do anything like that again."

Bagel was right behind Christine, skidding to a stop when he saw Pansy crying on the floor. "Oh no. Is Gerri...?" he couldn't finish the sentence and Pansy was sobbing so hard that she couldn't answer him.

Christine pulled a handkerchief from her pocket and handed it to Pansy. "Gerri's fine. Well, probably a little shaken up, aren't you girlie? But otherwise fine. Welling, the stubborn cuss, is finally gone."

A cheer went up from the rest of the crew, and Christine relayed the whole drama to those who hadn't been able to see or hear any of it. She was almost finished before Pansy finally got herself together.

"Did you get that on film?" Browning asked the MTV crew. He was all but jumping up and down, his nylon track suit generating its own current with all the static electricity he was creating. "This is amazing. The candles were fluttering, the trash was moving across the floor all by itself, and this girl," he pointed towards Pansy, "she deserves an Academy award for that performance."

"Yeah, we saw it," Clipboard Dude said, eyeing Christine.

"So how about it? You can film as many seasons as you want of one of your shows here at my little haunted hotel."

"Technically," Christine said, a cigarette already hanging off her lip as she searched her bag for her lighter. "Your hotel is no longer haunted."

"What?" Browning froze.

Christine lit the Virginia Slim and drew in a lung full before blowing it out from the corner of her mouth. "Well, you still have a few shades running around the place. There's nothing I can do with them, but they won't bother anyone. The other ghost you had here haunting the place moved on last week. As I just shoved your last ghost out the door by sheer force of will. You're officially ghost free."

"But you were talking to other ghosts. You said there were more."

"Those are our ghosts," Randy explained. "They're just along to help us out today, they don't live here."

"But they could, right? Like, I can pay you to keep them here."

"Absolutely not," Lee and I said at the same time.

"It doesn't work like that," Pansy told him.

"It doesn't matter," Briefcase Dude said. He unlatched the dark brown leather briefcase he carried and pulled some documents out. "Ms. Hermance, would you be interested in doing a series for MTV Entertainment? We'd love to follow you for a few weeks, get some real day-in-the-life footage, if you know what I mean."

"Never gonna happen, sonny," Christine said, blowing smoke directly at him.

Browning stepped in front of Christine. "What do you mean, sign her? You're here for me. I wrote to you. Give me those papers, those are mine."

Briefcase Dude pulled the papers away from Browning's grasp as they began to argue. The Mrs. joined in, interjecting several choice words to both the MTV crew and to Mr. Browning.

Christine left them to it and wandered over to where Lee and I were floating beside Pansy.

"Did the nurse ever tell you where she'd buried the body?" Christine asked her.

"No. She said that it took her several evenings to dig the hole, so it had to be somewhere close by, but somewhere no one would notice a hole."

"I think I know," I said. "There's a fallen down shed at the rear of the garden. I don't know if there was a shed there when she originally buried him, but I caught her out there just staring at it one day. It seemed like an odd place to woolgather."

"It could be worth digging him up to see if there's something in the grave that held him here. I'd like to remove whatever it was just to keep him from coming back."

"Can he do that?" I asked. The process had looked pretty definitive from my angle.

"I don't know, but I'd rather not find out the hard way. While I appreciated your take on why he was still here while you were taunting him, I'd bet there's something real and tangible there in his grave. I'll suggest as much to Browning once he's done having his temper tantrum. Maybe he can film himself digging it up and it'll make him feel better."

We all looked over to where the Brownings were now screaming at one another, words like idiot and divorce being bandied about at high volume. The MTV guys were slowly backing toward the stairs, trying to escape without the couple noticing that they'd gone.

"Yeah, or maybe we'll just send him another email," I said.

29

"Two chocolate shakes, on the house," Chandra said with a wink as Pansy and Bagel entered The Firefly Cafe the following Saturday afternoon.

"Oh, you don't have to…"

"Speak for yourself," Bagel said, interrupting Pansy's denial. "I never turn down free food."

They slid into a red vinyl booth and Pansy began digging through her bright orange backpack purse. "Is Lee here?" she asked me.

"Right here," I told her.

Pansy removed a paper envelope of photos she'd picked up at the drugstore in Trinidad that morning and began flipping through them to find the six shots she'd taken for Lee. She placed them across the end of the table and sat back with a grin on her face.

"Oh, that's gorgeous," I said, looking over the shots of Lee and Diane's elaborately carved double headstone. Pansy and Bagel, armed with his dad's weed eater and a bucket of bleach and water, had trimmed back the weeds from their grave and scrubbed the granite headstone to remove the moss and mildew growing on it. Pansy had left a bouquet of flowers for Diane and something else that I couldn't make out for Lee.

I squinted. "Are those... pencils?"

"Yeah, I left him a bouquet of pencils," she confirmed. "I thought he'd appreciate that more than flowers. Does he like it?"

I took in Lee's stunned expression and watched as he lightly traced his wife's name in the close-up shot of her side of the headstone. "I think you've done the impossible, Pans. The old man is speechless."

"I think I am too," he all but whispered. "This is completely unexpected, but really and truly appreciated. Tell them I said thank you."

I relayed his message to the living and tried to change the subject to give him a few minutes to look over the photos by himself.

"So, while you were at therapy this morning, Randy and his trusty metal detector had some luck up at the hotel." After their massive blowout, the Brownings had wasted no time packing their belongings and vacating for parts unknown. It was doubtful that they'd left together, but when Lee and I had gone back the day after the seance to see what they planned to do, the carriage house was empty. A quick search had confirmed that the motel room where the business partner had been staying was also empty. Had they all left together or ran in three separate directions? Either way, the gate had been left open and the security camera had been disconnected.

Pansy had called Randy after school on Wednesday to update him, and he'd hypothesized that the Brownings would need all the head start they could get to escape the huge amount of money they owed. With no MTV contract and no ghosts to lure in new investors, there was no way they could finish the renovations. If they were smart, they'd have cleared out whatever they had left in their bank accounts and headed to Mexico.

Since no one was home, and since Christine had left the PPS instructions to dig up Welling's body and burn whatever was left, the PPS had taken the day to go on an impromptu archaeological dig. Lee and I had gone with them because that was way more interesting than anything else we had going on. Chandra had to open, Pansy had gone to therapy, and Bagel claimed he wasn't able to get out of his shift at Foodarama. I figured he was happy to have an excuse to not find any more dead bodies.

Chandra delivered the milkshakes to the table herself and spotted the photos set out on the end. "What is this? Oh, did you guys clean up Lee's grave? That's so nice of you."

"Well, he can't get in to see it, so we took some photos," Bagel said.

"So, have you heard anything yet about what the guys have found?" Chandra asked while pulling two straws from her apron pocket and tossing them onto the formica table top.

Pansy shook her head. "I had a therapy appointment this morning and just got back. Gerri was telling us about it."

I told what I knew. "Okay, well, Jessica really did bury him at the edge of the rose garden right where that shed was. It took the guys a while to move all the debris out of the way, but they found him about two feet down. There was a rusted iron cross laying on top of what was left of the body. Most of the bones had disintegrated, but his shoes were still intact, as well as the buttons from his shirt and pants. Randy thinks it was the iron cross that held him to the property."

Chandra tapped her pen against her order pad as Pansy relayed the update. "You'd think someone would have noticed an unexplained hole in the rose garden."

"Unless she covered it with something," Pansy said with a

shrug. "Or the gardener was sick for a few days. Or on vacation. However she did it, she obviously got away with it."

"True," Chandra conceded. "Well, one thing I do know, we can expect a new article on all of this from Randy in the next issue of Paranormal Today."

Pansy rolled her eyes. "As long as he leaves my name out of it."

"Speaking of paranormal things," Bagel asked after sucking down four inches of his milkshake in one go. "Did Christine say when she was coming back?"

Pansy nodded. "Yeah. She said she had some clients to visit up north but that she'd be back through in a few weeks. She promised to stop by and work with me before she heads home. She said she wants to test out what all I can do."

"That is awesome, Pansy," Chandra told her. "I've got to get back to work, but tell Gerri I said thanks for the update."

Bagel slurped up the rest of his shake and leaned back in the booth. "So what's next?"

"Well, tonight is the investigation at that motel in Barton and then next week is graduation," Pansy said.

"I don't mean on our social calendar. I mean, what's next on your list? What cool new trick are we going to test out on Gerri and Lee? What mysteries do we have left to solve?"

"Honestly, I think we've covered most of our list. Of course, there's still Thomas. We haven't had any luck tracking down his family," Pansy said.

"I haven't even been able to track *him* down, yet," I said. "But we've got all summer to devote to that task."

"Yeah. One more week of school to get through and then we'll have all summer to relax and be lazy before we start college."

"As long as we don't find any more famous dead people," Bagel grunted.

"You're fresh out of bodies, aren't you Lee?" Pansy asked.
"He says he is," I confirmed.
A lazy summer sounded perfect.
Of course, it didn't work out that way.

A SNEAK PEEK AT BOOK 3: A SPIRIT OF SUMMER

If this was a John Hughes movie, the rain would be gentle and the multicolor lights of open shops would be reflected across the sidewalks down Main Street. I'd be soaking wet with my makeup still perfect, and a boy that I'd had a crush on since junior high school would be running down an empty street toward me to proclaim his love. But this was not a teen movie from the eighties. The rain was torrential, the shops were all closed because nothing in Perth stayed open after nine, and I was dead. Never needing an umbrella didn't balance out the fact that I would never fall in love with the perfect guy. I would never have a career, get married, or have kids. My sister, who had been by my side since our birth, had crossed the graduation stage without me a few short hours ago. I was throwing myself a pity party.

It wasn't her fault that I wasn't joining the Class of '96 as they matriculated from Perth High School. It wasn't even her fault that I'd come back as a ghost three days after the traffic accident that had caused my death, although she still blamed herself. It was maybe her fault that she could see and hear me, although that was like, a total bonus. She couldn't see or hear any of the other ghosts we'd met, but there was a glimmer of hope on that front. A few weeks ago a real, honest to god psychic medium had helped us dispatch a corrupted spirit to the great beyond, wherever that may be, and Christine had been really impressed with the promise Pansy showed at Medium work. It wasn't exactly a skill one could put on their college admissions application or anything, but we thought it was pretty cool.

Perth was a small town and our senior class consisted of about ninety kids, most of whom did not, in fact, find Pansy cool in any way, shape, or form. She'd been in the papers uncovering too many dead bodies for them not to take notice. First had been Christopher, who we suspected had been drowned by his mother. Then the body of missing country music star Stuart Mayes, who my friend Lee, also a ghost, had actually found, but Pansy and my best friend Bagel had 'discovered.' We hadn't known it was someone famous at the time, so the news coverage she and Bagel received shocked us all. Then there was Doctor Welling. Pansy hadn't even been present when the Perth Paranormal Society had dug up the grave of Mister Evil Doctor Dude who'd been haunting our last case. That didn't stop the local news from slapping her photo up on the screen every time they talked about the burned pit of bones and shoe leather that they'd filmed after the PPS had set fire to his grave. It was like they loved to make her look as crazy as possible.

I was thinking about ways to haunt the reporter when I noticed something moving out of the corner of my eye. I'd been staring at the reflection of the hardware store's neon 'closed' sign in the growing puddle of water backing up on Main Street and I couldn't figure out, at first, what had caught my attention. A crack of lightning lit up the street and I saw a scraggly orange tail disappear around the low brick wall that surrounded the elementary school. What self-respecting cat would be out running around in the pouring rain?

I floated across the street, over the wall, and with the next flash of lightning located the orange ball of sopping fur curled under a metal playground slide. One green eye stared me down as I drew closer. Only one eye, I realized, because Harvey was missing the other one. This was Summer's cat who lived a life of leisure batting at suncatchers and windchimes in her shop across the street. Sarah, Summer's twenty-something assistant, had been running Wild Harmony since Summer had left - had Harvey escaped earlier in the day without her noticing?

"What are you doing out here, buddy? Don't you know that it's raining? How'd you get out?"

Harvey gave a plaintive meow, which in no way answered my questions. Had Summer returned home? She'd been gone for almost six weeks with no word about where she'd gone or when she'd be back. It wasn't like her. She'd told Chandra, our fellow PPS member, that there was a family emergency and that she had to go home. She hadn't left a phone number and it wasn't until after she'd gone and the group started talking amongst themselves that they realized that no one knew where her family lived or even where she'd grown up. It was straight up like an episode of Unsolved Mysteries. What could we do but wait for her to eventually call or come back?

Despite Summer's mysterious disappearance, Harvey was my immediate concern. Even though I could now pick up small objects and make things move for short distances, there was zero chance I was dragging a fourteen pound cat out from under a playground slide and carrying its unwilling butt all the way across the street.

"Hey, buddy. I'm going to go get Pansy. I need you to stay here so we don't have to look too hard for you, okay?" He stared past me and I wondered for the hundredth time if he could actually see or hear me. Either way, I hoped he stayed put.

I floated across the street to the Wild Harmony and up to the second floor to see if maybe Summer was home or if Pansy would need to call Sarah to get the key. I hoped she was home. She'd missed out on the conclusion of our last investigation and we had, like, a metric crap ton of stuff to tell her. I hoped to float into her apartment to find the electric kettle steaming and maybe some Stevie Nicks blasting from the ancient stereo system. But the lights were off, and the only illumination came from the security light in the back parking lot. The sheers covering the window overlooking the lot were blowing in the breeze on a curtain rod that was now bent and hanging by one bracket.

I searched the area around Summer's end table, finally locating one of her lamps, now on the floor, and managed to push the switch. The light cast crazy shadows since it was leaning at a strange angle, but the scene before me would have been bad even in normal lighting conditions. The whole place was trashed. It looked like a scene from a teen movie where the parents go out of town and the kids throw a wild party. Everything was either knocked over, broken, or both. What had happened?

"Strange things are afoot at the Circle K," I muttered to myself.

The curtain sheer blew into the room, and the shards of broken glass scattered across the floor caught the light. Well, this answered the question of how and why Harvey was outside in the rain. Poor baby. The storm must have seemed less frightening than whatever had gone down in here. I floated out the back wall to check the parking lot and found it empty. I booked it over the ravine that ran behind the shops on Main Street and across our neighborhood until I came flying through our front door. Like, literally.

"Pansy!" I yelled at the top of my lungs. I could hear voices in the living room, but that was just the parents entertaining Grandma and Aunt Bev who'd driven up from Red River for graduation. It was exactly where I'd left them an hour ago, and I considered having Pansy enlist their help for a second, but they rarely saw one another and this shouldn't take long. Pansy just needed to alert the police and then they could take care of the situation.

Floating upstairs, I headed straight for our bedroom, the large room at the end of the hall that we'd shared since our birth. Pansy was still wearing the pink slip dress she'd worn under her graduation gown, the knee length scrap of fabric shimmering as she danced to Walk Like an Egyptian. Someone must have broken out the Greatest Hits of the 80s CD after I'd left.

"Pansy," I yelled again to be heard over the music.

She froze with elbows akimbo, one arm up, the other down in her Egyptian pose when she heard me.

"I need you to call the cops."

"What?" she asked out loud before remembering that she wasn't alone. But the music was loud and since Amber, Anne, Chrissy, and Jenny were all still singing and dancing along, her outburst went unnoticed.

I moved closer to yell in her ear. "I just found Harvey running around outside in this storm, and when I went to see if Summer was maybe home I found the whole apartment trashed. You've got to call the cops."

"Gotta go pee girls, give me a minute," Pansy said to the room as she made her way out of our bedroom and hustled toward the upstairs bathroom.

"How am I going to call the cops? I'm here and there's a

room full of witnesses that I haven't left all evening. How would I know what's going on at Summer's apartment?"

"I don't know, but we've got to call it in. The window is broken and her carpet and drywall is going to get ruined if they don't cover it up."

"Is whoever broke in still there?" she asked

"I...I don't know. I didn't hear anyone moving around, and the back parking lot was empty. I didn't notice anyone parked in front of the shop, but I didn't look down the street. It's possible someone was out there and I didn't see them."

"Crap," she said, tapping her pale pink fingernails against the bathroom counter while she did mental gymnastics. "Okay, I'll say, I don't know, uh... that I need to go get more ice. I'll drive over and say I thought I saw something."

"I told Harvey to stay put, for what that's worth. He's under the big slide on the elementary playground. You could say that you saw him and stopped to see how he got out."

"Okay, but what if he's gone by the time I get there?"

"Well, I also left a lamp on in Summer's apartment," I offered.

"Okay. Okay. That's good. I'll say I was driving by and saw Harvey run across Main Street and behind the building. So, I drove back there, and then saw a light was on upstairs. Since Summer's Bug wasn't there, I stopped to look around. I'm assuming it's the window off the fire escape?"

"Yep."

"Okay, so I'll tell them I saw the curtain blowing and realized the window was broken." She tapped her nails twice in confirmation, nodding her head in response to some internal conversation. "That should be believable. Crap. Why tonight? Why can't we just have one normal evening?"

I wanted to tell her that she was the only one having a normal graduation evening, but I bit my tongue. I needed her and she didn't need the guilt. Summer also needed her, even if she didn't know it yet.

"Okay, let me go get my keys and my purse. I'll meet you there."

"Don't forget your cell phone."

I watched as she went back into her room and made some excuse about needing to run out and get a bag of ice. I heard several offers for company, but she finally convinced the others to stay dry and continue having fun without her. As she darted from the front door out to the street where her bright yellow Geo Tracker was parked against the curb, it occurred to me that I should have told her to bring an umbrella and maybe a towel. She was definitely going to need a towel, but she should have figured that out on her own.

Can I help it if that gave me my first real smile of the evening?

COMING SOON

A SPIRIT OF SUMMER

A.B. Hooser & The Henlo Press - 2025

ACKNOWLEDGMENTS

First, I want to thank all of the Kickstarter supporters - that leap of faith is always so appreciated. It makes me absolutely DANCE knowing that people love and want to support our little ghost story.

I'd also like to thank my beta readers, Amber, Dawn, and Anna. Their advice is always invaluable and provides perspective when I can't see the forest for the trees. I appreciate your unpaid labor so very much!

And as always, I want to thank my fabulous publishing team at The Henlo Press. Thank you to Chandler for making the grammar go and wrangling the commas, Courtney for always being game for my crazy ideas and contributing a few of her own, Tiffany for proofreading and cheerleading, and Chad for designing my beautiful covers. Love y'all.

ABOUT THE AUTHOR

Author A. B. Hooser lives in Huntington, WV with her family and two dogs. Artist, gamer, writer, she lets the ADHD lead her into every new adventure. She tells people that she has mastered the art of procrastinating by creating an entire sticker business to avoid nishing the multiple books she has half- written.